THE IRON HUNT

I stepped back and slammed the door. As if that would save me. I stood, staring, expecting the demon to burst through. I also expected the boys to close ranks, but they watched the door, as well. Unmoving. Eyes huge.

'*Zee*,' I hissed.

'Maxine,' he said, expression inscrutable, ears flattened against his bristled skull. Raw and Aaz dug their claws into the floor, the spikes in their spines fanning out with a clacking sound, violently trembling. Dek and Mal also quivered, their breath rattling hot in my ears.

None of them looked ready to fight. And that was wrong, had never happened. It could not. My blood was their blood. My death, the same as their suicide. The boys lived only because I did. It was supposed to be an incentive. Beyond friendship. Or loyalty.

'Zee,' I said again.

'Open the door,' he whispered.

By Marjorie M. Liu

The Iron Hunt
Darkness Calls

THE
IRON HUNT

MARJORIE M. LIU

ORBIT

First published in the United States in 2008 by The Berkeley Publishing Group
First published in Great Britain in 2010 by Orbit

A CIP catalogue record for this book
is available from the British Library.

ISBN 978-1-84149-800-3

Typeset in Times by Palimpsest Book Production Limited,
Grangemouth, Stirlingshire

Printed and bound in Great Britain by CPI Mackays, Chatham ME5 8TD

Papers used by Orbit are natural, renewable and recyclable
products sourced from well-managed forests and certified
in accordance with the rules of the Forest Stewardship Council.

Mixed Sources
Product group from well-managed
forests and other controlled sources
www.fsc.org Cert no. SGS-COC-004081
© 1996 Forest Stewardship Council
FSC

Orbit
An imprint of
Little, Brown Book Group
100 Victoria Embankment
London EC4Y 0DY

An Hachette UK Company
www.hachette.co.uk

www.orbitbooks.net

*To my mom, who taught me to play by ear,
and my dad, who told me not to . . .*

ACKNOWLEDGMENTS

My deepest thanks to my editor, Kate Seaver, whose unwavering support, insight, and kindness made this book possible.

I would also like to thank my copyeditors, Robert Schwager and his wife, Sara.

Oh these deceits are strong almost as life.
Last night I dreamt I was in the labyrinth,
And woke far on. I did not know the place.
                                    —EDWIN MUIR

PROLOGUE

W HEN I was eight, my mother lost me to zombies in a one-card draw.

It was not her fault. There was a blizzard. Six hours until sunset, lost on a twisting county road. Bad map. No visibility. Black ice, winds howling down.

I remembered. Slammed against my seat belt. Station wagon plowing into a drift, snow riding high as my window. Metal crunching: the edge of the bumper, the front tire, my door. Beneath us, a terrible reverberating crack.

Lodged. Busted. Dead on our wheels. More than dead. My mother showed me spikes packed into the snow and ice. Tiny metal stars, so sharp the points pricked my palm when I bent to touch one. She pointed out the tires, torn into scrap, ribbons of rubber. Told me not to worry. Called it a game.

My mother cleared the road behind us. I watched from the car. Face pressed against the cold window, fogging glass. She juggled stars and spikes for me, and did not wince when the sharp points bounced off her tattooed hands. She danced in the falling snow, eyes shining, cheeks flushed with the blood of roses, and when I could no longer bear to sit still, I joined her and she held my wrists and swung me in great circles until we fell down.

I remembered her laughter. I remembered.

I remembered that I did not want to go with her. I wanted to stay with the car. I wanted to stay home with the wreck. Listen to the radio. Play with my dolls. My mother would not let me. Too dangerous. Too many weirdos. I was too little to handle the twelve-gauge stashed beneath the passenger seat, or even the pistol in the glove compartment; and the boys were still asleep. Anything could happen.

So we bundled up. Slogged backward in the dull silence of snow and the endless winter bones of the white forked trees. My mother carried me on her back. I saw: silver clouds of my breath engulfing the tattoos on her neck; that lazy red eye, Zee, tracking my face in his dreams. I felt the bulge of knives beneath her black wool coat, too light and short for a blizzard, for anyone but a woman who did not feel the cold. I heard the song she sang over the crunching beat of her boots on the empty road. 'Folsom Prison Blues.' Voice like sunshine and the rumble of a slow train.

A mile behind us, some local bar. Lonely way station. Out in the middle of nowhere, just a shed, neon lights shaped like a naked woman flickering on and off through the dirty tinted glass. Nipples winking. Pickup trucks in the narrow, shoveled, salted lot. Scents of fried food and burned engine oil in my nostrils.

My mother hesitated when she saw the place, just as she had hesitated earlier when we passed it in the car. Wavered, shoulders hitching. Both of us covered in snow. I could not see her face, but I felt her tension. Breathed it. Looked down and saw Zee struggling sleepily against her skin. Tattoos begging to peel.

We entered the bar. My mother let the door slam shut behind us. I could not see: too dark, too smoky, loud with laughter and rocky music. Warm as an oven compared to the blizzard chill. I clung, face pressed to my mother's neck. She did not move. She did not speak. She stood with her back to the door, so very still I could not feel her breathe, and all around us those voices faded dead within a hush, and the music, the low, rolling wail of electric guitar, snapped, stopped. Silence descended. Slow, cold, heavy as snow. Pregnant – a word I would have used. Expectant, full, with something living and turning, *gestating*, in that dark smoky womb.

'Hunter Kiss,' said a deep low voice. 'Lady Hunter.'

I peered over my mother's shoulder, past the loose black curls of her snow-riddled hair. She squeezed my leg. I did not listen. I could not help myself.

3

It was still difficult to see. Just one lamp on the bar, casting a glow, a ring of fire that did not touch the handful of men and women scattered like fleas in the smoky shadows. Still. Poised. Coiled. Dressed in flannel, jeans, weighed down with thick overcoats, dull and torn. Hats pulled low. Eyes like old wells – dark, hollow, with only a glint of reflected light at the very bottom of their gazes. Auras black as pitch. Anchored and straining. As though crowns of ghosts rested upon their heads.

Only one man stood before my mother. He wore a blue suit and a striped tie that shimmered like the steel in his shadowed eyes. Wavy blond hair. Square jaw. Handsome, maybe. Handsome devil. Zombie.

All of them, zombies. Human shells. Living. Breathing. Possessed.

My mother made me slide to the floor. I clutched the hem of her coat. I tried to be small. I knew danger. I knew threats. I knew a demon when I saw one.

My mother raised her hand. Metal sparked between her tattooed fingers. A star from the road. Bristling with spikes. The zombie smiled. He also raised his hand. In his palm, a deck of cards.

'All we want is a look,' he said. 'Just one. You know how it is.'

'I know enough.' Her voice was so cold. She could not be the same woman, not mine, not my mother. Her hand tightened around the spikes, which dug into her skin but did not puncture, no matter how hard she squeezed. I watched her hand, the straining tendons. I heard metal groan.

The zombie's smile widened. 'One-card draw. Highest wins.'

'If I refuse?'

'Now or later. You know the rules.'

'You pervert them,' said my mother. 'You pervert this world.'

'We are demon,' said the zombie simply, and stepped sideways to the battered bar, its surface scarred and mauled by years of hard elbows and broken glass. Ashtrays overflowed. Bottles clustered. Everything, sticky with fingerprints; even the air, marked, cut with smoke and sweat.

My mother watched the zombie. She watched them all and shrugged her shoulders. Her jacket slid off slowly, falling on the floor beside me. She wore little. A tight white tank top, a harness for her knives. Silver tattoos roped down her arms, glinting red. Eyes. Open and staring.

No one moved. Even the zombie in the suit went still. I watched their auras tighten, pulsing faster, harder. My mother's mouth curled. She took my hand. Squeezed once. Led me to the bar where the zombie waited, leaning on a stool. His smile was gone. He looked at her tattoos. His eyelid twitched.

My mother tapped the bar. 'Last time it was chess.'

'You were ten,' he replied, tearing his gaze from her arms. 'And that was your mother's game. You're not her.'

Her mouth tightened. 'Show me the deck.'

The zombie placed it between them and stepped back. My mother fanned the cards. Her gaze roved, flicking once to me.

She shuffled. So did the zombie. Three times each. The slap of the cards sounded like gunfire. My mouth dried. My heart thundered. I clutched her leg, and her fingers buried deep into my hair. She held me close. The zombie tapped the deck and slid one card to the side. My mother did the same.

'Two of diamonds,' she said. Voice hard, like she wanted to kill. The zombie remained silent. He flipped his card and pushed it to her. My mother stared. Her hand tightened in my hair. Her jaw flexed.

'You run,' said the zombie softly, 'and it will be worse next time. I think you remember.'

'I think you ask too much.'

'We ask for so little, considering. Just one glimpse. Painless.' The zombie leaned in. 'Do *not* be your mother.'

She shot him a cold look. He slid from the stool, and the rest of the room shifted, shadows crawling like worms – zombies scuffling from their chairs to cross the floor. Closing in. Eyes black. Auras writhing. My mother faced them. I did not see her hand move, but her fingers flexed, and a knife suddenly glinted, held loosely. No hilt. Just blade. Razor-sharp. In her other hand, that barbed star.

The zombie loosened his tie. 'You can't kill us

6

all. Not without injuring our hosts. Innocents, all of them.'

My mother said nothing. So still. Hardly breathing. Her fingers squeezed the blade, and she turned, blocking the entire room from my view. She looked down at me, and her gaze was hollow, impossibly grim. Her eyes, black as a demon's tongue, and just as cold.

'Do not be afraid,' she whispered.

I tried to hold her to me, but she slipped away, and zombies took her place. So many. Shoulders broad as mountains. Packed tight. Breath hot. Stinking with sweat and winter wool. I could not see faces for shadows, but the zombie in the suit leaned close. Crooked his finger like a hook. I remembered cold shock. Hammers in my heart. I had thought they wanted my mother, but it was me. They wanted me.

'Frogs and snails and puppy-dog tails,' murmured the zombie, his eyes glinting silver. 'Sugar and spice, everything nice.'

He grabbed my jaw with one hand. Squeezed. Pushed down until I was forced to kneel. I could not breathe. I felt my thoughts bleed – for sunset and the boys, my mother. I wanted her to save me. I wanted it so badly, so hard, wished so much to understand.

I wanted to understand.

I could not forget. Consumed and hunted – *I know what it is to be hunted* – feeding those creatures my fear and pain, dispensed like so much sour candy. Demons in their stolen human skins staring with

7

darkling eyes, searching for weakness, a way into my mind. Wanting to make me one of them. Zombie. Infected with a parasite.

I fought. I must have. I remembered voices in my head. Whispers and howls. Zee and the boys, raging in their dreams. I remembered my heart. My heart, opening like a bloody mouth, tasting my terror—

—And then biting it out of me. My heart, shedding the fear and tossing it away. Letting something else slip into its place.

Something from me. Of me. Born in the roots of me. A darkness deep and vast, forever dead, forever cold – and in my soul a slow, shuffling resurrection, a terrible yawning hunger, rising through blood and bone as though every cell of my body had been born empty and frozen and now – *here* – nectar and milk and honey.

Mine to take. Mine to steal. Mine to kill.

I never felt so clearheaded as I did then. Never so strong. I could have killed those zombies. I could have killed them all. Eight years old. Ready to murder. Starving for it. Skin, pulling. Muscles stretching from my bones. All of me, reaching with my soul. Grasping at demons.

The zombie let go of my face. He let go, and I grabbed his hands. I held him to me, and a gray pallor spread – like stone cracking beneath his skin, cold and dead – and I stole him. I stole him away and felt the taste of demon in my blood, rich and sour, like bitter, bilious honey.

And the darkness grew, and I could see it – I closed my eyes to bear witness – and saw it was not a mere void, but a body, turning and turning beneath my skin – glinting like obsidian touched by moonlight, shiny and slick and sharp.

The zombie's eyes rolled back. His friends grabbed him, hands appearing under his arms, across his chest, in his hair – pulling him, hauling hard. My fingers could not hold his wrists. He slipped free. Everyone stumbled back, and I followed. Something inside me wanted to follow.

My mother slipped between them, catching me. Holding tight as I struggled, still trying to chase the hot stink of those zombies – those scared little demons – burning me blind and hungry. My mother said my name, my name – *Maxine, Maxine* – and placed her hands on my face, forcing me to look at her. The boys, those tattoos sleeping on her palms, kissed my flushed cheeks.

They swallowed the darkness. Wrapped themselves with treacherous tenderness around my soul and knitted shut my heart like a door – a door never opened, never seen. They ate the needle and thread, consumed the key. Murder and hunger and death – obsidian and moonlight – nothing more than a bad dream.

A bad dream. Less and more than dream, after all these years. I remembered my mother in that moment – her breathlessness, the softness of her face – and behind her, that zombie in his suit, stretched on the ground, his skin gray and his eyes open and staring.

His whisper, the slow, churning hiss of his breath as he said, 'She passed. She's strong enough to kill the others. She's strong enough for *them*.'

My mother said nothing. She held me closer. I felt her heart pound. The other zombies backed away, lost in shadow – less flesh than shadow – and only that zombie with his shining hair and cracked skin tried to stay near, rising slowly to his feet, lurching one step closer. He watched me, and behind my heart, something rattled, wanting out. My mother's arms tightened. She backed away, toward the door, carrying me. The zombie followed, bent over, holding out his hand. My mother shook her head. 'I played your game. You had your test.'

'This was not part of the test,' he whispered, pointing at himself. 'This was not part of anything that should *be*.'

My mother turned, and he grabbed her shoulder. She let him. She stood still as ice as he pressed his mouth against her ear and whispered words I could not understand, whispered long and low and hard. I watched my mother's face change.

The zombie pulled away. Skin peeled from his face in strips. Fresh blood dotted the corners of his eyes. He swayed, like he was weak. Dying. 'Do it, Hunter. It's not worth the risk. *Kill her*. Have another child. You're still young.'

My mother's mouth tightened. She set me down and rubbed my head. Gentle, reassuring. At odds with the death in her eyes.

A knife appeared in her hand.

She moved fast. Opened the door of the bar and shoved me outside, into the snow. I fell on my knees. The door slammed shut behind me. I tried to go back inside, but the knob would not turn. Locked. I banged on the wood with my fists, screaming for her. Screaming and screaming.

Men screamed back. Women howled. I heard pain in those voices, terror, and now – now I realize – death. I listened to my mother murder. I stumbled back, breathless.

Silence was worse. I did not know who would come through that door. And when it opened and I saw my mother, I still did not know who had come through. Her hair was wild. Her face spattered red. Eyes dark and burning.

I did not know what I said. I did not remember. I was sure I stared. That much, I stared. I tried not to flinch when she knelt and looked into my face. She held up her hands for me to see. Blood glistened on her fingers. Blood that slowly disappeared into her tattooed skin. Boys, drinking up. Feeding.

'I don't want you to remember this,' she whispered, touching my forehead. 'Baby. My baby.'

She stole from me. Memories, hidden behind dreams. I did not know how I lost so much – how she did it – but I blame my youth. I was so young. I forgot it all – even later, when I saw more. So much more. Even then I did not remember those zombies, that bar – my mother and the darkness, caged.

11

So naïve. I thought I was wise. I thought I knew everything. But thirteen years after that moment in the snow I watched my mother get shot in the head. And I finally understood. I remembered. I got it.

I got it all.

CHAPTER 1

I was standing beside a former priest in the small secondary kitchen of a homeless shelter, trying to convince an old woman that marijuana was not a substitute for sugar, when a zombie pushed open the stainless-steel doors and announced that two detectives from the Seattle Police Department had arrived.

I listened. Heard pans banging, shouts from the other kitchen; the low, rumbling roar of voices in the dining hall, accompanied by classical music piped in for the lunch hour. Tchaikovsky's *Sleeping Beauty*. My choice for the day. Sounded pleasant with the rain pounding on the tin eaves, or the wind sighing against the cloudy window glass.

I heard no sirens. No dull echoes from police radios. No officious voices grumbling orders and questions. Some comfort. But on my skin, beneath the long sleeves of my leather jacket and turtleneck, the boys tossed in their sleep, restless and dreaming. Today, especially restless. Tingling since dawn. Not a good sign. When Zee and the others slept poorly, it usually meant someone needed to run. Someone, being me.

'Impossible,' Grant muttered. 'Did they say why they're here?'

'Not yet. Someone could have called.'

'Any idea who?'

'Take your pick,' Rex said, the demon in his aura fluttering wildly. 'You attract busybodies like gravity and a 34DD.'

The old woman was still ignoring us, and had begun humming a complicated melody of show tunes from *South Pacific*. A tiny person, skinny as a scrap of leather, with a nose that had been broken so many times it looked like a rock-slide. Pale, wrinkled skin, long hair white as snow. Wiry arms scarred with old needle tracks and covered in thick plastic bangles.

Mary, one of the shelter's permanent residents. A former heroin addict Grant had found living in a gutter more than a year ago. His special project. An experiment in progress.

I watched her lean over a red plastic bowl, filled to the brim with brownie mix and chocolate chips. Her right hand stirred the batter, a pair of long, wooden chopsticks sunk ineffectively into the mix, while her other hand held a glass jar packed with enough finely crushed weed to make an entire city block high for a week.

She peered through her eyelashes to see if Grant was looking – which he was, even though his back was slightly turned – and we both flinched as she dumped in another lump of the green leaves and started stirring faster.

'You need to get rid of that stuff,' I said. 'Split it between the garbage and the toilet.'

Grant's knuckles turned white around his cane. 'It could be a coincidence the police are here. Some of them stop to chat sometimes.'

'You willing to take that risk?'

'Flushing evidence won't take care of the basement.'

I looked down at the old leather of my cowboy boots, pretending to see past them into the cavernous underbelly of the warehouse shelter. Furniture used to be manufactured in this place. Some of the big sewing machines and leatherworks still gathered dust in those dim, dark spaces. Lots of places to hide down there. Rooms undiscovered.

One in particular, hidden behind some broken stairs. Found by accident, just this morning. Filled with heat lamps. Packed wall to wall with a jungle of carefully cultivated, highly illegal plants. A makeshift operation. And one old lady hip deep in the middle of it, singing to her green babies. Knitting little booties for real babies.

Crazy, charming, sweet old Mary. I had no idea

how she had managed to pull off an underground farm. She might have had help. Or been manipulated. Maybe she was just resourceful, highly motivated. Either way, there was a mess to clean up – and not just for Grant's sake, because he owned this shelter.

He liked Mary. He liked her enough to bend his moral backbone and risk his reputation – hold her hand and try to make things better. I felt the same. The old woman needed someone to make things better. No way she would survive jail. I knew it. He knew it. Not even handcuffs. Not a glint of them. Mary was like a butterfly wing. Rubbed the wrong way, and it would be scarred from flying.

'Sin is in the basement,' she warbled sweetly, oblivious. 'Turn on the light, Jesus. Shine, Lord, shine.'

The zombie laughed. It was an ugly, mocking sound, and I stared at Rex until he stopped. He tried to hold my gaze, but we had played this game for two months. Two months, circling each other. Fighting our instincts.

Rex looked away, leathery hands fidgeting as he adjusted the frayed red knit cap pulled low over his grizzled head. The high collar of his thick flannel coat hugged his coarse jaw. His host's skin was brown from a lifetime spent working under the sun. Palms callused, covered in fresh nicks and white scars. He wore his stolen body with ease, but the old ones, the deep possessors, always did. Wholly demon, in human flesh.

16

He was afraid of me. He hid it well, his human mask calm, but I could see it in the little things. I could taste it. Made the boys even more restless on my skin, but in a good way. We liked our zombies scared. We liked them better dead.

Grant gave the zombie a stern look and swayed close to my elbow, leaning hard on his carved wooden cane. Tall man, broad, his face too angular to be called pretty. Brown hair tumbled past the collar of his flannel shirt and thermal. His jeans were old, his eyes intense, brown as an old forest in the rain. He could be a wolf, another kind of hunter, but not like me. Grant was nicer than me.

'Maxine,' he rumbled. 'Think you can handle Mary?'

Sunset was still two hours away, which meant I could handle a nuclear blast, the bogeyman, and a vanful of clowns – all at once – but I hesitated anyway, studying the old woman. I grabbed the front of Grant's shirt, stood on my toes, and pressed my mouth against his ear. 'She likes you better.'

'She adores me,' he agreed, 'but I can deal with the police.'

I blew out my breath. 'What do I do with her?'

His hand crept up my waist, squeezing gently. 'Be kind.'

I pulled away, just enough to see his mouth soften into a rueful smile, and muttered, 'You trust me too much.'

'I trust you because I know you,' he whispered in my ear. 'And I love you, Maxine Kiss.'

17

Grant Cooperon. My magic bullet.

And it was going to kill me one day.

'Okay,' I told him weakly. 'Mary and I will be fine.'

He smiled and kissed my brow. Mary's singing voice cracked, and when I glanced around Grant's broad shoulder, I found the old woman glaring at me. She was not the only one. The zombie looked like he wanted to puke.

Whatever. My cheeks were hot. I cleared my throat and glanced at the flute case dangling over Grant's shoulder. 'You going to use your voodoo-hoodoo?'

'Just charm,' he said wryly, kissing me again on the cheek before limping from the small kitchen, his bad leg nearly twisting out from under him with every step. Rex gave me a quick look, like he wanted to say something, then shook his head and followed Grant past the swinging doors.

Faithful zombie, tracking the heels of his Pied Piper. My mother would turn in her grave if she had one. All my ancestors would. They would kill Grant. No second thoughts. Cold-blooded murder.

Stamping him out like any other threat to this world.

I glanced at Mary. She was licking brownie mix off her chopsticks – watching me warily. I tried to smile, but I had never been good at holding a smile, not when it mattered, not even for pictures, and all I managed was a slight twitch at the corner of my mouth. I gestured at the jar in her hand. 'Probably ought to put that away.'

Mary continued to stare. Zee stirred against the back of my neck – a clutching sensation, as though his tiny clawed heels were digging into my spine. It sent a chill through me; or maybe that was Mary, who suddenly stared with more clarity in her eyes, more uncertainty. As though she realized we were alone and that I might be dangerous.

She had good instincts. It made me wish I was better with words. Or that I knew how to be alone with one old woman and not feel homesick for something I could not name, but that made my throat ache as though I had been chewing bitterness so long, a lump the size of my heart was lodged like a rock behind my tongue.

'Mary,' I said again gently, and edged closer, wondering how I could get the jar out of her hand. I did not want to scare her, but I had to hurry. No matter what Grant said, I did not believe in coincidence. Odds were never that good. Not when it mattered.

Zee twitched. I ignored it, but a moment later my stomach started churning, like my bowels were going loose, and that was odd enough to make me stop in my tracks and listen to my body. Except for nerves, I never got sick. Not a single day in my life. Not a cough, not a fever, no vaccinations needed. I had an iron gut, too. Give me a food stand in Mexico with local water, old meat, some questionable cheese – and I would still walk away without a burp.

But this felt like the beginning of something. I rubbed my arms, my stomach. Zee shifted, tugging on my spine, then the others joined him – all over my body – and every inch of me suddenly burned like I had been dipped in nettle oil.

I swayed, leaning hard on the table. Mary flinched. I could not reassure her. I could not think. I was too stunned. And then I could do nothing at all, because pain exploded in my eyes, like a razor shaving tissue from my eye sockets. I bent over, pressing my fingers hard against my face. Digging in. Breathing through my mouth. My knees buckled.

Then, nothing. Pain stopped. All over my body, just like that. No warning.

I huddled, breathless, waiting for it to return. All I felt was an echo, burning through my skull and skin like a ghost. My heart hammered so hard I wanted to vomit. I was light-headed, dizzy. My upper lip tasted like blood. My nose was bleeding.

I sensed movement. Looked up, vision blurred with tears, and found Mary staring, chopsticks pointed in my direction like chocolate hallucinogenic magic wands. Her blue eyes were sharp. My knees trembled. Blood roared in my ears.

'Devil always comes knocking like a bastard,' she whispered.

I heard footsteps, the rough click of a cane. I snatched the jar of weed from Mary's hand, and ignored her squeak of protest as I hurried to the sink and dumped its contents down the trash disposal.

I turned on the faucet, flipped the switch – and while the disposal rattled, I dashed water on my face.

My gloves were still on. I grabbed a paper towel to swipe the blood from my nose and crumpled it in my fist, turning to face the swinging doors just as Rex pushed through.

His aura sang with a dark crown so thick and black it pulsed like a cloud of crude oil. Amazed me, again, that anyone in this world could be misled by his kind, that demons could take hosts and move so freely amongst their human prey and not one person blink an eye. I could not fathom such blindness. The danger of it.

Or why I let Grant continue his experiments with them.

He was just behind Rex. His eyes were wild, fierce, edged in shadow. Something had happened. When he walked in, his gaze slipped immediately to the crown of my head, searching. I knew he could tell from my aura that I was hurting. Grant started to speak, but I heard more footsteps, and he gave me a warning look just as two men walked in after him.

The detectives. I recognized them, even if I did not know their names. They were in their thirties, with close-shaven hair and neat suits. I was familiar with their faces because they stopped by the Coop every now and then to see Grant. Checking up on people. Using him as a sounding board. Once a priest, always a priest. Folks still trusted him to lend an ear.

The men stood a moment in silence, studying Mary and Rex. Then me. I tried to stay calm even though I felt like a deer caught in headlights. I disliked most

21

police. Not on principle. Most did good work. That was the problem. I had broken too many laws over the years to be comfortable around anyone with a badge.

I hoped I looked appropriately docile. I had cleaned up that morning, and my hair was pulled back. A bit of lipstick, some mascara. Nothing heavy. Not that I was trying to impress. I thought they had come for Mary. I was almost certain of it. I was scared for her. And Grant.

But I got a surprise.

'Maxine Kiss?' asked the detective on the left, a slender black man who kept his thumbs hooked lightly over his belt. He looked too by-the-book for such a relaxed posture, which made me think he wanted his hands near his gun and Mace. 'My name is Detective Suwanai, and this is my partner, McCowan. We have some questions for you.'

I stared, still feeling ill, head hurting. This did not help. The detectives should not have known me – or that I lived here. They might have spent some time at the shelter, but only a handful of people in Seattle, not including zombies, knew my real name. I had a fondness for aliases. I thought I made a good Annie. Reminded me of Sandra Bullock in *Speed*. Cheerful and competent. I was working on the cheerful part.

'I'm listening,' I said, fighting for composure. Very worried. Thinking, maybe, I should have denied being Maxine Kiss. No proof, no reality. But it was too late. My big mouth.

McCowan was several inches taller than his partner and about ten pounds heavier. Pale, cute like a frat boy, with a soft jaw that was going to drop into his neck within the next several years. His gaze flickered from Grant to me. 'What's your relationship with Brian Badelt?'

'I don't know who that is,' I replied.

'You've never heard of him?'

'Never.'

Detective Suwanai made a big show of pulling a photograph from his pocket. He flicked it toward me, and I leaned in. I was not surprised to see a corpse, but I was not happy about it, either. A headshot, taken on a stainless-steel examining table. Badelt was an older man, with a lean face and white hair. Straight nose, strong chin. He looked like a hard-ass even in death, but I might have liked him. Nothing wrong with being straightforward.

'I don't recognize him,' I said.

'What's this about?' Grant asked, and there was a melodic quality to his voice that I recognized. Power. Zee told me once that his voice tickled, but that was a gentle way of putting it. Anyone who could control a demon, who could change the very *nature* of a demon, did more than just . . . tickle.

It concerned me. I always worried when Grant used his power. There were too few lines before a push became possession. Such small lines between dark and light. Grant was still learning that. I suppose we both were.

23

Suwanai and McCowan stiffened slightly, an odd light shifting through their eyes: a trace of emptiness, a deep hollow. It lasted only a moment, but when they started blinking again, Suwanai said, 'Badelt's body was found in an alley off University Avenue. He was shot to death.'

Grant looked down, jaw flexing. I briefly closed my eyes. 'Why come to me?'

McCowan hesitated, but Grant made a low noise in his throat, a soft humming tone, and the detective shook his head, frowning. He touched his brow. 'There was a newspaper in his pocket. One of the daily Chinatown rags. Your name was written on it. We're following up.'

Suwanai also rubbed his forehead. 'Where were you last night, Ms Kiss? From midnight on?'

'I was here,' I said.

'With me,' Grant added.

'You're sure?' Suwanai pressed.

'We were naked,' I told him. 'I remember.'

McCowan grunted, glancing at Grant with some surprise. Then his gaze returned to me, flickering up and down my body. Assessing.

I kept my mouth shut. A man was dead. A man I did not know, but who had written down my name. And now I was a suspect. None of that made me feel good. Or particularly sexy.

Grant gave McCowan a hard look. 'Who was Mr Badelt?'

'You don't need to know that,' Suwanai replied.

24

'You're aware I have contacts. I could help.'
Grant's voice was calm, persuasive. I folded my arms
across my chest, hiding the tension in my hands.
Mary stood very still, doing an excellent job of
looking like a sane, innocent, elderly woman, while
Rex hung back by the refrigerator, blending with the
shadows. Watching. No doubt hoping I got stuck in
the slammer.

McCowan said, 'Badelt was a private investigator.'

Pressure gathered behind my eyes. I wanted to ask
who he had been looking for, but the name on the
newspaper was bad enough. The fact that he was
dead, worse.

McCowan stepped toward the kitchen doors. He
looked confused, a bit uneasy. I did not blame him.
Suwanai seemed more together, but maybe he was
just a better pretender. He smoothed down his suit
jacket with his dark, elegant hands. 'Ms Kiss, do you
have any idea why a murdered private investigator
might have your name in his pocket?'

'No,' I said firmly. 'I do not.'

Suwanai hesitated, studying my eyes. I let him. I
had not killed anyone in Seattle. Not yet. Not anyone
human, at least.

After a moment, he inclined his head. 'If we have
any more questions . . .'

'Of course,' Grant said gently, ever the upstanding
citizen. The detective nodded, still frowning, rubbing
the bridge of his nose as though the gesture comforted
– or pained – him. He did not look back as he pushed

25

open the kitchen doors, but McCowan did. Just once, at me. A furrow edged between his eyebrows. I met his gaze, unblinking, and after a moment he ducked his head and let the doors swing shut behind him.

I remained very still, afraid they would come back – but when they did not, I slowly, carefully, released my breath. Grant limped near, wrapping his arm around my waist. He drew me back against his chest. I stayed there, grateful.

'This is all wrong,' I said quietly. 'Not just the murder, but the fact a dead man had my name.'

'And that the police found you here,' Grant replied.

We both looked at Rex. He stared back, holding up his tanned, scarred hands. 'I had nothing to do with it.'

'You must know something.'

'No way. I'm not in the loop anymore.'

'You're all in the loop,' I muttered. 'I don't care how dried up your umbilical cord is.'

Rex stared at me like I was viler than a splat of diarrhea. 'You just don't care, period. You're still looking for an excuse to kill me, Hunter.'

'I don't need an excuse.' I tugged sharply on my gloves. Mary stared, but I no longer cared if she saw my tattoos.

Rex, despite his bravado, stepped back. Grant grabbed my arm. 'No time, Maxine.'

I did not relax. 'I need to find out what Badelt wanted, why he had my name.' I hesitated, thinking hard. 'He was in that alley for a reason.'

A man who worked for himself would not waste his time in a part of town that had no good bars, entertainment, or restaurants only a poor university student could love. It had rained last night, too – a hard, cold rain that had pounded most of the garden into a limp green shag of grass and leaves. Not good weather for walking the street just for the fun of it.

Grant seemed to read my mind. 'A lot of homeless live on University Ave. Someone might have seen Badelt. Or we could track down his office first, look for answers there.'

That was the smart thing to do, but I needed air, some time alone. My skin still crawled, and not just because of the boys. 'I'll head down to the university. You make the call. No one's going to tell you much, though. Confidentiality issues.' Not unless Grant went in person. His special brand of persuasion did not work over the phone.

'It wouldn't have been one of us,' Rex chimed in, and I knew what he was really saying. No demon, no zombie, would hire a private investigator to hunt me. It would be like paying money to find Mount Everest. If Mount Everest had teeth and claws and could eat people.

Which meant someone human wanted to find me.

Or maybe I had already been found.

I thought about my mother. Her lessons. She had taught me not to keep friends, to avoid roots. Born a loner, trained to be one. Safer that way, for everyone. No home but the boys.

27

But here I was. Hunter and hunted. With friends. A home and roots. My taste of the forbidden fruit. And I could never return to what was, what had always been – what should have been. I knew the difference now. I was too weak to give it up.

I stood on my toes, kissed Grant hard on the mouth – and glanced over his shoulder from Rex to Mary, who still watched us, eyes narrowed. Withered mouth creased into a frown.

'I'm sorry about your jar,' I said to her, and she hitched up her shoulders, the crease between her eyes deepening.

'Go with Gabriel,' she whispered. 'Gabriel's hounds will guide you.'

I had no idea what that meant, but Grant gave her a sharp look. A chill swept through me. My stomach felt odd. I had the terrible feeling I had just been thrust upon the proverbial crossroad, and had stumbled blindly onto a path that fairy tales warned about, the hard kind that showed the way to an enchanted castle, a forest of brambles, quicksand, and pits full of hungry dragons. A path that led to either death or glory. Neither of which interested me.

I had seen enough death. I had suffered glory.

Now I just wanted to be left alone.

CHAPTER 2

EVERY now and then while I was growing up, my mother would turn down the radio, and say, 'There's one thing you need to know about demons, baby. It may keep you alive.'

I would listen, even though I knew what was coming. I loved listening to my mother. She tried hard, even though our lives were frightening, to control the horror. To feed it to me in bits and pieces so that I could sleep at night and not dread the next forty-odd years of my life. And though she left some things out, she managed to tell me enough, in her own way, to keep me going.

My mother was a lady. And while she almost never used foul language, when she shut off the music, that was the one time she always broke her rule.

'Demons are bad motherfuckers,' my mother

29

would say. 'And as such, must be handled with care. Ourselves included.'

I drove the Mustang in the rain. It was only late afternoon, but the clouds were so thick and dark with storm, the headlights from opposing traffic burned like lighthouse beacons in my newly sensitive eyes. I rubbed them, remembering pain. I could still taste my blood.

Seattle in winter was an awful place to be. Always wet, hardly a glimpse of the sun except on rare days when it burned briefly free and rained down rays of precious ghostly light; or at night, when clouds slivered and stars glittered, and the moon, when it rose, glowed.

The only good thing about the weather was that it suited my wardrobe: long sleeves, high necks, jeans, and gloves. I never showed skin. Nothing but my face, and even that was a concession to vanity. My face, from the top of my neck to my hairline: the only part of my body not covered in tattoos. Part of my deal with the boys, the same deal generations of my ancestors had made. Our way of blending in with society. An illusion of normality.

I stayed under the speed limit. The Mustang was a target for traffic cops: red and gleaming like Snow White's poison apple. Classic sixties fastback, with a backseat custom-designed to be more comfortable for the boys. Leather buckets, retrofitted stereo, chrome detailing. An engine with thunder in its veins. Very sharp. I loved my car.

Teddy bears filled the back, most of them dismembered. Empty bags from various fast-food joints covered the floor, along with a sack of nails, bolts, and screws. Snack food. Tasty, I had been told, with jalapeño sauce and fries.

Steve Perry wailed on the radio. I turned down the volume, and the rhythmic beat of the windshield wipers took over. I was still in the warehouse district, a crumbling neighborhood of pale concrete, shattered sidewalks, and broken windows. Too much chain link. I had lived here almost two months and seen businesses come and go – artsy types, mostly. Cheap rent. Bare-bones revival and decay. The Coop, Grant's homeless shelter, was one of the few living fixtures in this fringe area of Seattle's downtown.

Zee tugged on my skin as I drove. All the boys did. Felt like bits of my body trying to peel away. Not a good sign. Like I needed another. I touched my nose, rubbing the outer edge of my left eye. My heart beat faster. I saw words in my head, my mother's neat script. She had kept journals. Big ones, leather-bound, with thick heavy paper that still smelled like incense and rosewater. I hauled them around in the Mustang for five years after she died. Now they sat in a carved wooden chest on the wooden floor of a warehouse apartment.

I knew every word. Every syllable and curve. I could still feel the imprint of her fingers through the indents of ink on the stiff pages, and the grooves –

sometimes, when I was very nostalgic – felt sacred. As though her soul resided in paper.

I recalled that my mother wrote about pain. Odd, unordinary aches. She kept copious notes. It was probably time I did the same. Not for posterity, but survival. One day someone else would need to learn from my experiences. Written words would be my only voice after I was murdered. The only thing I could pass on, besides the boys.

Such as this fact: My mother suffered only one bloody nose in her entire life. Accompanied by temporary blindness, sharp pain in her eyes.

She wrote that down, made a point of it. A separate chapter. Because afterward, a lot of people died. Afterward, she almost died.

Unfortunately, except for those small tidbits, the rest of the story was lost. She had gotten rid of it, ripped the pages out. Before I was born, I suppose.

But not everything. One line, just before the break in her discourse. Like a ticking bomb found under an airplane seat, or cold laughter when you thought you were alone.

The veil opened, wrote my mother. *The veil opened, and something slipped through.*

SOMETHING always slipped through.

No good explanation. Just that long ago, demons lived upon the earth. Many demons. They killed and consumed, and there was a war. People fought back. Humans. Others who were not human. They built a prison out of air, a prison made of layers and rings and boundaries, and they placed the demons inside, separating them by strength and viciousness and intelligence.

And then they sealed the demons up. Forever.

Except, nothing lasted forever. Not even the boys, though they had spent the past ten thousand years giving it their best shot.

Someone must have figured as much. Someone who could make a difference. Someone who created the Wardens, men and women with the speed and power to guard this world against a break in the prison veil. Humans, constructed to fight demons.

Humans, destined to save the world.

But the Wardens had not survived, either. They did not have the boys.

Leaving me. The last.

The women in my family had always been the last.

And the veil had opened.

Again.

HERE was another truth: I had spent my entire life on the road. I never went to school. My mother taught me, and based on some things I had seen over the years, I would say she did a pretty good job. We always hit the bookstores and libraries in every city and small town, and I learned to tell a lot about a place by the kinds of books that were carried, or the attention given a library. The best I had ever seen was in New York City. The worst in Paoli, Indiana.

Seattle was not so bad. But the bookstores downtown cared more about literary fiction than commercial reads, and that was indicative, I thought, of the social atmosphere. Yuppie, a little too pre-occupied with what other people thought, and only superficially friendly.

The number of homeless kids was another strike against the city. University Avenue was the worst. Maybe not as bad as Rio de Janeiro, but for the United States, it was up there. And two hours after leaving the Coop – two hours spent walking the streets in the rain, trying to uncover answers – I found myself in a dark alley off the Ave, near the sprawling Gothic splendor of the University of Washington, a child huddled near my feet.

A lot of children. Rain had driven them into door-ways, under tattered awnings, or here, in alleys, under cardboard and garbage bags. I smelled dog, and saw a ruffed brown tail sticking out from under a slicker, alongside gangling limbs and pierced noses and glit-tering eyes. Tattoos rocked the shadows. Not mine. My clothes still covered me from neck to toe, my fingers snug in my gloves.

I had ten minutes left. Sunset was coming. I could feel it on my skin. Streetlights were already on, sour fluorescent lines seeping into the alley. Storm clouds had not abated, and were so low and thick with shadow and rain and fog, it could have already been night.

I blinked rain from my eyelashes and crouched.

34

Peered into a box shoved tight against the Dumpster, and found a pair of eyes like snow and stone: white and gray, framed in black eyeliner. Boy. Hardly fourteen. Not old enough to grow more than a weak black fuzz on the tip of his chin. He wore a thick coat and jeans with holes in the knees.

His aura was clean. No demon inside his soul. Not a zombie. Just messed up, all regular.

'Hey,' I said gently, wishing I had a photo of Badelt. One taken while he was alive. 'I'd like to ask some questions, if that's all right.'

The boy had sharp eyes. Old as dirt. He studied me, and I held still, unblinking, counting seconds as my skin tingled and tugged. Sun going down. Somewhere, beyond the dark clouds.

'You're not a cop,' said the boy quietly.

'Kid,' I replied carefully, 'the last thing I am is a cop. But I *do* need information. A man was murdered around here last night. His name was Brian Badelt. White hair, long face.'

Just five blocks away. Yellow police tape still in place, and a cruiser parked at the entrance. Forensics team not done yet, apparently. I had walked past, collar pulled up, and gotten a quick look – just as any curious passerby might. Seen nothing except slick concrete and shadows, and the memory of a dead man's face. No answers in that. Nothing that could help me understand why he had my name, or whether he was looking for me. And if so, why that search had brought him here.

I wanted to know if he died because of that search. Because of me.

Maybe the crime-scene investigators already had the answers. Or not. Over the past two hours, I had learned that police had already approached most of the transients living on this street. Based on the almost nonexistent levels of cooperation I had received, I doubted Suwanai, McCowan, or their crew had discovered much. Not unless they played dirty, something I was unprepared to do. Adults and kids had enough problems, homeless or not.

But I saw something in the boy's eyes. Gave me a feeling the others had not. He had a softer gaze. Like the streets had not quite driven the sweetness from him. Made my heart hurt. Made me want to do something I should not.

'I saw him,' whispered the boy, and all around us, eyes slit open, glints of cold steel in wet shadow. His admission surprised me more than it should have. So much that I had to take a moment and replay those words in my head, testing them for what I thought he had said. *I saw him. I saw, I saw.*

My skin prickled. My skin moved. I rocked back on my heels and wanted to close my eyes and hug the boy, hold my breath in case he turned to smoke and disappeared. 'What did you see?'

He hesitated, and though tucked at the back of the box, I was certain he felt the other children staring. All of them, listening.

Plastic rattled. Feet shuffled. His gaze flicked past

my shoulder. I glanced behind and found a young woman. She had skin the color of a ghost, pale and flawless, with studs running the rims of her ears, in her nose, inside her tongue. Black eyes, black spiked hair dripping with rain. Canvas fatigues hugged her body. Brass knuckles flashed. So did the edge of a blade. Tough chick. Nice style.

I turned my back and peered into the box. I had minutes at most. No time for a pissing contest. Not with a kid.

'Help me, and I'll help you,' I told the boy. Rain seeped down my collar, against my skin. I did not feel it. The water absorbed too quickly into my tattoos. Faster now. Heat spread beneath my turtleneck and jacket, down my stomach across my legs. My fingers burned.

The boy stared, gaze torn, cheeks hollow. Like a ghost, biting the edge of living; unseen, unknown, unsure. Something hard tapped my skull. Brass knuckles. I ignored the girl and continued watching the boy in the box. He knew something more than just the murder. I could see it in his eyes. He knew.

The girl hit me again. I felt no pain, just the impact against my shoulder, which sent me down, gloved palms slamming into wet cement. If I were only human, she might have broken something with that blow. Rain ran into my mouth and eyes. I licked my lips.

'Stop asking questions,' hissed the girl, leaning near. 'Or you'll stop breathing.'

I turned my head and looked into her eyes. Beyond the girl, at the alley mouth, cars passed in the pounding rain, headlights shining. Men and women appeared fleetingly, walking fast with hands full of backpacks and umbrellas, heads bowed. *See no evil. Suffer none at all.* Such a thin veneer, between there and here. So easy to cast illusions. Especially when people were afraid to see the truth.

I could see the truth in the girl's eyes. She was scared, but serious. She would hurt me if I did not walk away. She would make life difficult. Made me wonder if something similar had happened to Badelt. I wondered, too, what she would do to the boy for talking. What someone *else* would do.

I blinked, and the girl flashed her teeth. Then her knife. It was very small, not much longer than her palm. Hardly a toothpick. She saw me studying the weapon and smiled, like she had won.

Inside me, the sun. Going, almost gone. No time. Not for niceties. No time to be kind.

I grabbed the knife. Snatched a fistful of blade and it punctured my leather glove. Steel scraped my tattooed palm and made a terrible sound. The knife snapped. Hit the cement between us, but the rain drowned the clatter, and the alley was dark.

The girl saw, though. She saw and stared, and I grabbed the back of her jacket, moving fast, marching her to the mouth of the alley. She tried to fight me. Slammed my ribs with her brass knuckles. Made an impact like a baby's kiss. I dragged her to the sidewalk and rain ran down my face. My skin hissed. Sunset. The sun.

'Why are you doing this?' I asked the girl harshly. 'Who has you scared?'

'Fuck off,' she snarled, and grabbed my breast, fingers digging in and twisting. I felt no pain, but it shocked me. It was a surprisingly dirty tactic for a kid so young. Maybe one that had been used on her. The possibility made me sick.

'I can help you,' I said, but she spat on me, a big, fat goober on my jacket, and that was it. No more time. 'Fine. Walk away. Don't look back.'

She hesitated longer than she should have. Something to lose, something driving her. I wished I had time to ask. I wished I had a choice, but I could not stay here and keep an eye on the boy. I could not risk the girl continuing to engage me. Not now.

I squeezed my fingers until she cried out, and forced myself to hold on, making certain she got the message.

Be more afraid of me.

She was. I saw the shift when it happened: in her eyes, in her mouth. Her whole demeanor, small like a kitten in the jaws of a Rottweiler. Bitterness filled me. I hated this. I hated it all. Monster, me. Scaring little girls, little broken girls. All of us, lost little girls.

I loosened my fingers. The teen broke away without a word. She turned, walked fast, and did not look back. Neither did I. I ran like hell, furious at myself. Sick at heart.

I did not go far. I had burned that bridge thirty minutes ago by not returning to the Mustang and sitting in the parking garage, twiddling my thumbs over a book or talking to Grant on the phone, digging up dirt, putting our heads together. I pushed. I waited too long. Now I was in public.

It was dark for sunset, unusually so, which was all I had in my favor. I slid between the bumpers of two parked cars – a battered Volkswagen and muscular SUV – and slumped on my hands and knees, the ends of my hair dipped in rainwater. No streetlights in this section. No windows full of light. Only shadows – and me, just one more shuddering body collapsed on a street full of them. I heard people walk past. No one slowed. I hoped no one saw. I hoped they were blind. I hoped I was not screwed.

Somewhere, the sun went down. I felt the horizon swallow, the push of heat in my own throat, as though inside me the darkness, the vast space of night and the stars spinning between my ribs. My tattoos began to peel. The boys woke up.

Hurt like it should. Skin tearing. Flayed by smoke and shadows. I swallowed bad noises, throat aching, and tore off my gloves. Shook so hard my teeth chattered. Minutes ago, tattoos would have covered my hands – fingers, palms, even my nails – black and etched with lines. But now bodies writhed, silver skin dissolving into a mist that poured from beneath my clothes, and I felt hearts pound that were not my own. Slender, muscled limbs slid hot and heavy through my hair. Small fingers caressed my cheeks. Melodic whispers mated with the patter of rain.

Endless rain. Chilling, soaking my clothes, heavy and tight. I felt discomfort. Acute discomfort. The cold and wind, an ache in my knees from the hard concrete. My palms were frozen. My nose ran. I could hardly think.

My skin was human again. So very human. Hit, I would break. Stabbed, I would bleed. Shot, strangled, drowned: I could be killed now. I was human, until dawn. Vulnerable, until then. Mortal.

'Maxine,' whispered Zee. 'Sweet Maxine.'

I sat up, scraping my shoulders against cold, slick car bumpers. Three little bodies crouched before me, lost in the dark wet shadows. Zee, Aaz, and Raw. Skin the color of soot smeared with silver and mercury, lean and warm. Steam drifted from the razor scales of their bristling spines and spindly arms – two arms, two legs – claws instead of fingers and toes. Their feet were vaguely human, as were their rakish faces, angular to the point of pain. I smelled fire, leather – something else I could not name, but which smelled like my mother. A scent that had always been home.

My home. Their home. Until it was time.

Never enough time. I tried to stand, but my body ached. I took a moment. Purrs rumbled against my ears, little tongues scraping skin. Dek and Mal, their long serpentine bodies wrapped around my neck as they snaked under my jacket to fish through my inner

41

pockets. They had no legs, and only two arms – vestigial limbs good for little more than grasping my ears. Heads shaped like hyenas, with smiles to match. Best little bodyguards on earth.

Dek and Mal found the teddy bears I had stashed for them – dopey little things the length of my finger, attached to key chains. I heard crunching, wet smacks. Tiny giggles. The boys liked to eat bears. I had to order in bulk. I never took them to the zoo. Poor damn grizzlies.

Zee hugged my arm, rubbing his cheek against my coat as the silver needles of his hair shimmered and cut the leather like butter. 'Bad dreams, Maxine. Bad as bones.'

'Tell me.' I watched Aaz and Raw slink away on their bellies, red eyes blinking lazily. They could have been dragons, wolves; or both, caught in limbo. Perfect twins, except for the faint patch of silver on the tip of Raw's chin. They disappeared beneath the SUV. I pulled several Snickers from my jacket. Tossed them into the shadows and heard a faint cheer.

I gave one to Zee. His claws dragged trenches in the concrete as he swallowed the bar whole, wrapper and all.

'Your dreams,' I reminded him. 'They hurt me this afternoon.'

He hesitated. 'No choice. Something in the air. Something coming. Had to warn you.'

'The veil.'

'Cutters. Hot slicers.'

Demons. Something larger than zombie parasites. I had already guessed as much. I looked him in the eye. 'Give me more.'

'More,' he echoed softly, tearing his gaze from mine. 'More is coming. More is ending. Maxine. Sweet Maxine.'

He stopped. His silence was final. I unclenched my hands. No good pushing. Zee had a habit of riddles. Unfortunately, he was the only one of his brothers who could hold a human conversation. Far as I knew.

I glanced over my shoulder, shoving the gloves in my pocket. People were coming. I heard laughter, the slap of shoes in puddles. Rain on umbrellas. Nice. Normal.

'We're hunting,' I told Zee. 'Big trouble.'

'In Little China,' he crooned. Such a goof. He loved movies. Missed the eighties. And the Crusades, though I had yet to figure out that one. Might have been the armor. He had a thing for crunchy meals.

Zee flashed white teeth, a tongue long and black, and melted into the shadows beneath his feet. Gone in a wink. No idea what lay on the other side of a shadow but had a feeling I was better off not knowing. I did not worry about whether Raw and Aaz would follow. The boys had a system.

I stood. Got some looks from passersby. Nothing serious. No one ran or screamed. No one ever had. I gave a good face, dressed nice, stayed clean – kept the demons and tattoos out of sight. It took so little

43

to hide the big secrets. Not that anyone would ever imagine an army of demons living on one woman's skin. If they even believed demons existed.

I thought of Badelt. Got a bad feeling in my gut.

I walked back to the alley. Dek and Mal remained sleek and heavy on my shoulders, the turtleneck collar hiding their bodies while their sleek, tufted heads stayed tucked out of sight within my hair. A sharp observer might see some glint of a red eye, but only as a figment of light and fancy. Not demon. Not animal.

I looked for zombies. Checked auras for dark spots. This was a good part of town for parasites. The human crush, seeping with heartache. All the pain a dark spirit required to stay alive.

Emotions made energy. Energy was food. That violence could beget violence was no joke. It took a particular breed of demon to create zombies, but the cracks in the veil had grown over the last century, making it easier for them to slip free from their prison in the first ring of the veil. Once here, they infected humans who were emotionally vulnerable. Turned them into puppets, living tools. Mindless shells. Good for trouble, abuse – self-inflicted or dished out. Charmers, all of them. Subtle.

A zombie would kill you with a smile. Smiles made everything sweeter.

Dek and Mal hissed in my ear. I glanced over my shoulder and saw a man and woman some distance behind me, strolling down the sidewalk. Despite the apparent differences in gender, they both wore dark slacks and slick wind blazers that strained against their broad shoulders. Intense eyes stared from thick faces with ruddy cheeks. Identical bulges distorted the sides of their jackets.

Really big cell phones, maybe. Urban missionaries, roving the night to aid the helpless. Innocent. Utterly harmless. Wonder Twins.

I reached the alley. Stopped, staring. I had been away less than five minutes.

The children were gone. All of them. Bodies had huddled against the brick and concrete, and now those same spaces were empty. Plastic bags fluttered like ghosts; cardboard boxes stood battered and crushed like stormed castles. An eerie absence, cutting. I wanted to hold my stomach.

A man stood in front of me. He was young and blond, like the others, and smelled of cigars. Built like a bull. Would have looked more at home in furs, with a club in one hand. Modern times were not for everyone.

He told me not to move. He had a Russian accent. I did not say a word. I could not have cared less about conversation. I was thinking about those kids, especially the boy. I had gotten him, maybe all of them, in trouble. I had brought shit down on their heads.

The man pulled out a cell phone. He spoke into it. I did not understand Russian, but I got the drift. I felt movement behind me and found the Wonder

Twins. They held guns. Nearby, Zee and the others watched from the shadows, red eyes glinting like rubies. Dek and Mal rumbled in my ears.

I took a step. Trigger fingers tightened. If they tightened any more, the Wonder Twins would be dead. I looked back at the fellow with the cell phone. 'The children. Where are they?'

He ignored me. A car engine roared, and a pair of headlights pulled in to the end of the alley. A limo. The door opened from inside. No one got out. I could not see who sat within.

Everything, my mother used to say, *is connected*.

And I could, on occasion, be a very patient woman.

The man gestured with his gun. Shadows filled the limo. The boys always liked going for a ride.

I got in.

CHAPTER 3

A N old man sat inside the limo. He wore a suit.
Thick black glasses perched on the end of his
nose. He was bald. He was a zombie.

The man with the cell phone began to get in after
us, but the zombie held up his hand and said a word
in Russian. The blond hesitated, backed away, and
shut the door. The limo started moving. I opened the
minibar and took out a ginger ale. I needed something sweet.

The zombie watched me, a smile curling the corner
of his mouth. He was a small, spindly man, swallowed by the immense seat across from me. His eyes
were cold, his aura black. Older and more deadly
than most. Higher up the food chain. But he should
have been running. Engagement with me was a death
sentence. Usually.

Which meant he had something on me. I had a bad feeling what that was.

'Hunter Kiss,' said the zombie. 'So infamous. How very interesting finally to meet you in the flesh.'

'Sure,' I replied, sipping my drink. 'I'm popular tonight.'

His smile widened. 'You look like your mother.'

My fingers tightened around the can. The zombie took off his glasses and rubbed the edge of his suit jacket against the lens. 'Your mother never cared for pleasantries, either. Beautiful woman. But then, your family has always been striking.' He slipped his glasses back on and blinked, owlishly. 'I assume your wards are nearby?'

I snapped my fingers. Zee, Aaz, and Raw coalesced from the shadows. They sat beside me, all in a row, legs too short for the leather seat. In unison, they swung their clawed feet, hands clasped in their laps. Deceptively prim. Little smart-asses. I opened the minibar, and Zee pointed to the whiskey and vodka. I passed out the bottles.

The zombie raised his brow. 'How endearing.'

'You have no idea.' I felt my heart sink into a dark, hard place. 'Are you responsible for the disappearance of those children in the alley?'

'I am responsible for many things. But not that.' He tilted his head, watching Zee and the others with a curious – and rather unnatural – lack of fear. 'I did, however, retrieve *one* of them. A boy. That boy you took such interest in.'

The zombie had been watching me. All that time, I never knew it. 'You think I care?'

He laughed. 'My dear, your mother had the heart of a lion, but you, merely a lamb. You care. You care too much.'

Dek and Mal poked their heads from my hair. Raw tipped whiskey into their small mouths. I wanted to take the bottle and smash it across the zombie's human head. And then exorcise the hell out of him.

'The boy,' I said. 'If you hurt him—'

'That would not be in my interest. He is my protection. Against you.'

'A man died last night. Were you involved in that, too?'

A faint smile touched his mouth. 'There are many players in the game, Hunter. How many watch you from the shadows, you may never know.'

That was a bad answer. I wanted to tap my foot, but kept my leg still. The limo felt like a cage. 'What do you want?'

'Conversation. Nothing more. You have my word, on the blood of my Queen.'

I leaned back. Zee stilled. 'Blood Mama sent you?'

The zombie's expression never changed, but his throat bobbed, and his aura flickered. 'She has concerns.'

I held my breath. Blood Mama was the ruler of the first prison ring, and a true zombie queen, more powerful than all her children combined – and she

49

grew more powerful with every soul her children inhabited. The pain they made was the pain she felt, and it fed a hunger that never ended, and never would.

I had met her. I had crossed the veil itself to face her presence. Given myself up, allowed my body to be dragged into the prison. To save Grant. Blood Mama had tried to possess him. She had come close. So close to taking everything I cared about. Again.

Blood Mama had ordered the murder of my mother.

She had ordered the deaths of all the women in my line. She would order my murder, when it was time. A decision entirely dependent on Zee and the others. My boys. My friends. Who would abandon me one day in favor of some distant, future daughter – whoever she might be. And when that happened, when I no longer had their protection, Blood Mama would know. All the zombies would know. I could almost hear the rifles being loaded.

Not that I let it get me down. Not that I had abandoned hope. I was not afraid. Not anymore – though I remembered those days. I remembered being terrified. Scared of possibilities. Some distant, future pregnancy, which would start the clock ticking down the seconds of my life.

Some in my bloodline had tried to avoid sex entirely, determined to elude their fates. But children were how Zee and the others survived. Celibacy was the same as their murder. And if a Hunter would not willingly procreate . . . the boys, so I had been told, would force the issue.

And that was something I tried never to think about.

'I want to see the boy,' I told the zombie. 'And give me the name of your host.'

'Edik Bashmakov.' He tipped his head to me. 'And you may *not* see the child until our business is complete. I cannot take the risk.'

Glass broke. Aaz was eating the vodka bottle. 'No trust? I'm willing to take *you* at your word.'

He shrugged; a delicate movement, infinitely refined. 'You are the Hunter and you have no bounds, no allegiance. No one you answer to. Your word has no honor.'

I imagined my hand on his forehead, sucking the demon free. 'And you? Possessing human bodies? Feeding on suffering? Is *that* honor?'

'It is survival,' he replied calmly. 'Do not judge us by human values. You, who pretend to walk amongst them. You, who are only half a breed, some glorified prison guard. You, lonely little Warden.'

Zee rested his claws against my knee and stared at Edik. The zombie lowered his gaze. 'This will not take long, Hunter. Then I will go, and you will have the boy. Agreed?'

I could have set Zee and the others upon him. Exorcised the demon from that human body and tortured it into speaking. My mother had taught me the trick. But I thought, perhaps, that was a line I did not feel like crossing tonight. And I did have *some* honor.

I drank my ginger ale. The boys pressed close, clinging. My eyes ached. Outside, the limo drifted into a neighborhood of warehouses, rusty steel. I smelled the ocean. I thought of Grant. We were near him.

'Tell me why I'm here,' I said.

Edik's aura flickered. 'The veil. It opened tonight. You felt it.'

'Do you know what came through?' It would not have been Blood Mama or her brood. Zombie-makers did not need to wait for the veil to open.

Edik said nothing; unmoving, not one muscle, not a twitch, though his aura burned. Either he did not know or did not want to say. I took another sip of ginger ale. 'What does your Queen want?'

The zombie slid his hands down his thighs, resting his palms on his knees. 'I think you know, Hunter. The prison is failing. When it does, this world will die.'

No mystery, no surprise. A logical conclusion, one I had been trying to ignore for the last decade. But I had never heard it said quite so bluntly. 'I can't imagine why you're warning me. You're a demon. Prison goes down, you win.'

Edik's flickering aura was the only thing about him not perfectly, coldly, calm. Even his eyes, hard as steel. If bullets could have been made from disdain,

52

I might have died in that moment from a shot through the head.

'You are so naïve,' he said.

'Am I?' I replied. 'Wow.'

Edik's mouth tightened with displeasure. 'You have no idea what rests in the prison rings. My kind are vermin to the others, less than demon. Rats chasing the tails of wolves.'

Demon politics. Something I had not considered. Maybe I was naïve. 'You think I care? All I want to know is what came through the veil.'

'Calculation,' he said mysteriously. 'A pawn, a scout.'

The ginger ale suddenly felt like acid in my stomach. 'What else? How do I find this demon?'

'Only my Queen knows.' Edik hesitated. 'She was used, Hunter. She was used in the service of another. Forced to make a bargain, to facilitate the passage of this pawn.'

'No one forces Blood Mama into anything.'

Edik looked away, a muscle twitching in his face. 'Our brethren in the veil will destroy us, you know. They will kill us when they break free. They will consume us. But before they do, before all the walls fall and the First Ward crumbles, and the Reapers rape the bones of this world, the others will have their way with your humans – and no matter what you think of Blood Mama and her brood, we are *nothing* compared to them.'

I said nothing. I sat very still. Except for my fingers,

making a dent in the soda can. Blood Mama had chosen well. Edik Bashmakov had talent. He was a true connoisseur, a professional, at the art of imparting bad news. I admired his skill. I no longer felt quite so eager to kill him.

More like I wanted to run screaming for the hills and never look back.

'Ten thousand years of peace.' Edik stared at his withered hands. 'The prison has been our blessing.'

I exhaled slowly. Tried to act cool, dispassionate, but inside, my gut roiled, and my muscles felt hacked with chills. I wanted to pull some covers over my head. Go find a tall mountain and hide in a cave. I wanted to call Edik a liar and a fool and pretend I was a normal woman, a blind woman, a deaf woman – a happy, ignorant, breezy woman.

I stared out the car window. Caught my distorted reflection: pale skin, dark hair. I wondered what it felt like to be possessed and not realize it, to have someone living inside your head, manipulating your mind until your body was nothing but a tool.

I felt like a tool. Like I was about to be used.

Zee and the others scooted close, resting their heads in my lap. I rubbed their razor hair and watched Edik's face, his aura. He had met my mother and survived. I wanted to know how, but I did not ask. I was becoming afraid of answers.

'What does Blood Mama expect me to do?' I asked carefully, never once doubting what he had told me was true. His aura could not lie. He had meant every

54

word. Something bad was coming. Something had arrived.

'Blood Mama did not say,' he replied smoothly. 'But as you are the Hunter, and better suited than most to killing my kind, you might consider the possibility that she expects you to continue what you are best at.'

My mouth crooked. 'I could start with you.'

He pushed his glasses up his nose, an effortlessly normal gesture, given the appallingly abnormal circumstances. 'Hunter, I am the least of your concerns. This is the end of the world.'

'And you're still holding something back.'

He hesitated. 'My Queen had another message.'

I waited a beat. 'And?'

He suddenly looked uncomfortable. 'It is for them.'

I stared. Raw stopped picking his nose, and Aaz sat up from my lap. Zee leaned forward, his scales cutting leather. Even Dek and Mal slid from my hair, their tails tightening around my throat as Raw reached back to stroke their soft heads. I slid the ginger ale into a cup holder and said nothing.

Edik looked at the boys. Sweat beaded on his brow, and his feet shifted against the limo carpet. Zee stretched close. Watching him felt like the first blush of a hurricane. He curled when he moved, pulsed and glided and shimmered like wet silk woven from mercury threads, quicksilver and deadly. All of them, the same: mouths made for death, merciless, without conscience. Splice together every predator, steal from the past and present and future of some murderous natural world – borrow from the unholy – and if you wrapped that up into a sharp tight package, you might find a shadow, a glimpse, of what they were.

My boys. My deadly little boys.

The old human host swallowed hard. He pressed his lips to Zee's pointed ear. Razor hairs brushed the zombie's face, slicing his pale wrinkled skin like a hot knife through butter. Zee could have controlled that. But only two people were allowed to touch him without consequences.

Edik bled profusely, but except for a quiver in his bottom lip, he showed no pain. Nor did he did speak long. Zee pulled back, red eyes shuttered, and the others crowded close, huddled like a churning mass of obsidian and knives. The little demon whispered to his brothers in their native tongue. I kept my mouth shut.

The zombie tapped the dividing glass, and the limo slowed. I glanced out the window and saw a chain-link fence, the outline of distant cargo ships.

Edik pulled a cell phone from the inner pocket of his jacket. He tossed it to me. 'I will call you with the boy's location.'

'The other children?'

'They scattered from the alley of their own free will. I promise you that, Hunter.'

I met Zee's gaze. 'And our business? Blood Mama's concerns?'

Edik's jaw tightened. 'Watch yourself.'

Not the answer I wanted to hear. I pushed open the limo door, slid out, and paused. 'Russian Mafia, Edik?'

His eyebrow twitched. 'This and that.'

I held his gaze. 'Keep your business away from children.'

'If I do not?'

'The boys have your scent now.'

I slammed the door. The limo pulled away. I watched taillights flash and hardly had the energy to think about what had just happened. But I did, and there was no comfort. Only questions, confusion, and the utter certainty that I was totally screwed.

The phone rang. I answered, and Edik said, 'Go east to the parking lot and find the white van.'

He hung up. I let Aaz eat the phone.

The old warehouse district was wasted and empty like a pile of bones. Night did not hide the scars. I saw floodlights in the distance, shining over the docks. Behind me, battered factories and broken glass, some bodies tucked into nooks, trying to huddle against the cold breeze that wound around my face. My hair was still damp from the early rain, and the sidewalk was rough. Patches of scrappy grass pushed up through the concrete. I heard the freeway, and the sounds of construction and night work at the shipyard.

I also saw the parking lot, half a block down.

I ran. The boys stayed close, loping alongside me, dancing between shadows. Zee reached up and took my hand. I gently squeezed his claws. He blinked out. By the time I reached the small crusty parking lot, he was already perched atop a white van parked near a ragged billboard covered by a peeling advertisement for Starbucks. There were very few cars in the lot. There was little of anything in the neighborhood.

'Is he in there?' I called up to Zee.

He nodded, surveying the area like a sentry on the watchtower. 'Little pea, little pod.'

I glanced at Raw, and he winked into the shadows. A moment later, the back doors swung open. I saw a mattress, and the boy. He was unconscious. Wrists and feet bound.

Raw sidled close and carefully cut the bindings. Hesitated, then trailed one claw down the boy's dirty cheek. Raw could cut through steel with his hands. He could make stone bleed. But the boy remained unharmed.

'Raw,' I said, and the little demon glanced at me. His eyes were mournful. Gave me a shock. I had never seen such emotion in his face. Not since my mother died.

Zee appeared. He stared at his brother, then the boy.

'Ah,' he murmured.

'What?' I asked.

'Sicily,' he replied, and patted Raw on the back. I had no idea what that meant, but it was clear the boy reminded the demons of someone. And it was not a good memory.

I leaned over the boy, smoothing back his dark hair. He looked younger with his face relaxed. He smelled sickly sweet, like chloroform.

But he was alive.

I slowly exhaled, and got out my cell phone.

CHAPTER 4

G RANT arrived in ten minutes. He drove his old Jeep, which had been rigged to accommodate his bad leg. Pulled up, opened the door, and reached out with one long arm to grab me close for a rough hug. He smelled like cinnamon and sunlight, warm as a fire in winter. Grant was always warm.

His flute was in the passenger seat. Weapon of choice. He let go of me and reached behind for his cane, then limped to the back of the van. I followed him. Heard his breath hiss.

'The boy saw Badelt,' I said.

'That's why he's here?'

'Hard to say. But he was used as a shield for a zombie.'

'Tell me,' he said, and I had to take a moment. Not because the story was hard. Went deeper than that.

Grant would never understand what it meant to me, to stand with another human being who knew me, all of me, and have a simple question asked with such casual expectant intimacy. No one could appreciate, except the boys, just how alone I had been, all those years. How alone I had thought I would be, for my entire life.

Or how important these small moments were. How much I loved them.

I explained what happened. Including Edik's message. Grant caught my wrist, his eyes dark, thoughtful. 'You okay?'

'No,' I said, and crawled into the van. I carefully hauled the teen into the cool night air and slung him over my shoulder. He was light for his age, and I was stronger than women my size. Most men, too. I had to be in order to handle the weight of the boys. They were dense, and their bodies weighed the same, whether flesh or tattoo.

The teen remained unconscious. I slid him into the Jeep. Grant glanced around to see if anyone was watching us, but it was just Zee and the others scouting the edge of the parking lot. Eating broken glass. In the distance I saw headlights. My face was wet. Rain.

Grant shut the back door. 'Is the boy still in danger?'

'I don't know.' I hesitated, thinking of the girl with brass knuckles. 'This is my fault.'

'No. Badelt, what happened to this child—'

'—wouldn't be an issue if I had still been on the move.'

He said nothing. Just looked down between us, the long fingers of his left hand twitching, like he was playing the piano or flute, thinking and seeing in melody. Which was the literal truth.

Grant had a neurological condition. Synesthesia. When he played music, heard voices – any sound at all, from the clatter of a pan to the song of a bird – he saw color. Color in people, too, regardless of what sounds they made. Reflections of souls and spirits, the essence of a human heart, mirrored in shades of light and energy. Auras, singing.

And when Grant sang back . . . things happened.

He touched the ends of my hair, delicately. The sensation, the sight, ran warmth down my spine, into my heart. I craved that heat.

'Sweet heart,' he murmured, and I could hear and see the separation in those words, because he wrote me notes like that, offhand scribbles when he wanted to remind me of something, or when he woke up first in the morning. *My sweet heart. My heart.*

Not sweet enough. I pressed my forehead against his shoulder, savoring the hard strength of his hand creeping up my waist beneath my jacket. I was so tired. Grant pushed back my hair to kiss my ear, and scratched under Mal's chin. Dek purred.

We got into the car. Grant drove. The boys sat at my feet, resting their bony cheeks on my knees as I stroked their heads. Zee crawled into my lap and

62

closed his eyes. I cradled him like a child. He stuck his thumb in his mouth. Someone needed to watch Yogi Bear tonight.

'I found Badelt's office,' Grant said. 'It's in Chinatown.'

I leaned my head against the cold window. 'Did you call?'

'I got an answering machine. Then I went in person. No one was there. Or at least, no one who wanted to answer the door.'

I nodded, threading my fingers deeper into Zee's hair. I would have to check it out. Men like Badelt did not stay in business without some kind of organization. There would be payment records, names, and numbers. Maybe an appointment book. Something that would lead to the person who had given him my name.

It was important. Too few humans had ever heard of me for it not to be. Not that I was invisible. I had bank accounts, a house in Texas. Apartments in Chicago and New York City. Lawyers in San Francisco and London who handled the various trusts and estates passed down from mother to daughter over the past five centuries, a process begun by an Italian Hunter, a noblewoman by marriage, who had understood that guarding the prison veil was not a call to poverty.

I had a different name on the paperwork, though. Not Maxine Kiss. Maxine Kiss had never existed for anyone but my mother and the boys. Some zombies. Grant.

Living off the grid. A paper trail would have felt like a cage.

Not that it had kept me safe from the Seattle Police Department.

Grant pulled in to the parking lot outside the homeless shelter, and we sat with the engine ticking, rain pattering against the glass. He glanced down at Zee and tickled the demon's belly. He was the only other person who could. 'What was the message? What did Blood Mama tell you?'

His tone was gentle, but strained. He had his own issues with Blood Mama: her attempted possession, how she had almost killed him just to weaken his mind. No other demon could have done it. Grant was too strong.

But the memory kept me up some nights. Grant was a good man. He would make a terrifying monster.

Aaz and Raw twitched. Dek and Mal stopped purring. Zee turned his face away, burying his head in my stomach. 'No. Private.'

Grant frowned. I shook my head. If the boys had made up their minds, nothing would change them. Scared me, though. All of it. Building in my gut, the same awful sensation that had crawled through me earlier, but without the pain. I did not like mysteries. Especially when they involved me. Too much about my life, my bloodline, was already a question mark.

The teen made a small sound. I reached for his hand. Grant whispered, 'Come on. Let's get him in.'

Inside, home. Grant lived above the shelter: three

adjoining warehouses bought years ago with money inherited from his father. Local and national newspapers published regular stories about the place, though I suspected that had less to do with raising awareness, and more with the fact that the reporters were women and Grant was dead hot. And a former priest. Some chicks dug that.

Green grass and young oaks covered the grounds, along with winding sidewalks and small benches illuminated by old-fashioned pewter lanterns. There was a garden, part of which had been converted from an adjoining lot. Some of the homeless regulars had green thumbs. Grant let them work their magic. No flowers blooming this time of year, but the roses had just been pruned, and the smaller, native plants nestled in the transplanted roots of evergreen and cedar were green and lush. Less than an acre, but an oasis, sheltered in the city with a hush.

Grant moved fast with his cane. Kept his flute tucked under his arm and clipped up a short path that cut through the southern corner of the garden. The boys slid between shadows. The damp air smelled cold and sweet. I heard glass break some distance away, and drunken shouts. Bad night for someone else.

Grant had a private entrance to his apartment. He unlocked the door, and I walked past him, carrying the boy up the stairs. A lot of stairs. Grant said it kept him in shape, helped his balance. I thought he was a masochist.

The apartment took up the entire upper floor of

the southern warehouse. Good views of the city, soft wood floors, brick walls, and miles of bookshelves. Other things, too: a motorcycle, a grand piano, my mother's battered oak chest of journals and other artifacts. Lights were on, and the air was golden and warm. I glanced at Grant as he limped up the final steps, his breathing slightly rushed, and he pointed to the spare bedroom near the kitchen.

No one had used the room in the two months I had lived here. Grant did not have many visitors; fewer now, I supposed, since my arrival. Zee and the others would have made it difficult for guests, even if the boys stayed out of sight.

The spare bedroom was just that, though: spare, almost empty except for a bed and nightstand, and a battered oak wardrobe that had been bought from an antique shop. Grant pulled back the covers. I laid the boy down and took off his shoes. He did not respond, or make another sound.

'He's hurt. In his heart.' Grant leaned hard on his cane, staring at the teen. His left hand made a fluttering motion. 'Something is . . . off.'

'Good or bad?'

Grant's frown deepened. 'He's not going to go looking for the kitchen knives. But he might run. He's not going to trust us.'

'Some psychic you are.' I lightly punched his arm. 'I could have told you that.'

A smile flitted across his mouth. 'I can try to heal him. Or at least take away some of the fear.'

'Not yet. Not unless you think he's going to hurt himself or someone else.'

'He won't.' Grant pointed at the boy's chest. 'He's got a soft spot, right there. I wish you could see it, Maxine. It's a light, pulsing, above his heart.'

I wished I could see it, too. 'Means good things, I assume.'

'Means there's hope,' he said quietly. 'Means he's a good kid, deep down.'

I had thought as much. 'I need to check Badelt's office.'

Grant said nothing, not right away. Just regarded me with that silence I had come to think of as another kind of music, his quiet voice. A faint smile touched his mouth. 'You've got that soft spot, too, Maxine.'

I looked down. 'Probably the size of a pin.'

'Try the sun,' he said. 'Bigger and better than the sun.'

Heat flooded my face. He bent and kissed my cheek. 'I'll stay with the boy. Just in case he wakes up.'

I rubbed my hand against my thigh, still thinking about his words, how he affected me with them. 'Try not to let him get away.'

'Don't let this bum leg fool you.'

'Like greased lightning,' I said, trying to smile, and failing. I peered up into his face, wanting to ask him if everything would be okay, if we would survive even past the end of the world, but that was stupid and sentimental, and saying it out loud would have frightened me. I wanted to be here, in the moment, and not worry about the future. Because even if Edik was wrong, and the veil remained until my death, I was still going to die. Everything ended. Nothing lasted forever.

'Better go,' Grant said. 'Before you scare me into keeping you here.'

I hesitated. 'I'm that obvious?'

'You can't hide your soul, Maxine. Not from me.' His gaze grew strained. 'Go. Call if you need help. Keep the boys close.'

Close, or death. No alternative, not in my life.

Not in theirs, either.

I missed the Mustang, but it was – hopefully – still parked by the university, and the Jeep had a good engine. Little hands appeared from the shadows by my knees to fuss with the radio. The boys found the eighties station. Whitesnake wailed, then rocked into AC/DC. Dek and Mal boogied, the tips of their tails thudding against my collarbone. I drove fast.

I reached Chinatown in ten minutes and found the address Grant had given me. It was a small brick building crammed between the glowing neon lights of a crowded noodle place that had red Chinese characters emblazoned on the steam-clouded front window; while on the other side, pounding with loud music, was a movie rental shop plastered with international posters, yellowing with age.

Badelt's office was on the second floor of the narrow brick strip. Front door locked. I saw postal boxes through the glass pane and glanced down at Aaz. He flashed me a grin and faded into the shadows. A moment later, the front door opened from the inside. I walked in, Dek and Mal still humming 'Is This Love' in my ears.

I did not encounter anyone on the stairs, and except for the sounds of the restaurant next door, heard faintly through the walls, the building seemed quiet, empty. I passed a small law office on the first floor, and on the second found two doors advertising a MR CHEN, ACCOUNTANT and a MABEL LEE, HERBAL MEDICINE. At the end of the hall, farthest from the stairs, was a battered wooden door and a placard that read, BRIAN BADELT, PRIVATE INVESTIGATOR.

I hesitated, still listening, and checked the corners of the dimly lit hall and ceiling for cameras. Seemed safe enough. The largest shadow was the one my own body cast, and the boys used it as a conduit to pour free into the hall, gathering around me like wolves. Only Aaz was missing – until Badelt's door opened, and Aaz peered out with a sharp grin.

The office was small. One room, one window. No space for a secretary. The air smelled like cigarettes. No plants, no pictures on the walls. Just one filing cabinet, a desk, three chairs – two in front of the desk, one behind – and a phone and fax machine. Simple. Man of action, not frivolity. Maybe no money for frills, though I remembered his picture – thought *hard-ass* – and decided this was just his personality.

'Coppers been here,' Zee said, sniffing the floor. 'Been all over.'

I figured as much. Man dies from gunshot wounds, you check his work and home. That, and Badelt's desk looked messy, paperwork scattered. He seemed like the neat type, too fussy to tolerate disorder. I walked around the desk and sat in his chair, listening to the boys prowl. Tried to imagine myself as Badelt, sitting here, gazing over my domain. Looking at my name.

'Zee,' I said. 'Check out the filing cabinet.'

He snapped his claws at Raw, and the two of them started pulling drawers. I slid on my gloves, leaned forward, and checked the desk. In the first drawer, I found an unlocked metal box. I opened it and looked down at a box of bullets. No gun.

The drawer beneath held a framed picture of Badelt. He stood beside a small middle-aged Chinese woman who had her arm draped around his waist and a smile on her face that was so big and happy it could have melted stone. She was strikingly beautiful, unusually so. Most women who looked like her lived only in the movies, or on magazine pages. Badelt seemed just as happy. No big smile, but his eyes were crinkled with warmth. A good look on him. Better than death, that was for sure. I wondered if the woman had been his wife, but if she was, his keeping their picture in the drawer of his desk was probably not a good sign.

I heard the boys muttering at each other from the

filing cabinet, and placed the couple's picture back in the drawer. Nothing else was in there. I started pushing papers around the top of his desk. Toward the bottom, something caught my eye. A newspaper, date from yesterday. I hesitated, then unfolded the paper, scanning the pages. Outside, the wind picked up, rattling against the window at my back. Dek and Mal stopped singing.

I turned, looked out, but saw nothing unordinary. Zee and the others were still messing with the filing cabinet. I focused on the newspaper.

It was, as Suwanai had said, a local Chinatown rag. I saw them all the time, especially when Grant and I came to the area for lunch or dinner. There was an edition published exclusively in Chinese, but this was the English version, a slim paper that dealt with local news, politics, and announcements, most of it related to the Asian community.

Made sense that Badelt would have found it an interesting read. His office was in Chinatown. Stood to reason most of his work might be community-based, as well.

I almost missed it. I was flipping fast, a sense of wasted time creeping up on me, and my eyes skimmed over a photograph at the bottom of page four. I started to turn past, then froze.

The photograph was old, but clear. Based on the caption, it had been taken in 1957. Front and center stood a young white man who looked big and strong, ruggedly attractive, with a sunny, healthy virility not

71

often seen in the modern male species. He was dressed in simple clothes, and looked cheerfully dirty. Behind his right shoulder I saw a giant stone Buddha set in a craggy hill, and at its base, white tents. His hip leaned against a table set amongst rocks and sand, its surface covered in small artifacts: pottery shards, small pieces of metal.

JACK MEDDLE, read the caption. ARCHAEOLOGIST.

But it was the woman on his left I could not stop staring at. She was slender, dressed in a simple blouse, long pants, and tall boots. She wore gloves, and a kerchief knotted loosely around her neck. Fine, delicate features, high cheekbones, full mouth, flawless skin. Hair pulled back. She had striking eyes, filled with a defiant raw strength that seemed to reach out of the photograph – daring, haunting. The eyes of a fighter. A Hunter.

My grandmother.

My lungs ached. I forced myself to breathe. Felt little bodies crowding close and leaned back as Zee and the others took a look.

'Oh,' Zee said, very quietly.

Took me a moment to speak. 'What is this?'

'Silk Road,' he said, as the others all shared a long look. 'After the big boom.'

Big boom. The bomb. My grandmother had been in Hiroshima during World War II. Never learned why, only that she was lucky: The bomb fell at 9:15 in the morning. Sun in the sky. Tattoos secure. The boys kept her alive. Covered her face and breathed for her until she could travel to safety. Anything, everything, to survive.

I looked at the caption again. Her name was listed only as Miss Chambers, an alias I was unfamiliar with. Miss Chambers. Adventurer. That was her title. Appropriate, I supposed.

I scanned the article, which discussed how Dr Jack Meddle had, while on a Silk Road expedition, stumbled upon an ancient temple buried in the sands almost one hundred miles north of Xi'an. A place of diverse worship, for Christians, Muslims, and Buddhists.

Now some of the artifacts unearthed from that temple were being displayed at the Seattle Art Museum, as part of a traveling exhibition of ancient Asian antiquities. The grand opening, according to the newspaper, was tonight. Part of a gala celebration timed to coincide with the Chinese New Year, fast approaching.

Jack Meddle was going to be there.

I sat back in Badelt's chair and closed my eyes. I did not believe in coincidence. Meddle had known my grandmother, and here I was, looking at a photo of them together, found in the office of a private investigator who had written down my real name.

I looked at my grandmother. Studied her gaze, so much like my own, and felt, too, that I was staring at my mother. An eerie sensation.

I also saw something else that was curious.

My grandmother was standing very close to Meddle. So close, in fact, she might have been holding his hand. Or his waist. Maybe his ass. Hard to say. I could not see their hands, which were hidden behind their backs. Shoulders pressed together like glue, bodies turned in, just slightly. The two of them looked comfortable, like they were used to being close. Working together.

I checked the date again – 1957. No specific month.

A chill swept through me. My mother had been born in 1958.

'No,' I said out loud, and looked at the boys, who stared back like choirboys: far too innocent, little devils. Zee shuffled his feet. Dek and Mal lay curled, very still, on my shoulders.

No. It was impossible.

But it also made sense. Or maybe that was wishful thinking. The women in my family never talked about fathers. Or grandfathers. No record of them in the journals. One would imagine storks got involved for all my mother had ever spoken about sex and men and babies. It was a sore subject.

I checked my watch. A little after eight, and the gala ended at eleven. I still had time. I took another long look at the photo, then carefully folded the newspaper and stuck it into the back of my jeans. Helped the boys return the files. They were quiet, subdued. So was I.

I knew my grandmother only through photographs and her journal: just one, her writing and language spare, to the point. I thought of all the other women who had come before, countless women who had fought the demons, a chain unbroken from mother to daughter for more millennia than I cared to contemplate. I knew even less about them.

I wondered if Zee and the others would miss me when I was gone.

When Badelt's office was back in order, I looked at the boys, reached up to pat Dek and Mal, and said, 'Is that man in the picture my grandfather?'

Zee said nothing. Raw and Aaz stared at the floor, little claws digging into the wood, spikes flat against their scaled skin. No way to tell if that was a yes or a no, but it was obviously another subject not meant for discussion. Too many of those tonight.

I gave them a hard look. Walked to the door. Opened it.

And found a demon waiting on the other side.

CHAPTER 5

*E*XPECT *the unexpected*, my mother once said. *Because the unexpected most certainly will be expecting you.*

The demon was taller than the doorframe, so tall my neck hurt to look at him. He was wrapped in a cloak that billowed and heaved in the still air of the hall, the cloth – if it was cloth – whipping about his body with such violence he could have been standing in a hurricane. I saw shadows in the winks of those folds, bottomless, endless – like oubliettes for souls.

Little of the demon's face was visible; a wide-brimmed black hat swept low over his eyes, revealing only white flesh, a pointed chin, the long masculine line of a hard mouth. Black hair curled past his jaw, the very tips twining and writhing like snakes.

I saw no hands. And though his eyes were hidden

beneath the brim of his hat, I felt him looking at me. His stare, like a brand upon my face, the heat of his gaze pushing through me with unfathomable strength.

I lost my mind. It had been a long time. Most demons I encountered tended to be of the spirit variety, wearing human bodies. Substantial as a breath of bad air. The ones made of flesh and bone were rare. Harder for them to pass through the veil. Took an opening. But more than that, it required another level of escape, through the rings, the ascending prison dimensions. Power was needed to achieve freedom. Determination. Which meant the ones who did break free, as my mother would say, were bad motherfuckers.

The boys and I had fought our share. Some had been on earth for centuries, merely hiding until our paths crossed. I had no way of knowing just how many escapees there were. It was a big world. Only one Hunter.

I stepped back and slammed the door. As if that would save me. I stood, staring, expecting the demon to burst through. I also expected the boys to close ranks, but they watched the door, as well. Unmoving. Eyes huge.

'*Zee*,' I hissed.

'Maxine,' he said, expression inscrutable, ears flattened against his bristled skull. Raw and Aaz dug their claws into the floor, the spikes in their spines fanning out with a clacking sound, violently trembling. Dek and Mal also quivered, their breath rattling hot in my ears.

None of them looked ready to fight. And that was

wrong, had never happened. It could not. My blood was their blood. My death, the same as their suicide. The boys lived only because I did. It was supposed to be an incentive. Beyond friendship. Or loyalty.

'Zee,' I said again.

'Open the door,' he whispered.

'You're going to get us killed.'

'Never, Maxine.'

'You're wrong.'

'Never,' he snapped, and there was heat in his voice, anger. Not directed at me. I could feel that much. I could taste the truth. The boys had never steered me wrong.

My heart hammered. I opened the door.

The demon was gone.

I did not waste time. I ran down the hall and jumped the stairs, three at a time, feet pounding. The boys followed, loping through the shadows, disappearing entirely as I burst onto the sidewalk and skidded into a crowd just leaving the noodle restaurant. I ignored their yells. My skin prickled. My stomach hurt. Bile in my throat. Big fat target.

GoMaxineGoGoGo.

I ran, fled, tripped over my own feet racing down the street to the Jeep. I had a vague plan. Lead the demon away. Find some high ground. Isolated. Away from people. Hope like hell the boys helped.

Just before I reached the Jeep, Dek and Mal hissed in my ears. I faltered. Felt air move against my hair, and turned just in time to see a dark blur slam into the sidewalk behind me. Concrete cracked. Like a thousand spines breaking, and I looked down and saw feet shaped like knives; literally, blades; or claws that might have been blades, long and straight, shining quicksilver. The demon stood on those feet like a dancer, *en pointe*, and took a step. His toes clicked as they cut the sidewalk. His head remained bowed, cloak shimmering like dark water.

'Hunter,' whispered the demon. 'Such a long time, Hunter.'

His voice was smooth and warm as some lava kiss, a slow bath in liquid fire. I could not look away from his small, perfect mouth, which barely moved as he spoke. Terrifying. Eerie. My heart pounded so hard I felt light-headed.

I staggered backward into the same crowd that had left the restaurant. Nothing happened. The men and women did not notice my presence. They scattered around my body. Gazes slid past my face. Still talking to each other, having a good time. They walked past the demon without batting an eye, parting on both sides of him like a river accommodating an island.

The demon's mouth tilted into a sharp smile, eyes hidden beneath the brim of his black hat. Zee and the others poured from the shadows. Watching me, not the demon. Watching me closely. Like they expected me to do something. As though I needed no protection. I tried to summon them, but my voice caught. I choked on words.

And then, I just choked.

I was dense. Took me a moment to realize what was going on, and it felt like a lifetime, my skin hot, tears springing to my eyes. I tried to suck in air, but it met a wall in my lungs, and I could not breathe. I could not breathe.

'We *are* your breath,' whispered the demon, and I felt it. I felt his smile in my lungs. And still, the boys did not save me. They stared as though held on the end of some terrible tether, and I wanted to scream at them, but I could not make a sound, and the boys, Zee – *my family*—

'Do not fight,' whispered the demon. 'Hunter.'

I fought. I fought hard, and felt a flutter behind my ribs, familiar and haunting. A cold sensation. Cold as snow. Cold as a backwoods bar on some Wisconsin country road. Cold as my mother's knives. Darkness, stirring.

The demon smiled. 'Yes. You remember.'

Zee barked a sharp word, and the demon inclined his head. I went down hard on my knees, stars pulsing in my eyes. I thought of my mother, the boys. Grant. Everything went dark.

Then it ended. Ten hours, ten seconds, no idea. I found myself on the ground, almost blind. Alive and breathing. Boys were on top of me, little traitors, Dek and Mal twined around my neck while Raw and Aaz clutched my hands, cushioning my skull. Zee licked my forehead, rough tongue rasping my skin. I wished he would catch the tears racing from my eyes. So many tears. I could not stop crying. There was something inside me. Something burning my heart. I was burning.

My head lolled. I saw the demon facing me. Eyes still hidden behind the brim of his hat, cloak and hair snarling through the shadows. I grabbed the back of Zee's neck.

'Kill him,' I ordered breathlessly, daring him to defy me.

He did. He remained unmoving, and there was a story in his eyes, in all of them. I could not stand to see it. I could not. I pushed myself up, breathing hard, and faced the demon. That demon with his smile. My knees quavered, but I had my fists. I was breathing. That was something. Maybe.

Oh, God. Oh, fuck.

Zee grabbed my wrist. 'No, Maxine.'

I resisted. He pulled hard, tugging me behind him, then barked an order. Raw and Aaz tore spikes from their spines, wielding them like spears. I looked down the street and saw people coming, laughing and talking. No one seemed to see us.

'Oturu,' Zee snarled. 'Enough.'

The demon tilted his head, just so, and his body twisted, flowing like the skim of a shark through water. He danced when he moved; on the city street, wrapped in shadows: a kiss on the eyes, a devil's ballet, and only his feet moved, only his cloak had arms; and his hair, rising and flowing as though lost in a storm. I heard thunder, and when his toes sliced

81

spirals in the concrete, I listened to the wind bury winter; and when I tasted his grace, his grace had no name; only, night became something else in his presence, as though darkness had a soul, here, swaying to heartbeats roaring.

I could not look away. The demon swayed to a stop before me, so close we could have touched. Zee, Raw, and Aaz gathered near, spikes clutched in their fists.

'Hunter,' he said. 'We have missed your face.'

'I don't know you,' I whispered, every instinct in my body singing and raw.

The demon's smile grew a deeper edge. 'Blood holds no dominion, Hunter. You know us *well*.'

I knew nothing. Less than nothing. I thought of my mother. She would have been kicking ass right now. She would have taken one look at this joker and ripped a new hole in his face. Whether Zee helped or not.

Tendrils of hair drifted near. Mal snapped, hissing. I reached into my own hair, and Dek curled around my wrist and fingers. The demon leaned close enough to kiss.

I slammed my fist into his face. My fist, wrapped tight in the body of another demon. I did not need brass knuckles. Dek left spikes in the demon's jaw and took a chunk from his cheek, leaving a hole that gaped and smoked and burned. The demon danced from me, hissing, cloak billowing sharp.

'Stay away from me,' I snarled. The demon turned

just enough to show his profile, and the nimble ends of his hair plucked Dek's spikes from his face, dropping them one by one into his cloak, which absorbed the bone fragments like some ravenous abyss. His cheek began to knit closed. Raw trembled against my leg, but I did not think it was with fear. His gaze, like Zee's and Λaz's, was hard and cold and hungry.

Men walked past. One of them, a stocky fellow with a chunky belly and a bag of takeout swinging in his fist, almost walked right over me. Oblivious. Laughing with his buddies about some girl's ass. I felt like a ghost.

'Hunter,' whispered the demon unsteadily. 'You are still too new.'

I glanced at Zee, who stared at the demon with a familiarity that frightened me almost as much as the creature himself. 'What do you want?'

His eldritch hair coiled in the air. 'You woke us. Your soul reached for us. Inside the abyss, we felt your call.'

'I did no such thing.'

'*They* know.' The demon's cloak billowed briefly toward the boys. 'We can be here for no other reason.'

'You came through the veil.'

'We are not of the veil,' said the demon. 'But it opened. It is weakening. Something came through. You have . . . need of us.'

I felt rain on my face, and the newspaper digging into my back. Jack Meddle, I thought. My grandmother.

I did not have time for this crap. 'I don't need *anything* from you. You're a demon.'

He smiled faintly, but this time with a wry humor that was horrifying in its slip of humanity. 'As are you.'

Zee said a sharp word. The demon inclined his head and stepped back. The gesture was oddly respectful.

'Hunter, born again,' he whispered. And then his hair lashed out, faster than I could blink, and I felt a sting against my face in the sweet spot between my jaw and ear. I flinched, dancing back. Reached up and felt no blood – just an indent, a small series of lines.

Zee slammed his fist into the sidewalk. The demon bowed his head and stepped sideways into rain and shadow, the tips of his sharp toes digging trenches into the concrete.

'We are yours,' he whispered. 'But, Hunter, you are *ours*, as well.'

'No,' I began to say, but it was like watching a living abyss fold itself into one breath, one hollow. The demon moved – and disappeared. Vanished. So completely it was as though the world had opened its mouth and swallowed him.

I stared, my eyes nothing more than two holes burning in my head. I looked at Zee, Aaz, and Raw. Heads bowed, staring at their feet. Dek and Mal were silent, quivering. Sorrow. Shame. I could feel it in them, and it hurt. Broke my heart. I wanted to cry again, but there was no time. I had no place for tears.

'What just happened?' I whispered, but Zee said nothing. None of the boys would look at me. It hurt more than I could have imagined.

I touched his shoulder. 'You refused to fight for me. You betrayed me. I want to know why.'

'Sorry,' Zee breathed. 'So sorry, Maxine. From the heart, sorry.'

I brushed my hand across my eyes. More people were coming down the sidewalk; cars driving fast along the slick road. Music pounded from the rental shop, and the smells from the restaurants, the grease—

I bent over, gagging. Dek and Mal crooned in my ear. I turned back to the Jeep, numb, fumbling for the keys. My head pounded. Tears leaked from my eyes. Zee touched my knee, and I shook him off.

I got in the car, started the engine, and pulled away without waiting to see if the boys followed. For the first time in my life, I did not care.

CHAPTER 6

IF I had been thinking clearly, it might have occurred to me that a gala event at the Seattle Art Museum would be a black-tie affair.

But I was preoccupied. Mostly with hot shame. I felt useless, worthless. I was alive, but not because of anything I had done. The demon had not wanted to hurt me – simple as that – and the idea that I had been at his mercy made me sick. I could not even blame the boys. This was my fault. I had become complacent. Always with Zee and the others at my back, knowing they would take care of me, best as they could.

False confidence. My delusion. My mother had always worked so hard: martial arts, weapons training, games of strategy and deception. Keeping her mind and body sharp. She had trained me, too – but she had also been dead for five years, and I had let things lapse. I was rusty. I was an idiot. Relying on the boys was one thing – being lazy, something else entirely.

The boys sat very quietly in the backseat. No music. No fidgeting. I glanced back once or twice and found them with their hands folded in their small laps, little clawed feet dangling above the floor. Ten minutes of listening to them sniffle made it impossible to stay angry. Hurt, maybe, but I could not hold a grudge. Not with them.

'I need answers,' I finally said. Zee made a small hesitant sound that was distinctly uncomfortable, and I added, 'You owe me that much. I thought I was going to die.'

'No,' Zee said firmly. 'Not death.'

'I thought we were family.'

'Thick as thieves.'

'Then *what* is going on?'

'Can't,' Zee whispered, and a moment later melted from the shadows into the passenger seat beside me. He clutched his sharp knobby knees to his chest.

I searched his gaze. 'Why?'

Small fingers tugged the bottom of my jacket. Raw and Aaz squirmed around the gearshift, under my arms, into my lap. Made it hard to drive, but I did not have the heart to push them away. Zee hugged his knees a little tighter. 'Secrets, Maxine.'

'You promised not to tell me what's going on?'

'Promised not to tell *anyone*.' His voice was soft, almost childlike. 'Promised on our blood.'

My hands tightened around the steering wheel. Demons might be morally deficient – by human standards – but they kept their word. Always. I did not know what would happen otherwise, but it was important business. And the boys were no less demonic: Their word was law. But to bind it to blood was another matter. Blood was life. Blood passed on. Blood lasted until you died.

But the boys never died – and that was the life span of a promise.

'Someone made you promise not to speak about that demon we just met? What about Jack Meddle? That message Blood Mama gave you?' I felt like a broken record asking those questions, but I stared at him, waiting – then slammed on the brakes as the light in front of me turned yellow. We all plowed forward, Dek and Mal tightening their tails around my throat. Aaz smacked his head against the horn, and the Jeep blurted out a fat little sound.

'All connected,' Zee said, which made me want to beat my head against the horn, too. 'Mommy told you.'

My mother said a lot of things. Brush your teeth. Read the first three chapters of *War and Peace*. Always keep a twelve-gauge handy. But I think I would remember something about demons with knives for feet, or private messages between the boys and Blood Mama. I think she would have drilled that in.

I grabbed Zee's hand. 'You have to give me more. I'm out of my league.'

He shook his head. 'Never. You are the Hunter.'

I felt like a nobody. I ran my fingers along the short razor spikes of Zee's angular cheek. Felt like silk grass. He leaned into my touch, eyes half-lidded.

'Did you do this to Mom?' I asked him. 'Keep these secrets?'

He did not answer. I controlled myself, barely. 'The demon?'

Zee sighed. 'Oturu. He is Oturu. Also . . . a hunter.'

'Not from inside the veil. Not what I felt come through.'

'No.' He peered up at me, as did Raw and Aaz. Dek and Mal licked the backs of my ears. 'Never would have made you dead, Maxine.'

'I was scared.'

'All of us scared,' Zee whispered. 'But not because you might die.'

Chills beat through me. The light turned green. I hesitated, then accelerated through. I was downtown, and the museum was close. I found parking on the street, thought about asking more questions, but gave up. Later. I needed air. I needed to think about something else. I felt like a dog running in circles, chasing its tail.

Jack Meddle, I told myself, walking fast toward Union and First Avenue. Maybe I could learn something from him. Like whether he had hired Badelt. Or slept with my grandmother.

It was almost nine thirty. I had an hour and a half to stalk the man.

If I could get through the front door.

The Seattle Art Museum had recently undergone an expansion; the new building, attached to the former gallery – a curved art deco monolith – was an upward sheet of glass and steel that glittered on the night street with its own austere, sophisticated vanity. Regular museum hours were over, but I saw bodies milling inside – tuxedos, black gowns, the glitter and tinkle of glass and diamond.

My jeans were dirty, my hair a mess. I still had bits of sidewalk on my face, and my mascara had probably run. No time to clean up and nothing to change into. I had not worn a dress since my mother's death, and heels would probably kill me faster than a zombie.

The young man out front, stationed at a podium, was squat and round and wore an ill-fitting tuxedo that bunched at his waist and hung awkwardly on his shoulders. Temp job, or maybe a museum employee roped in at the last moment. He took one look at me, then glanced at a nearby security guard, who started ambling over with a self-important strut that made me want to stick my boot in his backside.

'You need an invitation,' said the man dismissively, smoothing back his slick brown hair. 'And some personal hygiene.'

'This is urgent,' I replied. 'I need to speak to Dr Jack Meddle.'

'I'm sure.' The man fussed with his sleeves and glanced again at the security guard. 'But not now.'

I was not in a good mood, and I felt like crap. 'This is a family matter. A family *emergency*, you might say. And his cell phone is turned off.'

'I am *not* going to interrupt—'

I stepped around the podium into his personal space, so close our chests briefly touched, and held his gaze like a snake charmer: unblinking, cold, and hard. His voice choked. I whispered, 'Do you really want to explain why the guest of honor was *denied* access to an important personal message, merely because the messenger did not conform to the dress code?' Several women in evening gowns, exiting through the doors, glanced at us with both curiosity and consternation. I ignored them. 'What's your name?'

The man hesitated, his stuffiness deflating. The security guard began edging away. 'I don't see how—'

'Your name,' I said coldly. 'Don't make me explain why I want it.'

He frowned, trying to maintain his cool, and took a step back. I let him. Watched as he made a maddening show of looking me up and down.

Then, in a very loud voice, no doubt meant to impress upon the exiting guests that he was doing a massive favor that in no way violated the rules of his employment, announced, 'Yes, but do take only a moment while you relay your *urgent, family-related message* to Dr Jack Meddle. He has many people wanting to speak to him tonight.'

'Thank you,' I said. 'I'll try not to leave greasy

fingerprints on the paintings, or toss chicken bones over my shoulder while I look for him.'

The man rolled his eyes. I brushed past.

Confidence was always the key to looking like you belonged, no matter how elite and froufrou the circumstances – or how run-down. And though I might have just had my ass handed to me by a demon, I still knew who I was – and I walked like it as I strode through the museum, head held high, back straight, with a sway to my hips that I hoped, but kind of doubted, any supermodel would envy.

The gala had drawn a good crowd. I passed beneath a discomfiting fleet of white cars hanging from the ceiling, twisted upside down amidst streaks of colored lights, and followed the trail of well-dressed indi-viduals to the old museum wing, where girls in tight uniforms carried platters of champagne and sushi.

I recognized some faces from the evening news, including several politicians who had recently stopped by the Coop for photo opportunities on the supper line with the other volunteers. I got some odd looks – from them, and everyone else who got out of my way – but I ignored them all and kept my eyes searching for the prize. Dek and Mal huddled in my hair, slipping deeper under my jacket. No telling where Zee and the others were, but I was certain they were close.

I glanced briefly at the artifacts on display. Most were made of pure soft gold, a rich deep yellow that looked like velvet made from the sun. Intricate metalwork, composed in an array of urns and ornaments and statues I wanted to spend more time appreciating. If these artifacts were the results of work my grandmother had participated in, then they were part of my history. I had so little of her already. I wanted to see the things she had touched. I wanted a taste of her adventure.

As it was, I almost plowed into Jack Meddle.

He was a big man, hard to miss, but I was momentarily distracted by a gold armband inlaid with onyx, a design that reminded me of the boys; as though the tattoos their bodies made had been pressed, in fragments, upon the jewelry. It was difficult for me to look away, but when I did, I turned too fast and rammed shoulders with the man I had been looking for.

'Oh,' I said, before I realized, then looked into his face and added, '*Oh*.'

It was him, no mistake. Jack Meddle had to be near eighty, but I could still see the man who had been in the photo. Tall, craggy, with that same lean charm and a sparkling, restless, intelligence in his clear blue eyes. He had nice eyes. Kind eyes.

Eyes that stared at me, amused surprise turning to puzzlement, then amazement.

'Jeannie,' he whispered, which gave me my own shock. Jean. My grandmother's real name. She had trusted this man with it. I started to tell him he was mistaken, but he shook his head, squeezing shut his eyes. 'No. You're not her.'

'She was my grandmother,' I said quietly.

'Yes,' he said, looking at me again, this time with wonder, a bewilderment tinged by hollow sadness. It made him look tired and old, and no matter how much I wanted answers, I suddenly felt bad for disturbing him; on this night especially, which was a celebration of his work. It was rude, and I was an interloper with no right to his time – no matter the mystery that had brought me here.

But Jack touched my arm, so gently; and then, before I could stop him, his hand slid around my neck, his fingers pressing against Dek and Mal. I froze, holding my breath. A moment later, the boys began to purr.

'Ah,' said the old man, sighing. 'I've missed the lads.'

I could hardly speak. 'You knew?'

Jack smiled, and stared deeper into my eyes. 'Of course, my dear. I am so delighted finally to meet you. Little Maxine Kiss.'

JACK made some excuses. We left the party. As we exited the museum through the front doors and passed the podium, I was not so distracted that I failed to note, with grim amusement, the dismayed expression on the man's face when he saw the both of us together.

'We can walk,' said Jack, pulling up the collar of his coat. 'My office is close.'

For some reason, it surprised me that he lived in Seattle. Under my nose this entire time. Made me feel odd, like I was a step out of touch with my life. 'You keep an office downtown? I thought you were an archaeologist.'

'Oh,' he said. 'This and that.'

He walked like a young man, with a smooth rollicking gait. I worked hard to keep up with him. 'My grandmother—'

'Jeannie,' he said. 'You look so much like her.'

'I saw a picture of you both.' I pulled the newspaper from my back pocket. 'In here. I found it in the office of a man who was looking for me. A private investigator.'

His pace faltered. 'Really.'

'Were you trying to find me?'

'Not I,' he said, his tone curious; halting and thoughtful. 'But I'm glad you were found.'

'I wasn't,' I said. 'The man was murdered.'

He gave me a sharp look. 'Murdered?'

'Shot,' I told him, and thought he must be lying about not searching for me. 'Just last night.'

Jack's jaw tightened. I glimpsed Zee, Raw, and Aaz in the shadows, the three of them standing apart, peering at us from under a car, from the mouth of a drain at the side of the road, and within the thin line cast by the pole of a streetlight. Red eyes glittered, the tops of their bristling heads pushing free of the slick darkness like demonic otters pulling free from water. The air tasted heavy with rain. Few people were on the sidewalk. I fought the urge to check the skies for figures in black cloaks, ready to descend.

'Did you know him?' I asked. 'His name was Brian Badelt.'

'I never met the man,' Jack replied, carefully. I felt like Suwanai, listening to my own answers.

'He knew my real name,' I persisted. 'He had it written down on a paper just like this. With that picture of you and my grandmother. How do you explain that?'

'My dear,' said Jack, 'I wish I could.'

'Then how did *you* know my name?' I fumbled for words, feeling awkward, ill at ease, thinking of my grandmother – Miss Chambers to the world – telling this man her name was Jean Kiss. 'We've never met.'

He smiled faintly. 'Not that you remember.'

I stared. Jack said, 'Here we are, my dear. The door just ahead.'

All I saw was the modern glass façade of an art gallery, a sleek presentation that screamed money and – I imagined – overly large paintings that no doubt consisted of black and white dots, or abstract imitations of tortured souls – meant to soothe the intellectual malaise of the very rich. Not the home of a treasure hunter, or a man who – if my grandmother had liked him – no doubt made his life outside the lines of normal society.

But Jack surprised me by stopping in front of the glass door, pulling free a set of keys from the pocket of his long black coat. An elegant script had been printed on the glass: SARAI SOARS: ART GALLERY.

He glanced at me and smiled. 'Oh, don't be so taken aback. Besides, this place belongs to my business partner.'

Sarai. I thought that must be her. I felt, for a moment, an awkward and unreasonable jealousy for my grandmother, that Jack Meddle could be involved with another woman. I had to remind myself, sternly, that Jean Kiss might never have been involved in the first place with the archaeologist – and that she had been dead for almost thirty years. I had to cut the guy some slack.

And stop with the obsession. All this fretting over one old man – when I had so much else to be concerned about – was a true waste of time.

But I was here. He knew my name. And the boys. That was enough.

The art gallery was smaller on the inside than I had thought it would be – and the paintings very different, even startling. My preconceptions, stretched beyond black dots and abstract splashes. I had to take a moment, staring. Baffled. Chilled.

Because the works of art hanging on the walls – every single one of them – were of unicorns.

Not the garden-variety unicorn, either. Not some Thomas Kinkade, dreamy-eyed, soft-lit fantasy full of white horses with big horns. Not a poster of some hot pink sunset with magic rearing on silver hooves like a prepubescent fantasy shot full of fairy-tale steroids.

None of that. I stood in the doorway of Sarai Soars

and stared at the most visceral incarnations of that creature I had ever seen in my life. I felt like I was thirteen again, when my mother had piled art books on me: the Pre-Raphaelites my favorites, English artists from the nineteenth century; like Rossetti, or Burne-Jones, their work sincere; themes romantic, classical.

These paintings held the same tone; strong lines and rich color, naturalistic detail: a unicorn upon a field of battle, crammed and crowded, sunk as though in quicksand by wild-eyed soldiers in medieval armor, trapped in a moment of death and violence, without end or horizon; merely bodies, tumbling upon each other, churning upon swords and axes splashed in blood. And the unicorn, braced amongst them, untouched and shining, lean as a starved tiger – staring out of the painting with eyes that reminded me of the demon: Oturu, his smile. Knowing and old and effortlessly powerful.

Masterful. Hypnotic. I wanted to buy the damn thing. I wanted to put a pillow on the floor and just lie there and stare.

There were other paintings, and each one felt like gazing at a truth. As though a unicorn *had* stood in battle, or upon the ramparts of an ancient desert citadel, surrounded by archers – or in the ocean, a gray specter of what seemed to be D-day, with the Allied forces fighting and dying upon the Normandy beachhead, and that fantastical creature nearly lost in the foaming waves, struggling with the men as they fought and died. I could feel it. In my gut.

The paintings themselves were few in number, probably because they were massive, and wall space was limited – but I was grateful for that. Staring at them too long made me feel as though my heart were being laid bare – and that something else might stare back.

'Remarkable, aren't they?' Jack murmured. 'Sarai does get inspired sometimes.'

'Yes,' I said, as Dek and Mal poked free of my hair to get their own good look. I tensed, aware of Jack studying them, but all he did was reach out and scratch under their chins. They giggled, purring, and it was just surreal enough to make me want to sit down and put my head between my knees.

But Jack suddenly stopped, and though he made no outward sign of alarm, his stillness was enough to make my hackles rise.

Cold air filled the gallery. Not a breeze or stirred breath, but an ambient rising chill, as if someone had just dumped a thousand pounds of ice beneath our feet. It was an unmistakable dip in temperature, a shock to the system – and not the malfunction of any air conditioner.

Heat was another kind of energy. Soak it up, leave only a chill. Like eating fire and pissing ice. All those archetypal images of Hell – brimstone and pits of lava, folks tap-dancing in flames – nothing but a manifestation of an old truth. Some demons liked it hot.

Dek and Mal rumbled. Zee and the others were still nowhere to be seen, but I felt them pressed within the shadows like sharp ghosts. I felt like I was looking for a ghost. I reached into my hair, fingers curling around a thick quivering tail. 'Jack, something's wrong. We're not alone.'

'It's nothing,' he said calmly.

'You don't understand.'

'But I do.' Jack glanced at a spot over my right shoulder, the corner of his mouth turning down. 'Let it pass.'

He knew too much. I should have found that exciting, but I did not. Maybe it was because I felt a hard ugly gaze boring into the back of my skull. I wanted to turn around more than anything, but I did not move a muscle. I pretended ignorance. Played the game. Trusted the boys.

And just like that, the cold snapped. Heat washed over us like the open door of a giant oven, but it was superficial. My bones remained frozen. My heart, arctic.

Dek and Mal stopped growling, but their straining tails were tense as tethers, and I patted them both as Zee poked his head from a shadow – directly behind Jack, out of the old man's sight – and shook his head at me. Whatever had been here was gone.

Jack said, 'I should keep more sweaters around.'

I exhaled slowly, trying not to shake. 'You sound used to this.'

He shrugged, utterly nonchalant. Or maybe it was an act. 'Certain associations draw unwanted attention. Nothing can change that.'

100

Certain associations. My grandmother. But he was too relaxed. I did not buy it. 'Jack. Who *are* you?'

Surprise flickered. 'Why, an archaeologist. You know that.'

'And I suppose, as a simple archaeologist, you're aware of . . . demons.'

'Well, no,' he replied, with faint exasperation. 'That has *nothing* to do with my profession.'

I stared, perplexed. Afraid for him, even. But Jack merely waved his hand and led me past a small rose-wood screen carved in sparrows and cherry blossoms. Behind, a narrow white door, and a narrow flight of stairs. We walked up to the second floor, which was so unlike the first, I had to take another moment just to get my bearings. And wonder whether I was going to be buried alive.

Tables surrounded me, long wooden surfaces piled high with paper and books. Mountains of them. Everywhere. Shelves lined the walls, but those were full, too, and the only way through – as the floor was also covered in books – was a long, narrow path that threatened to topple an avalanche of paperwork with every turn. I saw wooden crates filled with packing material and metal, statues upon the tables, and shards of pottery. I did not see windows. The room felt like being inside a big papery cocoon, warm and messy. Lamps, already on, filled the air with golden light. I heard Jimmy Durante singing softly.

'Make yourself comfortable,' Jack said, then: 'Zee, you can come out now. No need to be so formal.'

101

I bit my tongue. Zee appeared from beneath the tables, Raw and Aaz behind him. The boys prowled, sniffing the air, and Jack watched them with that same sad smile I had seen at the museum.

'Old Wolf,' rasped Zee.

'Little boy,' said the old man. 'Still the same.'

'Like you.' Zee flashed him a toothy grin. 'Silly skin.'

I folded my arms over my chest. Jack glanced at me and chuckled. 'I know that look.'

I frowned. 'I don't see how.'

'Jeannie.' Jack walked down the narrow path. 'And your mother.'

I had started to follow him, and stopped. 'You knew my mother?'

'Briefly. You were a baby.' Jack made some rattling noises, out of sight from me. 'Tea?'

'No,' I replied, still peevish about my close encounter downstairs. 'How come I don't know any of this?'

'My dear, I learned long ago never to question a woman in the rearing of her child, especially *you* particular women. You are ornery creatures.'

I had to sit down. My knees told me so. I perched on the edge of a table, my hip brushing paperwork and a glass jar of old pennies. Aaz rested his head on my knee, drooling slightly as I scratched behind his ears. 'Sounds like you knew them well.'

Jack made a muffled sound that I took to be a yes. I heard cups rattling. I wanted to ask him more – like,

Can I call you Grandpa? – but that was too much, absolutely crazy. But when I tried to ask something else, my mouth refused to form the words. My body wanted silence. So I obeyed, floating in gentle insanity, perusing the books I had been leaning against.

Most of them, surprisingly, dealt with northern European mythic traditions; specifically those of fairy, and, even more specific than that, something called the Furious Host, the Wild Hunt.

I was familiar with the concept. No expert, but I had come across it during all those trips to the bookstores and libraries. I had a vague impression of a man wearing antlers and a moss loincloth, leading ghosts and goblins and fairies on some spectral hunt through the woods. Not something I had focused on all that much. Hans Christian Andersen was more up my alley.

But I was nervous and needed to feel busy – and these texts were new to me, with inserts written by hand and typewriter. I found myself skimming, drawn to the words – one page in particular, which I thought must have been written in Jack's hand.

It is of us, I read, *this hunt, this wild raging hunt that takes upon itself the nature of an Age, and destroys so that others may be reborn.*

There was more, but Jack appeared down the narrow path between stacked paper. He held two steaming cups in his hands. 'Ah. You've found the light reading, I see.'

'It's interesting.' I closed the book – and the page. 'I thought you were an archaeologist only. Not a folklorist.'

'I am a man of many disciplines. And the two are not so dissimilar. There would be no cities to find, my dear, without the hearts that shaped them.'

I tapped the book. 'Fairy tales?'

'Dreams and portents,' he replied, and held out a cup. I wanted to ask him more, but kept my mouth shut and carefully set aside the book. I took the hot drink. Tea. The liquid was a dark rich red, and I sipped it, gingerly. Tasted good and sweet.

'Jeannie preferred sugar with hers,' said Jack. 'I thought you might have similar tastes.'

'It feels weird to hear you talk about her. I was shocked when I saw that photograph.'

'It's one of my favorites.' Jack leaned on the table opposite me and glanced down at Zee. 'There's a toolbox beneath the sink if you're hungry.'

Raw and Aaz looked at each other, ears perked, and disappeared into the shadows. Zee stayed where he was, regarding the old man with a thoughtfulness that made me nervous. I heard metal rattle. Dek and Mal chirped softly, and I reached into my hair to give them a gentle push. They winked off my shoulders, and the missing weight made me feel naked.

'My grandmother trusted you,' I said. Just as my mother must have trusted him. I wished I understood why she had never mentioned his name. Or why the boys had refused to discuss him when I first showed them his picture in Badelt's office.

I thought of the demon. Oturu. Jack said, 'We met in 1955. I had been working in Persia for some time, cataloging certain artifacts, evidence of cultural migration between China and the Middle East, and I happened to bump into Jeannie in the market. She was buying grapes, and was very angry at the price she had been quoted.' Jack smiled into his teacup. 'I came to her rescue.'

I found myself covering my mouth, hiding my own smile. I bit my bottom lip. 'What happened then?'

'She and I started talking. It turned out she had traveled extensively throughout Central Asia, and was quite familiar with certain archaeologically significant areas unknown to me – or any other outsider. She offered to take me to them. For a fee. She liked money, that one.'

'And the boys? How did you find out about them?'

'We were attacked.' Jack's gaze turned distant. 'Desert raiders. One of them shot at me. He was too close to miss. Jeannie . . . shielded me . . . with her body. Those bullets tore her clothing to shreds, but she remained unharmed. Scared the daylights out of the raiders, I can tell you that much. We were the only ones left alive.' He smiled again, but it was not quite as happy. 'She explained the rest. No choice, really.'

'How long—' I had to stop, and steadied myself with a sip of tea. 'How long were you together?'

'Oh, years.' Jack faltered, staring down at his tea. 'I assume your mother passed away.'

I hesitated. 'Five years ago.'

Jack's face was still turned from me, but his chin dipped deeper against his chest, and his hands tightened around the teacup. A tremor raced through him. So faint it could have been nothing more than a breath.

'You were so lovely,' he said quietly, and I thought he might be speaking to the memory of my mother until he added, 'Not a cry out of you. A sweet baby.'

I did not know what to say. Maybe he *was* speaking of my mother. Maybe me. Maybe, maybe. Too many maybes. 'She brought me to you?'

'Just after you were born. It was one of her last visits.' Jack set down his tea. 'Come. I have something for you.'

He stepped carefully down the path. I watched him intently, his words still ringing, said so casually. *It was one of her last visits.*

I started to follow, but Zee stopped me, holding up his hands. I swung him into my arms, and he pressed his mouth to my ear. 'We promised, Maxine. Mommy made us. No talking about the Meddling Man.'

'Why?' I whispered.

Zee hesitated. 'Look deep, beneath the skin. Meddling Man is all skin.'

A riddle. Not the worst. But it made me uneasy, when all I wanted was joy.

I found Jack on the other side of the room, around

a freestanding bookshelf that served as a dividing wall. I saw a sink, a stove, a dishwasher – four little demons eating the remains of a toolkit – a table that was, remarkably, only half-covered in books – one refrigerator that was twenty years too old, and a door to what I assumed was either a bedroom or a toilet.

Jack was mumbling to himself, and I tried to memorize every detail of the old man – still in a tuxedo, lost in a maze of books and paper. It was a treasure, a delight. Better than what I could have imagined.

I almost asked – right then, right there. The question almost slipped free. Took all my willpower to hold it in, but I was too scared not to. Too frightened of myself. Jack Meddle was a stranger. I had no reason to trust him. No cause to believe.

But I wanted to. I wanted Jack to say yes. I wanted him to be family, so badly I could taste it.

And if it was someone else, and not him . . . I did not want to know. Not yet. I could pretend, just for a little while.

'Here,' Jack said, smiling triumphantly. I still held Zee in my arms, and swayed close, peering at the object in the old man's hands. It was covered in a fine linen that he swiftly unfolded, revealing a round flat stone. A disc. Filled with deep concentric lines that seemed to shimmer, as though the stone itself was laced with veins of pearl.

My vision blurred. My stomach clenched. I leaned against the kitchen table. Zee's hands tightened around my neck.

107

'What is it?' I asked. My voice sounded strange in my ears.

'A gift,' Jack said slowly, 'from your mother. She said if we ever happened to . . . bump into one another . . . you should have it.'

'Bump into one another?' I rubbed my aching eyes. 'What were the odds of that?'

'My dear girl . . . you're here, aren't you?'

Raw and the others stopped eating. They sat on the floor, staring at the stone in Jack's hands. Dek and Mal collapsed from the shadows inside my hair to drape across my shoulders.

He held out the disc. I took it from him. My hand tingled. Zee seemed to hold his breath.

But nothing happened. It was just rock. Smooth rock, polished to a butter-soft shine. Sandstone, perhaps. It felt good to hold, and the design in its heart was simple. Those circles within circles. I touched the outer ring, dipping my finger into the carved line. I could not help myself. I began to trace it, and again, my skin tingled. I felt dizzy, and stopped.

'What is it?' I asked again.

Jack never answered. We both heard his door creak open, and then a woman called, 'Are you in there, Old Wolf? Something's happened.'

Zee vanished from my arms, while Raw and Aaz winked into the shadows beneath the sink. Dek and Mal stopped purring. Jack hesitated, as though he was seriously contemplating silence. 'Yes, Sarai. We have company.'

108

I did not hear the woman move through the other room, but suddenly she was there, at the corner of my eye. I turned.

And one piece of the puzzle slipped into place.

Sarai was the woman from Badelt's photograph. No mistake. She was slender, shorter than I, with long silver hair that framed a face so ethereally perfect, so lovely, I could only imagine Troy and Helen and one thousand ships, and think that *yes*, maybe such a thing could have happened, perhaps a woman could be that beautiful.

Sarai certainly was. A hundred times more beautiful in person, as if Badelt's photograph had captured only a rough copy of the woman – and though I guessed she was in her forties or fifties, I could hardly find one wrinkle, one flaw, in her skin. No makeup, either. She was unreal.

'You,' I said slowly. 'It was you who sent Badelt after me.'

'Oh,' Sarai said. 'Damn.'

CHAPTER 7

ODDLY enough, I thought of Shakespeare first. Part of a birthday present when I was twelve: a book of quotes from the Bard. Poetic maxims. My mother was big on those.

But they whose guilt within their bosoms lie,
Imagine every eye beholds their blame.

Maybe. But Shakespeare would have been waiting for a cold day in Hell before he saw guilt – or any other emotion – in Sarai Soars's eyes.

'He's dead, isn't he?' she said. 'Brian?'

I did not answer. I was too busy studying her reaction. My mother had kept her emotions hidden with most everyone but me. Survival, she called it, and maybe Sarai was the same – though I had questions that took precedence over personality. I wanted to know how she knew me. Or why seeing me would make her assume a man had died.

'He was murdered,' Jack said quietly. 'I'm sorry, Sarai.'

She closed her eyes and bowed her head. Silver hair fell around her face, and she pressed one finger against her brow, like she ached there. I suddenly felt more sorry for her – and wondered if that was a trap.

'You were close,' I said carefully. 'I was in his office. I saw the picture of you together.'

'We were married. Briefly. Years ago.' Her voice held little emotion; a faint sharp edge, nothing more. 'How did he die?'

'Shot. Last night.' I did not cushion the truth. Lying about the dead, when they had no voice to speak for themselves, had always rubbed me the wrong way. 'He had my name on him. The police found it. They came to me because they thought I might have killed him.'

Sarai's head remained bowed, but Jack's hands tensed. I gave him a long, hard look. 'What am I missing here, Meddling Man?'

The woman made a small choked sound. Her delicate hand, smeared with paint, passed over her eyes. 'Meddling Man. It's been years since I heard that name.'

'But you know mine.'

Sarai finally looked at me. Unshed tears glistened.

111

'Maxine Kiss. Hunter and Warden. Guardian of the prison veil. The last of your kind.'

My voice refused to work. The edges of the stone disc cut into my hands. Her gaze flicked down, across the object, and that careful mask slipped back into place. 'You should leave. Come back tomorrow. We can talk then.'

'No,' I managed, hoarse. 'I'm sorry for your loss, but I need answers.'

'You need nothing,' she snapped.

'Sarai,' Jack said firmly, and the woman spun away without a word, walking down the narrow, cluttered path of books with swaying, impossible grace. She did not look back.

I wanted to chase her down. I would have, except Jack's hand tightened. 'Let her be.'

I bit back a coarse response. 'You seem like an odd couple.'

'We've had years to work out our differences,' replied the old man, with a particular gentleness that made it impossible to stay angry.

I pushed back my hair, holding my aching head. 'How does she know who I am? Did you tell her?'

Jack did not answer. I looked at him. Found his gaze focused on the edge of my jaw, which was exposed now. Took me a moment, but I remembered Oturu, how he had hit me with his hair. I had forgotten about it, but Jack was staring – staring with a sick, slick flush in his cheeks. He had been so calm downstairs, so cheerful throughout all of this. I had hardly thought it possible to see that expression on his face.

But he looked at that spot on my jaw like it was a nuclear bomb, countdown sequence already ticking from ten seconds to one. A frozen, resigned fear, fat with dread.

As though he wanted to run – and knew it was too late.

I touched my skin and felt those marks. I looked for a mirror. Found one near the kitchen sink, next to a copy of Everett Wheeler's *Vocabulary of Military Trickery*, the cover of which was the repository for a dangerously rusty old razor and a wooden bowl of old-fashioned shaving soap, complete with bristle brush.

The mirror was delicate but heavy, framed in solid silver. The glass seemed to shimmer slightly as I looked into it, and I saw, below my ear, a small fan of lines that was almost invisible. No welts, no blood. Just indentations, as though a cold brand had been laid into me, pressed so hard it had left a permanent mark. The lines flowed into each other; fluid, as though unfurling, like the outline of a wing. Or a cloak. Or that demon's living hair.

I held my breath. Jack still stared, his gaze distant, hollow.

'You know this,' I whispered. 'What this means.'

He hesitated. 'No. But I know who gave it to you.'

I almost dropped the mirror. 'How is that possible?'

Jack's warm hand slid over mine, a brief contact

I was totally unprepared for, so much that I stood there, dumb, until I realized the only reason he had touched me was to take the mirror out of my hand. The old man set it down, very carefully. 'Tomorrow, my dear. We will be here.'

'We're here now,' I protested, part of my reluctance due to fear, an irrational dread that if I left the old man, I might never see him again. I felt weak for it, like a little kid, and squeezed the stone disc until I hurt. Pain was the only way I could remember myself, but even that was hollow.

Zee caught my leg, pleading with his eyes. All the boys were watching me. I hardly knew them, either.

I looked at Jack. 'Tomorrow. You promise?'

'Not a force on this world could make me break my word to you,' he said, with such solemn grave dignity I felt those words hang heavy and rich, as though a promise from Jack was something a person could mark on a treasure map and hold with an utter certainty of truth.

'All right,' I breathed. But before Jack could relax, I added, 'One more question. How does Sarai know me?'

Jack sighed. 'She also met Jeannie. And your mother.'

'Impossible. My mother, maybe, but not my grandmother. That woman is too young.'

'Not *that* young. You have to look deeper than the skin to know Sarai Soars, my dear. Much deeper.'

'Zee said the same about you,' I told him coldly. '"Meddling Man is all skin," he said.'

'Did he?' Jack smiled sadly. 'Well. You should listen to your friends.'

And with that, he walked me from his office.

I took my time driving home. Not a good night for pushing my luck. The boys were quiet. My head hurt.

I heard the piano while I was still on the stairs. When I opened the apartment door, Grant did not stop playing. He did not smile, either. His fingers flowed over a waterfall of Mozart, and I could feel the tension in every note.

I kicked off my boots, threw aside my jacket, and slumped beside him on the piano bench. My bones felt like jelly. So did my heart. Dek and Mal chirped, then disappeared from my shoulders. The apartment always felt safe enough to take a break from body-guard duty.

'Okay,' I said to the side of Grant's head. 'According to the zombies, the world is going to end, there's a demon who can choke me with his mind who claims I *summoned* him, and I may have found my bio-logical grandfather. Who seems to be living with Badelt's ex-wife.'

'Wow.' Grant did not stop playing the piano. 'All I've got is gas.'

I cracked a smile. 'Maybe you can pray real hard for it to go away.'

Grant lifted his hands off the keys. I took over,

115

playing 'Chopsticks.' He joined me a moment later, our duet growing increasingly complicated, until I was practically in his lap, our hands and arms tangled together.

'Apocalypse,' he finally said, when we stopped. 'That's old news. Tell me about the grandfather and ex-wife.'

So I did. And then I backtracked and described the demon, the reaction of the boys. Their refusal to fight the creature. Oturu.

Grant said nothing for a long time. His arms were heavy and warm around my waist. With all that had happened, I could not imagine sleeping, but my eyelids began to feel heavy.

'Don't pass out on me,' he said gently, kissing the back of my ear. 'The boy is awake.'

I straightened, rubbing my face. 'When?'

'Less than an hour ago. I convinced him to stay, but he's not feeling well. The chloroform.'

'He must be frightened.'

'He's scared of men. I couldn't stay in the room with him, even to talk. And no, I didn't try to . . . modify . . . him. Though I was tempted to take the edge off.'

I thought about that. 'Anything else happen? Suwanai and McCowan call back?'

'No.'

'Mary?'

'Rex is down in the basement, cleaning up the mess.'

'Personal zombie assistant.'

Grant grunted. 'I know he bothers you.'

'He's a human possessed by a demon.'

'He's reforming.'

'Does reformation include giving up his host?'

Grant said nothing. I turned in his lap to look at him. 'The demon and the man are not the same. One is still a prisoner of the other.'

'I can't kill Rex,' he said quietly, searching my gaze. 'I can't kill any of them, Maxine. Not while I know their natures can change.'

'Because you force them to.'

Grant shook his head. 'Because I show them another way. If they didn't want my influence, they could abandon those bodies, go anywhere in this world. You know that. They stay because it's their choice.'

Unfortunately, I did know that. And it wracked me. I killed demons. I killed them because I believed, unequivocally, that they deserved to die. I had been taught so from birth, told again and again that demons were irredeemable predators of the human race, and for my entire life had accepted that, without a single doubt, or question.

Until Grant. And now I lived under the same roof as zombies. My poor mother.

I scooted off his lap, but he caught my wrist and his eyes were dark, haunted. He very carefully turned my head to look at the mark beneath my ear, and after a long moment of silence, peeled down the collar of my sweater to examine my throat. I held still, eyes closed, trying not to remember what it felt like to choke to death. Wishing I could forget that cloak, or hair, those feet, and that smile.

Grant's lips touched my skin. His mouth was hot and gentle.

'I get left behind,' he murmured, alongside my ear. 'And I hate it. I pretend I don't. I pretend nothing ever goes wrong, but then you come home and tell these stories, and it terrifies me.'

'You hide it well.'

'You know me better than that.' Grant pulled away, holding my face between his hands. 'I'm going with you tomorrow. I'm not letting you out of my sight until this is resolved.'

'I can't let you do that, Grant.'

'You can't stop me.' His large, strong hands curled around the back of my neck, threading into my hair. 'We take care of each other, right? Isn't that what we promised?'

'Yes,' I said quietly.

'Okay,' he replied.

'Some priest,' I told him. 'You're so bossy.'

'Former.' His mouth softened. 'And look who's talking.'

I smiled, and heard a distant scuffing sound above us. Like gravel. Took me off guard. 'He's on the roof?'

'He said he needed air.'

'Any advice?'

'You don't need it.' His fingers danced a string

of notes across the piano keys. 'You always know what you need to do, Maxine.'

He was wrong, of course. Not that being down-right clueless had ever stopped me before. There was an art to living, and sometimes it required the in-exorable, relentless resolve just to keep plowing forward, one step at a time, no matter what the hell it was you were doing.

The rest usually took care of itself.

GRANT'S rooftop garden was accessible only through the apartment, and was, therefore, the one place we could relax together, outside, without worrying about covering my tattoos, or someone seeing the boys. It felt like an island on top of the world, and even though Grant did not have a green thumb like some of the other people in his shelter, he had managed to haul up some troughs of ferns and ivy. Anything with a sweet scent or dash of color had withered with winter.

The boy sat in one of two plastic lawn chairs, arranged near the fire pit, which was currently cold and dead. He did not seem bothered by the damp. He smoked a cigarette.

He saw me coming but did not stand. Just shifted his feet and looked down, tugging at his sweatshirt. I sat beside him in the other chair. Downtown towered before us, glittering like a string of steel and jewels. I heard cars and distant voices, the rumble of an airplane. I felt the boys nearby, in the shadows.

'Hard night,' I said.

119

'Had worse,' he replied.

'Good place to think.'

'I don't know anything,' he told me. 'About the murder.'

I studied his profile. 'That's not what you told me in the alley.'

He licked his lips and took a long drag on his cigarette. Blew smoke into the air, which I inhaled, enjoying the scent. The boy's silence stretched. I dug into the inner pocket of my jacket, swiped before coming up here, and found a packet of M&Ms. I tore open the paper and popped several in my mouth. Held out the rest to the boy. He hesitated, then took them.

Chocolate soothed. 'I'm Maxine.'

My real name. It slipped out before I could stop myself, and I felt frightened for a moment. Had to calm myself down. Not easy. I was losing my edge. I thought, maybe, I had never had one.

'My name is Byron,' said the boy. Real name or fake, but it suited him. His eyes were old. Like a poet's.

'I met his ex-wife tonight,' I said. 'Brian's ex. Her name is Sarai. She paints unicorns.'

'I didn't see anything,' he replied.

'You knew Brian Badelt. I could see it in your eyes.'

The boy stayed quiet. I held my own silence. We sat for a long time, and my stomach growled. No supper. Those lonely M&Ms made me thirsty. I could hardly hear the boy breathe. He was just a pale, skinny face surrounded by shadow.

'I'm sorry you got in the middle,' I finally said. 'I didn't know that would happen.'

'Maybe you didn't care.'

'I cared. I got you back.' Which was a little bit of truth, a little bit of lie. I wanted the boy to feel safe, though, and not because I thought it would make him talk. I just wanted him to relax. I wanted him to know that no one would hurt him. No pain, no price, no nothing that was not his own free will.

Byron's gaze flicked sideways at me. 'How did you do it?'

'The man responsible found me. We talked. He gave you back.'

'Couldn't have been that easy.'

'Does it matter?'

His eyes narrowed. 'You're not one of them.'

'No,' I said, unsure what *one of them* included; whether it was Mafia, or guys with guns, or just the miasma of society, bearing down on his head. 'I'm a lot scarier.'

His mouth twitched. I leaned forward, elbows resting on my knees. 'Badelt had my name in his pocket when he died. That's why I wanted to know more about him. I wanted to know why he was in that alley.' I studied the teen's profile, illuminated by the city lights. 'Was it to talk to you?'

Byron said nothing. I added, 'You probably won't believe me if I make you promises. Words are cheap.

But what I will say is this – I won't force you. You want to leave, you can leave. You want to stay quiet, stay quiet. But I could use your help.'

'Where are we?' he asked.

'The Coop. Maybe you've heard of it. It's a home-less shelter near Chinatown. The man downstairs is the owner. He's a good guy. You can stay as long as you want. Your own room. No strings, not unless you plan on doing drugs or having wild parties.'

He gave me a sharp look. 'That's a bullshit offer. I've heard of the Coop. No one gets their own room.'

'Some do. Special cases. You, if you want it.'

Byron put out his cigarette. 'Nothing is free. Besides, someone will report me to Social Services. They'll have to.'

'You have a good reason not to be at home?'

He shrugged and carefully tucked the butt of his cigarette into his jacket pocket. 'I'd be there, other-wise.'

Sure. Stupid question. I leaned back. The plastic chair was damp, though not nearly as much as I. I could have wrung a river from my clothes.

The boy fingered his sweatshirt, the edge of his coat zipper. His nails were painted black, and bitten down to the quick. I watched him, and the sky. Thinking about demons and the veil. Old men and women. Secrets.

I felt the boys all around us, watching from the shadows. I resisted the urge to finger the brand beneath my ear. My only scar.

122

Byron said, 'I can leave, anytime I want?'

'Anytime. We'll probably start nagging you about a GED after a while, or some other programs, but no one will force you. No one will kick you out.'

He did not believe me. I could see it in his eyes, but that was no surprise. Fourteen, fifteen, and living on the street with a gaze as old as dirt? There was a story there. Not a happy one.

He looked down at his hands. 'Brian brought sandwiches every now and then. He handed them out. Couple times he had coats and blankets, or even just comic books. Never wanted anything in return. It was nice.'

More than nice, given the sudden, stricken misery on his face. He did not look at me, but his eyes were red, and so were his cheeks. His right hand balled into a fist.

Grant had said Byron was scared of men. If he had trusted Badelt, that was a big deal. It would be a big deal for me. His grief was going to run deep.

'Did you see who hurt him?' I asked softly. 'Byron, what happened?'

He shook his head, rubbing his sleeve over his nose. 'Things have been getting rough. Some other people moving in. Guns. More drugs. There's money involved. The pretty girls have been disappearing. Brian gave me a number to call if I ever needed help. So I called. He was going to meet me. He said he had other questions. About something different.'

'Something different? Did he tell you what that was?'

Byron hesitated. 'He was interested in you. Someone named Maxine, anyway.'

'Interested.'

'Not like sex. Just . . . interested. Curious. If I had ever heard of you.'

Curious. About me. That made no sense, other than the fact that Sarai knew my name and face, and had been married to Badelt. And even that was no answer – just another question. This night, full of questions.

I set it aside. 'Tell me about the guns and drugs. The missing girls. Are the same men who took you responsible? Did they kill Badelt?'

Byron ate an M&M, his hand shaking. 'I was just leaving. The man who killed Brian had blond hair. He wore a long coat. Blue or black. Expensive. One of *them.*'

Again, that wording. 'Was he Russian?'

Byron shrugged, which could have meant anything. I sat back, thinking hard. The Wonder Twins and their cohort with the cell phone were certainly blond, but they had been dressed in cheap slacks and Windbreakers, not an expensive long coat.

And Edik, though unspecific about Badelt's death, had implied someone else was responsible. Someone watching me. Or maybe that was just another word game, meant to take the focus off him.

I hated this. My head still hurt, a low-grade

headache centered behind my eyes. I took a deep breath. 'Just one more question, Byron. Had you ever seen me before tonight? When we first met, I thought maybe you had.'

'No,' he said, looking me in the eyes. 'But you were familiar. I don't know why.'

Sicily, I remembered Zee saying. Sorrow in Raw's gaze.

I nodded. 'Thank you, Byron.'

He looked at me, uncertain. 'Now what?'

'That's up to you.'

Byron hesitated. 'Maybe I could stay tonight.'

'Okay,' I said. 'Try it out. You can keep the room downstairs, then in the morning we'll move you to one of the studios. Like a miniapartment, just for you.'

He looked at me like I had snakes coming out of my head, which might have been the case had Dek and Mal still been on my shoulders. The little demons, however, were behind the boy, draped around Raw's neck; the three of them peering around a barrel full of ferns.

'It's the truth,' I said. 'I can show you now.'

'No,' he replied. 'But I still think you're full of it.'

The clouds were clearing. I caught gasps of starlight and thought about the demon with his cloak, dancing on knives.

We have missed your face.

You woke us. Your soul reached for us. Inside the abyss, we felt your call.

125

Blood holds no dominion.
You have need of us.

I stood, savoring the cold breeze that swept over my face. I smelled the ocean and the docks, remnants of grease from Chinatown.

Byron stood, too. He was taller than I, but almost as slender; a hungry look on his face, starved for more than just food.

'How long?' I asked him softly. 'How long have you lived like this?'

I thought he was going to bristle, but then he took a breath, and his shoulders relaxed. 'About six months.'

'And there's no one?'

'There was,' he said, looking down. 'But he died last night.'

I nodded, silent. Started to walk away. Byron cleared his throat, and I stopped, looking back. He fidgeted, fingers worrying at his sweatshirt zipper. My stomach turned, uneasy. 'Yes?'

Byron looked like he was going to be sick. 'I wasn't going to tell you.'

I took a step toward him. 'What?'

The boy pressed the heel of his palm against his brow, as though in pain. His voice dropped to a hoarse whisper. 'The man who shot Brian . . . caught me watching.'

I stopped breathing. 'Did he hurt you?'

Byron nodded, face crumpling. My mind went to places I did not want to imagine, and shied away, wild. 'He let you go. You survived.'

Tears leaked down his cheeks. 'He said a woman would come asking questions. He said he would kill me if I talked. When I got taken tonight . . .'

I thought I was going to die, I imagined him finishing.

His entire body shuddered. I felt *myself* die, just a little. I wrapped my arms around the teen. Gingerly. I was not used to hugging, but he clung to me, crying, wracked with such violent grief I could not imagine all his emotion was from Brian's death alone.

He still thought he was going to die. I could feel it. I had given him a reprieve, that was all. Byron was terrified.

I saw the boys watching us. Zee had one fist knotted against his chest. Raw and Aaz, Dek and Mal – all of them, staring, deep in memory. I could always tell. It was in their ears, their mouths. Slack, distracted.

I held the boy. I held him a long time.

CHAPTER 8

I could not handle it on my own. Grant helped me put the boy to bed, and this time, I let him use the flute. I stood by the door and watched him sit in a chair by the nightstand and play his own music, his own creation. Invented on the spot for Byron's soul.

The teen's psyche sounded a little like the *Firebird Suite*, lilting and eerie and sad. I could not see his aura – only, ever, the shadows of demons – but I felt Grant's power course through me and sink into my bones. I imagined what it must be like to rearrange the colors of a boy's soul – color that reflected energy, energy that represented emotion. A nudge here, a prod there. Gentle. Subtle. Healing. The boy slept. Grant had done that first. To make it easier.

After a while, I left them.

Zee and the others were in the bedroom. Their

teddy bears were out, amputated limbs leaking trails of white cotton stuffing. The boys started humming 'Living on a Prayer' when I walked in, voices high like some demonic version of Alvin and the Chipmunks; but it was a mournful version, and when they started throwing scissors, they only halfheartedly aimed for each other's eyes. I watched them for a moment, then stepped over their current issues of *Playboy, National Geographic*, and the *Wall Street Journal* piled alongside coloring books and half-chewed crayons.

I stripped off my clothes on the way to the bathroom. Felt something heavy in my pocket, and remembered, suddenly, the stone disc Jack had given me. A gift from my mother. I looked at it, rubbing my palm over the smooth soft surface, my fingers trailing through the engraved circular lines, nestled within one another.

I laid it down on the nightstand, heart aching.

I did not look at myself in the mirror. I took a shower. It felt good. I tried not to think too hard. I also tried not to freak out, but I was just not that lucky.

I cried. I cried for myself, my mother. I cried for Badelt and Byron. I did not know why. I had seen people die. I had killed. But I felt like I was coping with my mother's death all over again, and that was more than I could bear. Even thinking about Jack Meddle was no distraction. Just another terrible ache.

I turned off my brain. Stayed under the water a

long time. Scalding hot. I could hardly see the walls for the steam. I was dizzy.

When I exited the bathroom, Grant was in bed. The lights were low. Boys, gone. I pulled back the covers. Saw a lot of skin. I dropped my towel.

Grant, very gently, said, 'I'll make it better.'

And he did.

I was a poor dreamer. I used to have nightmares – or better, visions of elephants soaring, crickets in top hats singing – but since my mother's death, my dreams had been bereft, bullish in their simplicity; my life so terribly bizarre, there was nothing left to conjure in my sleep. If I dreamed, then I was good at forgetting. Mostly, there was only darkness in my mind.

But when I fell asleep that night I dreamed of drums. I dreamed of a valley cast in moonlight, spread beneath me like round cheeks, and there were wing tips against my feet, like the cloak of a dragon, and a taste in my throat that was cinnamon and spice, and something worse, awful and metallic – creamy like butter made from blood.

I was not alone in my dream. The boys were there, ranged about me like wolves, and I was in the company of wolves, real and golden-eyed and sharp with silver fur. I wore fur. I wore gold and silver, and against my brow a slender crown that pricked my skin with thorns. In my hand, a sword.

And behind me, soaring against my back, a wall of darkness, a cloak writhing and twisting, a pale mouth smiling.

It is time, I thought. *This is blood*.
So it was.

WHEN I woke, my skin was covered in tattoos. Sunrise. I had survived the night.

My mouth tasted like cinnamon. I gazed down at my hand, nearly lost in the covers. Red eyes stared back, unblinking and flat. Raw, silver on his chin, distorted upon my skin. He had rested on my thigh yesterday, but the boys never slept in the same spot twice. I rarely let others see my tattoos. Some things were hard to explain.

A warm foot nudged my leg. I rolled over. Grant was propped up on his pillows, early morning sunlight warming his brown hair. He held the stone disc.

'Sorry,' he said, absently. 'I got curious.'

I lay on my stomach, tucking pillows under me, and caught him checking out my tattooed breasts, one of which was currently the bosom pillow for Zee. I looked down and found his mercury hand frozen against my sternum, middle claw raised.

'Well,' I said mildly, 'I know he isn't flipping *me* off.'

'Don't ask,' Grant muttered, and rolled the stone in his large palm. 'What is this?'

'Limited-edition garden ornament. The boys have been watching QVC again.'

His mouth twitched. 'Maxine.'

'Jack Meddle gave it to me. He said it was from my mother.'

'Just like that? Some coincidence.'

'You know how I feel about those.' I ran my finger against the hard, thick muscles of his forearm. 'Do you believe in fairy tales?'

Grant pushed deeper into the covers and turned on his side, placing the stone between us, on the edge of my pillow. 'I believe in you. And I know what I can do. I suppose that means anything is possible.'

I gazed at the stone, and in the morning light the edges of those circular lines resembled veins quickened with glints of lavender and silver – crushed pearls – and though it could have been a trick of the eye, I imagined a faint pulse, as though a tiny heart beat inside the stone.

'Why?' Grant asked.

'I don't know. It was in my head.' I turned, exposing my jaw. 'See anything?'

He peered closely. 'A tattoo extending out of your hairline. Dek or Mal, I'm not sure who. Just enough to cover the mark. I don't feel it anymore, either. Can the boys get rid of scarring?'

'Not to my knowledge.' I wondered why the boys would prefer to expose themselves than allow that brand to remain on my face. Or how Jack had recognized it.

Grant grunted. 'I talked to Zee last night. Tried to get some answers out of him.'

'And?'

'He told me they made some promises.'

132

I buried my head in the pillows. 'I got the same line. Did they give you *anything* useful?'

He smiled. 'Guilt. Something I'm well versed in.'

I could not laugh. 'When you were a priest, did you take confessions?'

'Sure. Have something you want to get off your chest?'

'Ha.' I rubbed the stone with my finger. 'Just wondered if you ever . . . encountered anything truly bizarre. So horrible you had trouble keeping it to yourself.'

'Haven't you kept secrets?'

'Not the kind that mess up a person's life.'

Grant pulled me close. 'Confession, the sacrament, penance . . . all of that is supposed to help sinners commune with God. Self-examination, with me, as priest, standing in for Jesus to exercise forgiveness. It was never my place to judge. And as for repeating what I heard . . . that's something I could never do, not even to save my life. Or anyone else's.'

'But you did judge. You acted.' I looked him dead in the eye. 'You knew you could fix the most troubled. And you used the confessional to find them.'

He did not deny it. He had said as much to me in the past, and it was one of the reasons he had left the priesthood. Too much conflict. Too much danger. Not from himself, but from the Church.

Grant closed his eyes. 'You just had to bring that up.'

'Sorry,' I said.

'Don't be. I just . . . couldn't let some of them go.

133

Not as they were. And maybe that was wrong of me. Could be everything I do is wrong. But you can't compare that to Zee and the others, what they're keeping from you . . .' He stopped, sighing. 'There must be a good reason for it. They love you, Maxine. And not just because they need you to survive.'

I hoped so. I picked up the stone and cradled it above our heads, trying to be careful. My mother had wanted me to have this. My mother. I could hardly imagine it.

I could not understand why.

'It's a labyrinth,' Grant said, tapping the edge of the disc. 'At least, I think so. It's a bit different from what I'm used to.'

I stared at him, surprised. 'You've seen something like this before?'

'The imagery is a mainstay of the Church. Symbolizes the path to salvation, enlightenment.'

Interesting. 'So what's different about it?'

Grant's gaze was sharp, thoughtful. 'A labyrinth has only one beginning, and one end. See where these lines meet the edge? There are nine of them. Nine ways in.'

'It's probably not literal.'

'I'm sure it isn't. But the symbolism is the same across cultures, from ancient Greece, to Iran and China. Relics have been found in pre-Columbian North and South America. Australia, even. And in all those places, labyrinths are depicted a certain way. Not like this.'

'Expert much?'

'Had to be.'

'You've got that glint in your eye.'

He grinned. 'It's a fascinating topic. And a very appropriate gift. Your mother knew what she was doing.'

'She usually did,' I replied dryly.

'But see, look at this.' He tapped the stone, tracing his finger around the concentric lines. 'There may be nine ways in, but there's only one way to the center, once you slip into this opening . . . right here. One single path. A unicursal maze. And all it takes is faith to reach the end. Not logic. Just endurance.'

'My mother would have appreciated the sentiment.'

'There's something else she would have liked more. The archetype of the warrior.' Grant looked into my eyes. 'If you study the myths associated with labyrinths, there's always a malevolent presence within it – the Minotaur, Satan, Khumbaba. But where there is evil . . .'

'There's someone fighting against it.'

'In the labyrinth, the warrior will defeat the darkness,' he said quietly. 'And win salvation for all.'

I closed my eyes, imagining my mother gazing at the stone and its engraving. Contemplating her daughter's future. 'That doesn't explain why she didn't just give this to me herself.'

'Part of the message?' Grant raised his brow. 'Leaving things to faith, the convoluted path? Maybe she thought it would mean more if you received it . . . later.'

After she was dead. A message beyond the grave. That, too, made sense. My mother had been esoteric in life; death, apparently, had not changed a thing.

'You know,' said Grant thoughtfully, 'from a human consciousness standpoint, a labyrinth is seen as a door between two worlds. Some also believe that prehistoric labyrinths might have served as traps, symbolic or not, for . . . malevolent spirits.'

I shook my head. 'I'm convinced. Message received.'

Grant's mouth twitched. 'Still doesn't explain the deviation in the iconography. The lack of order, the nine points of entry.'

I snuggled deeper into his side. 'You sound like a professor.'

'Does it turn you on?'

'Keep talking.'

He began to smile, but a faint line gathered between his eyes. He held up the stone disc, turning it in the light.

'What?' I asked.

'Something that doesn't make sense. I keep thinking it's my imagination.' He hesitated, still staring at the stone. 'A person in a coma has an aura. Deep indicators. But the longer and harder someone sleeps, the shallower that light becomes. And those who are damaged beyond repair . . .'

'They pulse,' I said quietly, reaching out to touch

the engraving, the glints of silver. I traced the lines, feeling something shift inside my mind; a dark flutter. 'Reduced to heartbeats.'

Grant stared. 'You see it.'

'Something.' My gaze was drawn to my hand: another kind of snarl, a jam of knots and complications, a maze of flesh and time and death. Each line in my skin, evidence of a life I was responsible for. No running, either. I was the bars of my own cage. Jailer and the jailed.

The phone rang. Grant did not pick it up. He pulled me close and leaned over my body until I was covered in his skin. I hooked my leg around his. I felt small when he held me. Safer than I should. Warm. Grant was the only thing the boys allowed me to feel when they slept.

'Listen,' he said quietly. 'This is not you, alone.'

'Okay,' I whispered. 'But we had this conversation.'

He leaned his forehead against mine. 'I mean it, Maxine. Please.'

'I know.' I kissed the corner of his mouth. 'Go figure.'

He smiled, though it was strained. I could not see his eyes. Made me flash back to the demon, Oturu, and I forced Grant away just enough so that I could look at him fully.

He hid nothing from me. Not one tremor. Not the heat, or the full beat of his strength, which was steady, calm. I did not know what he saw in my eyes, but I knew what I felt. It scared me.

'Don't,' he said.

'People get hurt because of me.'

'Faith, endurance.' Grant held up the stone. 'Listen to your mother.'

I laughed at the irony. 'If I listened to my mother, I wouldn't be here right now. And you would probably be dead.'

Grant made a face and rolled out of bed. I sat up, tossing aside covers. My body was dark with tattoos, even down to my toenails: the color of claws. No nail polish for me. Never stuck.

I thought about Byron and grabbed my jeans and boots, dragging a navy cashmere turtleneck from the closet. Grant yanked on a pair of jogging pants that slung low across his lean hips. I tossed him the cane. His eyes were sharp, his jaw set. Sexy beast.

I swiped the stone disc from the bed and shoved it into the back pocket of my jeans. The floors in the living room were slippery with sunlight. I glimpsed blue sky through the windows and grabbed a pair of gloves from the coffee table.

Byron was not in the spare bedroom. The bed was made.

I stood there, disappointed. Grant placed his hand on my shoulder. 'Maybe we should check downstairs. He might be eating breakfast.'

Or maybe he had run like hell. Not that I would blame him. I was the reason he had gotten hurt. He probably figured I was also the reason Badelt had been murdered.

138

I left Grant to finish getting dressed. There was no direct access to the shelter from his apartment. I had to go outside, and the morning air was crisp and damp, with only a faint scent from the docks to mar the breeze. Made me miss Wisconsin winter sunrises, with air so cold it cut the lungs like a knife. During the day, the only temperature I could feel was in my lungs. Gave a place some texture.

I entered the shelter near the kitchen and smelled bacon grease and coffee. Past the swinging doors, pots banged and the dishwasher rattled, competing with sounds of laughter. Smokey Robinson blared from the intercom that fed into the cafeteria. Folks liked some Motown with their cereal.

One of the volunteers staggered in from the loading bay, holding a trough of day-old glazed doughnuts, donated from a local bakery. I snagged one. 'Don't suppose you've seen a kid around, have you? Teen, pierced, black spiked hair and sweatshirt?'

'There's a dozen of them out there this morning,' grumbled the woman. 'Take your pick.'

I pushed open the swinging doors, peering into the cafeteria. Long tables filled the room, most of them packed. My gaze slipped over tired, worn faces, some cheerful smiles, and several tense men and women with quiet children sitting between them. I saw a group of teens, trying to be small over by the wall. But not Byron.

No zombies this morning, either. That was some relief. Too much tension when they were around.

139

And when newcomers showed up, initial interactions were always unpredictable. Especially if the zombie encountered me before Grant.

I finished off the doughnut, made a quick pass through the main halls, then went back outside. Took a walk through the garden. Smelled the sharp tang of cedar sap and grass. Felt the boys doing the same, in their sleep. Raw tugged on my arm. I paused, then started walking in that direction. My eyes ached.

On the edge of the shelter's grounds, near a battered chain-link fence, I saw a tiny figure standing by a tree. A little girl, alone. I could not see her face because she was staring away from me, at the road, but her hair was dark, and she was dressed in denim overalls and red boots. Cute outfit. I remembered having one just like it.

I looked for a parent – any kind of adult – but except for some lone figures standing outside the main shelter doors, I seemed to be it. Made my heart squeeze in a bad way. Sometimes people abandoned their children at the Coop. I had only seen it happen once, but Grant assured me that by the summer, we would probably have several more. Folks got tired, desperate. Thought it was the only way to take care of their kids and offer them a better life.

The boys started tugging on my skin as I approached the child. I rubbed my arms and slowed down, keeping some distance between the girl and myself.

'Hello,' I said.

'Greetings,' replied the girl, unmoving. I waited a beat, then walked a wide circle, unable to take my gaze off her face. My stomach dropped. Dizziness cut. It was hard for me to stand. Cold fear rode over conscious thought.

The girl was me. At eight years old.

I stared at her. Cars passed behind me. I heard seagulls and the bellow of a distant ship horn; coarse laughter by the shelter; the faint creak of leather as my gloved hands clenched into fists. Trying not to let them shake.

The girl did not look at me, but I saw the edge of her eyes: mine in shape and color, but cold, empty. 'I heard things, even in the darkness. Within the veil. Great tales of this world, sprung to life after our passage. Humanity, risen into an empire of enlightenment, unlike any other beyond the Labyrinth. Such wonders,' she whispered, her voice adult. 'Such desperate, terrible wonders.'

'And now you're here,' I said. 'Now you see.'

'I see,' she said. 'I am full of seeing, and still I hunger. You would not understand such hunger. For immortals trapped behind eternity, in the interminable prison dark, stories are currency. Stories are life. Stories are to be bartered, to become blood.'

Her appearance was an affront, no doubt meant to put me off balance. But it was her words that twisted me. 'You didn't cross the veil to hunt stories.'

The girl smiled, looking far away. 'On the contrary. I have come for nothing but. And oh, the tales I will tell. No Wardens. No Avatars. Humans, ignorant and squealing in their misery. Nothing protecting this world. This world, that is *nothing* as we believed. Empires squandered. Gold and iron, and no soul.'

'You sound disappointed.'

The girl's little hand slid from her pocket. Twine dangled. Or maybe it was hair, braided into a string. 'Memories compete. I am older than some. I remember other worlds. Dazzling worlds. I had hoped this one would earn its place in the pantheon. But what am I, except old-fashioned in desire? After we are done here, there will be other empires to admire. An infinity, beyond the Labyrinth.'

She was talking to herself. Riddles. 'You came here to see me. You know what I am.'

'You, Hunter,' said the girl disdainfully. 'Prison guard. Host to an army of runts. I have heard stories of your bloodline, as well, but you are not so much to reckon. Ten thousand years thins the spirit. And human flesh was ever so easy to carve.'

'Then you *don't* know me,' I said quietly, stepping close. 'And you're welcome to get in line.'

The girl smiled. 'One thing first, Hunter. Before we scrabble in the grass. Tell me of Jack. Jack and his Sarai Soars. The wolf and the unicorn.'

Expect the unexpected. But that question still clubbed my heart. I fought to keep my expression smooth, cold. 'How do you know them?'

The girl held up her hand. Skin shimmered, becoming so translucent I could look through her palm at her face. Like smoke. Or a ghost. Around us, the air cooled as though shaved by ice.

I gritted my teeth. 'That was you last night.'

Her hand solidified. 'My eyes are everywhere. And Jack and Sarai, no matter what they call themselves, are . . . old friends. Imagine my surprise to see you with them. Just imagine. If you had not been there, we would not be having this conversation. I would have . . . ignored you.'

'And now?'

'Now you are part of the game. Now, while I have been given a reprieve from my masters, I will seize the moment to settle old stories.'

'No,' I breathed coldly. 'You stay away from them.'

'Or what?' The girl regarded me with distant, imperious condescension. 'You are only *one*, and alone. The Wardens are dead, Hunter. And you will be the blood I use as ink, as I write *the end* upon my skin.'

I walked to the little girl, that demon wearing my baby face, and leaned down with ice in my veins. 'I never liked wasting time.'

'Nothing is ever wasted.' The demon grabbed my throat. She had a strong grip. Might have pulverized regular human flesh, crushed it into mush, but I just stood there while she strained, and silently stripped off my gloves.

I grabbed her wrist. Aaz dug in. I watched my own face – eight years old, demon me – slacken with

143

surprise. Hardened my heart and held tight, kneeling as all the boys got in on the act of absorbing her life into their bodies – using Aaz as the direct conduit. The demon's grip on my throat loosened, mouth twisting in agony. Her eyes shut.

'Thank you for not ignoring me,' I whispered.

The child snarled, facial features contorting, losing solidity. And then, with a snap like bones cracking, she dissolved completely – and disappeared into smoke.

Aaz could not hold on. Neither could I. In seconds, the demon was gone. But she reappeared just out of reach, a shadow of me – colors faded, washed out, as though standing on the other side of a black-and-white television screen.

'This is my world,' I said hoarsely.

'Mine first,' she breathed. 'Mine, again. You cannot stop that. The veil is falling, Hunter. And when the others learn what I have discovered—'

She stopped, a shudder ripping through her frame – and the face she wore, mine, trembled briefly into something older and far more expressive. Oturu's mark burned, throbbing to my heartbeat. I wanted to touch it, but dug my fingers into my thighs.

'Go home, demon,' I told her. 'Go back inside the prison. Or I *will* kill you.'

The girl's face stopped shifting, and she looked at me with glittering endless eyes, ancient and terrifying. 'That is not my home, Hunter. And I am *not* a demon.'

I lunged toward her. She disappeared again. Only this time, she did not come back.

I pushed myself up to my knees, staring at the spot. Boys restless on my skin. It took me ten minutes before I was strong enough to stand. Ten minutes before my thoughts settled into some echo of rational calm.

But my legs wobbled. My heart thundered.

I was scared. Really scared.

Just not for me.

CHAPTER 9

WHEN I was twelve years old, I watched my mother pull a man from a burning car. Freak accident on a stretch of Oklahoma highway. Not many other vehicles involved, but a semi changed lanes, colliding with a sedan, and things got ugly. Big fire, unconscious driver.

My mother never hesitated. She disappeared into the blaze and came back, clothes burning, hair on fire. A man draped across her shoulders; hurt, but breathing. My mother, totally unharmed. Sporting a new haircut. She dumped the man, and got back into the station wagon. Gunned the engine and pulled a hard U-turn on the median. Drove us out of there.

Never heard a peep on the radio, afterward – not even a segment on the news – though nowadays there would probably be a cell-phone video making our lives hell on YouTube. Not that it would matter, given the alternative.

'Exceptions to the rules,' my mother would say. 'There are always exceptions.'

Drawing attention for a good cause was one of them. Like fighting demons, even if it was in broad daylight. Lost opportunities, after all, were like wasting air while drowning a mile underwater. No matter who might be watching.

I turned around and saw Byron.

I did not know how long he had been standing there, but he was pale and skinny in his oversized clothes, and his eyes belonged to a kid who had not only seen some bad things, but might have just witnessed something downright crazy, like a grown woman tussling with a child that could vanish into thin air.

'Hey,' I said, awkwardly. 'I was looking for you.'

'I was on your roof,' he said, voice hollow, almost like he was talking on automatic pilot. 'Grant said you guys didn't check there.'

I nodded, then realized his gaze had dropped to my hands. I had shoved my gloves into a pocket. Forgotten to put them back on. Too busy thinking about the end of the world. And one old man who might be my grandfather.

I had to warn him. I needed answers.

I tried to play it cool as I pulled on my gloves, but I felt like the mask had been ripped off my face. All my secrets, naked and burning.

Byron swallowed hard. 'You got more of those?'

'Here and there,' I said shortly.

'You don't look like the tattoo type.'

'Told you I was scary.'

Some of the tension leaked from his shoulders. 'Scary's not bad sometimes.'

A smile tugged at my mouth. 'Thanks, kid.'

He seemed embarrassed and rubbed his nose, glancing past my shoulder. I looked, just in case, but saw no sign of a demonic mini-me. Found him checking me out again, though. I did not budge from the scrutiny, his searching gaze; emotions flickering in his face: doubt, fear, unease. Maybe some appreciation, though God only knew what that was for.

'You eaten breakfast?' I asked him.

'I was going to bail,' he said. 'I can't stay here.'

'Don't leave on an empty stomach.' I walked past him, trying to act more relaxed than I felt. 'Unless you're a vegetarian. In which case, you're screwed.'

I did not wait to see if he followed though my ears strained for his footsteps. I heard him, after a moment, and kept my mouth shut when he caught up, matching my pace. He walked with a hunched shuffle – bad posture, trying not to be noticed.

'Why do you live here?' Byron asked.

'Why not?' I checked around us for more demons, or pieces of the sky falling; maybe locusts and flying toads. 'Why do you live on the street?'

'Because it's there,' he replied.

I glanced sideways. 'Still haven't seen those

rooms. Locks on the doors. Your own key. Might be able to swing you a job here, or somewhere close by.'

'Whatever,' he muttered, but I could tell he was interested. I did not have much practice at dealing with kids his age – kids at all, period – but I thought I was doing okay. He was not running yet. No matter what he might have seen.

We reached the main doors of the Coop. Byron cleared his throat, his hand sliding up to finger a bruise at the side of his neck. I had not noticed it the night before. I wanted to ask where the injury had come from – if there were more – but I thought I knew. Just one more thing to feel sick about.

Byron caught me looking, and his hand froze. I pretended not to notice. Just kept walking. Jack and Sarai floating at the back of my mind.

Old friends.

Old friends with a demon. Or whatever that creature might be.

I patted my back pocket and felt the stone disc. My mother and her secrets. My grandmother.

'Fuck,' I muttered. Byron glanced at me, and I added, 'Sorry.'

The teen shrugged like it was nothing, but I still felt embarrassed. I was not a brilliant example for good behavior. Not for a kid. Not that Byron cared, I suspected.

The main kitchen had a volunteer lounge where all the folks who kept the Coop running could go and chill out. Eat, read, watch some television. Byron and I grabbed trays and plates and squeezed in between the servers on the main line to grab some breakfast. I did not feel hungry – I had to hit the road, like *now* – but the boy was walking wounded. I could see it in his eyes. If I ran off, he might not be here when I got back. And I wanted him to be. I needed him to be safe, almost as much as I needed to see Jack and Sarai.

No good reason for it. Something in Byron just hit me the hard way. Or maybe that was guilt. He had gotten hurt because of me. Badelt and his questions.

I forced myself to eat, and halfway between the second and third bite, my stomach started growling happily. Byron tucked in more food than I, but not by much. Both our plates, piled high with scrambled eggs and bacon, hash browns smothered in ketchup; toast, butter, jam. Another doughnut.

'I'm gonna puke,' Byron said, toward the end of his plate. He stuffed another piece of bread in his mouth.

'You could eat like this every day,' I muttered, dialing the information services number on my cell phone. I asked for the Sarai Soars Art Gallery, but according to the man clicking away on the other end of the line, such a place did not exist. Or if it did, was unlisted.

I slammed the phone into my jacket pocket. Byron stared at me, a piece of bacon hanging limply in his fingers. 'Brian was married to a woman named Sarai.'

I suddenly felt sorry I had made that call in front of him. 'He talked to you about her?'

'Said she was beautiful.' Byron shrugged, and dropped the bacon back on his plate. 'Also said she was a pain in the ass, but that most women were.'

Sounded like the man in the picture. 'Was she the one who hired Badelt to come looking for me?'

'Don't know.' Byron rubbed his hands on his jeans. 'You're not going to tell the police I saw anything, are you?'

'No,' I said firmly. 'Far as they know, you don't exist.'

He nodded, jaw tight. Like maybe he really was feeling queasy. I pushed back my chair. 'Let me show you that room.'

The private wing was on the second floor of the middle warehouse, between the dining hall and the common rest areas. Grant had set it up in order to accommodate those special cases he occasionally encountered – families or individuals who were particularly close to getting back on their feet, but needed that extra push – or even folks who were not remotely near success, but who would benefit from the confidence of having their own place.

It was a closely guarded secret. A tricky balance. Grant was good at it.

My key chain was full. I let us into the wing, and we walked down a long corridor that had been painted a pale sand color with white accents. Track lighting and a simple tile floor lent an upscale quality that

151

helped residents forget they were living in a home-less shelter. I stopped halfway down in front of a white door. Opened it and let Byron in.

It was the same size and shape as a hotel room, with a bathroom directly to the right of the door, and just beyond, a bed and dresser. A telephone sat on the narrow nightstand, along with a pad of paper and a pen. One window faced southeast. Sunlight trickled through the sheer curtain. The walls were white, the furniture simple, in some cottage style.

Byron stopped in the middle of the room, staring. His back was to me. I wanted to see his face, but I was afraid to move. 'It's yours, kid. No rent, though most people volunteer downstairs to make up the difference. And like I said before, no drugs, no parties. We'll nag you to get your GED.'

He said nothing. I thought of Jack, the demon, and crept close, behind him. 'Byron. I need to go take care of something. Will you be all right if I leave you here?'

He nodded. I held out the door key, over his shoulder. 'This lock is the same as the main wing door. We'll change it if you decide to stay.'

Byron looked down at the key, then took it, almost gingerly. Raw tugged on my hand, rearing up toward the boy. He wanted me to remove my glove. I ignored him. I backed away from Byron, shoving my protesting hand into my jacket pocket.

As I began to leave the room, the boy turned, just slightly. 'Maxine.'

Maxine. It felt strange hearing him say my name. He spoke so softly I could hardly hear him. I still could not see his face.

His hand hung down at his side, clenched around the key. 'The man who killed Brian . . . he was one of them. You know. Part of the group selling drugs and taking girls.' Byron paused. 'You asked yesterday. I never answered your question.'

'Thank you,' I said heavily. 'You just helped me.'

The back of the boy's head moved in a jerky nod. He looked very small and slender inside his ratty clothes. I had the overwhelming urge to take him shopping, which meant it was time to get out, fast. Holy crap. My mother had been right. Stay in one place too long, and you just might lose your mind.

I shut the door and left. All I had to deal with now was Grant.

I found him at the chapel. He was playing his flute, perched on the edge of a chair beside the pulpit, his cane leaning against his thigh. More than half the seats in front of him were filled. Already deep into his morning inspirational, something the regulars liked to call a 'quirk of the man.'

It was an informal thing. Grant might have left the priesthood, but the priest had not left the man, and he liked saying a few words in the morning to anyone who showed up to pray. Nothing sugary, or full of fire and brimstone. Just a gentle sentiment or two, mostly about being optimistic, finding joy in life. Followed by a bit of music. Always, music.

He was performing 'Danny Boy' this morning, pouring out its sweet mournful tones. Power tickled over my skin. The man at work. Grant was the only other person I had ever met who straddled the lines of the mundane and the supernatural. He did it easily, with grace. Playing his music, masking it as brief entertainment – right now, shifting the auras of the congregated in subtle, quiet ways. Leaving folks with a lightness of the spirit, a sense of possibility, hope. An easing of despair.

Grant, able to create joy within anyone. Except me. The only person he could not affect. Which was for the best. I had my own way of being happy – a reliance on smaller moments. Flashes etched together in my memories like a quilt, or scenes from a movie – a Western, some lone gunfighter standing against an entire army. Bad attitude, terrible odds. Hard to kill.

I saw some zombies in the audience, rapt.

You are playing with fire, I thought at Grant, unable to shake the old uneasiness, my fear for him – that he could change souls and demons with nothing but a song.

I was afraid one day he would change himself.

I heard feet pounding down the hall, and stepped outside in time to see Mary racing helter-skelter toward the chapel. She had giant sunflowers on her dress, and cats the size of soccer balls adorning a giant shapeless sweater that came down to her knees. A streak of red lipstick had been applied haphazardly across her withered mouth. She almost ran past me into the chapel, then stopped, fixing me with a fierce look. 'Someone is committing sin.'

'Sin,' I said.

'Sin,' Mary hissed impatiently, and pointed behind her. 'Murder.'

I blinked once, brain on the fritz. Then ran.

I had no idea where to go, but I strained to hear, and caught a shout somewhere in front of me, at the end of the winding halls. Glass shattered, floating on startled gasps. Sounded like it was coming from the lobby. I raced around a corner in the hall, brushing past ragged women who looked over their shoulders, dragging children.

At the end of the corridor, by the front volunteer desk, I saw a big man dressed in loose gray pants, his body dwarfed by an immense brown coat that made him look like a bear. His beard was dirty, tangled and damp, his hairy hands shaped like baseball mitts.

He was also a zombie. One of the regulars, a convert to Grant.

Byron was on the ground in front of him.

My focus narrowed to a knifepoint. Painful. The boy was conscious, but badly hurt. Unable to stand. I watched in horror as the man slammed a heavy boot into his back. I was too far away to stop it.

Others tried to intervene, but the zombie was too big, crazed. Rex was in the middle, grappling to get between him and the boy. His leg was torn, bleeding. Glass all over the floor. Anger in his eyes. Anger and hunger. Feeding, soaking in pain and fear – slips of raw energy. I could almost see the straw.

He saw me coming, and his expression shifted. He shouted again at the other zombie, but this time it was a warning.

Too late. Rex threw himself to the side as I barreled into the zombie. I hit him so hard he flew off his feet, slamming into the wall. I heard a crack, a rumble, felt plaster rain down on my head – but the zombie kept fighting, his eyes bulging, crazed. I had never seen one of them so blind with rage.

He stood, and I followed, gritting my teeth as he grabbed my arm, shaking me hard. He did not stop. He started screaming, and the boys stirred, restless, dreaming violence. Dreaming the zombie's scent.

I grabbed his crotch and twisted with all my strength. Demonic parasites felt pain while inhabiting their human hosts, and the man beneath me screamed. I squeezed harder. His loose pants made it easy. He let go of my arm and tried to hit me, but I sidestepped, still pulling, and that only hurt him more.

He dropped. I yanked so hard he fell backward, like a tank. The floor shook. I stepped on his neck before he could curl up on himself, and when he did not look at me, I slapped his cheek and grabbed his beard. He trembled, red-faced, breath rattling.

Sober now, cut sharp as a nun. Staring at me as though he realized he was about to die.

I controlled myself, barely. 'Rex. Get these people out of here.'

'No,' Rex said. 'Hunter.'

I snapped my head around and stared into his eyes. 'Do it, or you're next.'

'I'd listen to her,' said Grant. I looked over my shoulder and found him standing behind us, quiet as a wolf. His knuckles were white around the head of his cane. In his other hand, the flute.

The zombie bucked beneath me. I dropped, slamming my fist into the floor by his head, shattering the tile. 'Do not even *think* about fucking with me. You try anything, you even *think* about standing up, and I will have you shitting out of your dick so fast you'll *beg* me to rip it off.'

The zombie froze. Everyone was quiet. Dark spots danced in my eyes. Rex said a few low words, and I heard feet shuffling, a halting murmur. I looked sideways and found Byron near me, eyes closed. Unconscious.

Everything inside me stilled. The boy's face was a wreck. Left eye swelling, bruised veins streaking into his lower cheek. His nose was broken, blood flowing across his upper lip, and his brow was covered in cuts and scrapes, like a bootheel had rubbed off the skin. Did not seem real. I could still see him standing in that damn apartment. He had been out of my sight for only ten minutes.

Rex knelt. 'Nine-one-one's already been called.'

I forced myself to look away. Grant leaned near, as far as his cane would allow, gazing at the zombie sprawled beneath me.

Grant said, 'You beat that child.'

His voice was impossibly soft, terrifyingly cold. The zombie sucked in his breath, shuddering; his eyes bloodshot, chest heaving. 'I forgot myself. Please. *Please* don't let her kill me. I saw him and forgot. *I forgot.*'

I did not care for coincidence. Byron was too specific a target. 'Why the boy? Did someone put you up to it? Edik? *Blood Mama?*'

The zombie looked from Grant to me, and shook his head, desperate. Words spilled from his mouth, demonic words. Rex drew near, and the zombie shifted to English.

'Tell them,' hissed the possessed man. 'Rex, *tell* them.'

Rex looked away. 'No, Scotty.'

The zombie looked incredulous. 'But . . . he's a *skin.*'

'Skin,' I echoed sharply. 'What do you mean by that?'

Scotty clamped his mouth shut. Rex turned away, walking to the corner of the reception area, no purpose to his movement; simply, as though he needed the distance. I glanced again at Byron. The boy seemed to be breathing, but he was still as stone.

'Answer her question,' Grant said. 'Why did you use that word?'

Scotty refused to speak. I said, 'He crossed the line. You know that.'

'Maxine.'

158

'No. He's *mine*.'

Grant closed his eyes. I stripped off my gloves. The zombie wept, no longer fighting; only begging, begging so hard. I felt no mercy. I had found demons in grandmothers and kindergarten teachers, in police officers and politicians. I had exorcised children and the dying. The demons were all the same. Pain was the guarantee, no matter what the package looked like.

I placed my hand against the zombie's brow. 'Any last words?'

'Bargain,' he gasped.

'No. Give me free words, and I'll make it fast. Promise me no one made you do this.'

Scotty said nothing, which was all the answer I needed. His aura began to pull away from his head; the demon inside, preparing itself for a quick escape.

Like hell. I pressed my hand even harder against his brow and spat out the words my mother taught me. Old words, ancient. The demon inside the man shook loose in moments. I trapped it in my hand. Just a wisp, a smoke signal. The little demon screamed, his voice like a high, piercing whistle.

And the boys, in their sleep, sucked its body into my skin – and ate it.

Ten seconds from start to finish. Grant still had his eyes closed. I was afraid to touch him, but as I pulled away he grabbed my hand, raised it to his cheek, and held it there. I started breathing again, and kissed his shoulder.

Beneath me, Scotty groaned. I stepped off his body and crouched by Byron. I touched his hair, but that was all. I did not want to hurt him. Fear made me sick. So did rage.

Grant said, 'Rex. We'll need help here.'

The zombie said nothing. He left the reception area. Grant leaned down and sang a soft melody under his breath. Power prickled. On the floor, the man's breathing calmed. Grant did not stop humming. I did not know what he observed in the man's aura, but his melody shifted, and I could almost imagine a jigsaw puzzle: a rearrangement of fragments, slipping new cues into place.

Possession, whispered a tiny voice in my head. *Grant is no different.*

But he was. I would never believe otherwise.

Grant stopped humming. His silence was profound, as cutting as his song. He leaned heavily on his cane, thoughtful, and glanced at some of the men who walked into the reception area. All of them were regulars to the shelter, fellow homeless, big strong guys who were studying for their GEDs. I knew, because every now and then I tutored a class. They knelt by Scotty and helped him sit up.

I sat down on the floor, feeling like a German shepherd, and guarded the boy until the ambulance came.

THE shit hit the fan at the same time. EMTs, police, sirens wailing so loud I heard babies crying. Some

160

of the guys who had been helping with Scotty scattered fast. No one wanted to be around a badge and uniform. Including me.

I had to talk to the officers. No sign of Suwanai or McCowan, but word would leak back. I could only imagine what they would think, but all I hoped for was that no one linked Byron to Badelt. A can of worms I did *not* want to deal with. Not through official channels, anyway.

EMTs carried Byron out on a stretcher. He wore a neck brace. Grant limped close, haggard. 'I'm going to have to call Social Services. If I don't, the hospital will.'

I pressed my knuckles against my forehead. 'I should have been more careful. I promised that kid everything would be okay. Now he's practically in a coma.'

Grant sighed. 'He's faking unconsciousness, Maxine. He's awake.'

I froze. 'You're kidding.'

'I was distracted. Didn't notice the mark in his aura until ten minutes ago, but there were too many people around to call him out. The EMTs will figure it out soon, if they haven't already.'

'You think he heard me kill that demon?'

'Don't know. But no matter how badly he's been hurt, I doubt he'll stick around that hospital long enough for the police to question him. Or for Social Services to take custody.'

I felt sick, like a monster, for not being able to

protect the boy – or keep the rug firmly under his feet. 'Someone needs to be with him.'

'Why do I get the feeling I've been assigned the job?'

'Because you're the only one I trust. Scotty called Byron a piece of skin. Nothing but *a* skin. Zee used that word last night to describe Jack Meddle, and here it is again, out of the mouth of a zombie. A zombie who just so happened to attack a boy who knew Badelt.' I closed my eyes, hands tapping against my thighs. 'Byron said that Badelt was murdered by the same people running drugs through the university district. That would be Edik's group.'

'And he answers to Blood Mama,' Grant said grimly, then looked on as the police led Scotty out of the lobby.

It was terrible. The big man seemed so lost. Human again . . . and now this. I wondered how long he had been possessed, how much had been stolen from his life. Certainly, his freedom. If I had exorcised the man as I should have the first time I met him, all this could have been avoided.

Made me angry. At myself – and Grant. Though it was hard to hold that anger when I looked into Grant's face and saw something cracking, breaking. He watched the police take Scotty like he was the one in handcuffs. He listened with awful tension as the big man protested he did not remember committing a crime.

I grabbed his hand. 'Don't.'

'Don't,' he echoed bleakly. 'Don't soften it. You and I both know how this happened.'

'Sure,' I replied. 'But the boy's a target. If not Scotty, then someone else. No good looking back.'

Grant rubbed his thumb over the back of my hand. 'I hadn't planned on letting you out of my sight quite so soon. I seem to remember making an impassioned speech last night.'

'It was a good speech,' I told him; and then, gently: 'I'll be fine.'

'You're talking to me, Maxine.'

'I will be fine,' I said again, more firmly. 'Really. I'm more worried about the boy. And you.'

Grant shook his head. 'I would say, *I'll be fine*, but then we'll just start all over again. And we'd both be lying.'

'Go,' I said, feeling miserable. 'Be careful. I'd do it myself, but there's other trouble.'

He gave me a sharp look. Rex approached. His aura was dull, his expression guarded. Grant leaned in and whispered something in the zombie's ear. Rex looked at me and shook his head, but Grant grabbed his arm and the dark spittle of Rex's demon aura fluttered, gasping under the power of Grant's touch, the barely audible melody of his voice. That was all it took. It helped that Rex was willing.

Convert. Goody Two-Shoes. Demonic son of a bitch declaring himself free for the light. Weaning himself from pain. And Blood Mama. There might have been twenty other zombies, male and female, who felt the same. All of them rotated through the shelter, coming in for regular musical *treatments*, personal sessions with Grant that allowed him to modify the energy patterns in their demon spirits. Mornings in the chapel were icing on the cake.

Not that Scotty could be called a success story.

Some of the people in the reception area still watched us. I disliked the scrutiny, but Grant caught my hand and pulled me close. '*You* be careful,' he whispered. I nodded dumbly, swallowed up by the intensity of his gaze. There were promises in Grant's eyes. Always, promises.

He backed off, slowly – gave Rex another hard look – then limped down the hall.

I watched until he was gone, then turned to the zombie. He stood with his hands shoved in his pockets, a demon staring from those human eyes. He was a man of all trades in this place. He helped people, was well liked. But he still fed on pain – even if he did not cause any.

Rex did not move. Neither did I. Behind us, people began talking again, laughing uneasily. I heard a broom, the tinkle of glass. Somewhere, the dulcet croon of Smokey Robinson. I smelled blood, but Rex seemed unconcerned by his injury.

'Let's go somewhere else,' I told him.

We found a bench down the hall and sat. Rex stared at the wall across from us, painted butter yellow and covered with fat butterflies, painted by the children who used the day-care services the shelter

provided. I saw tulips, fairies hiding in red petals –
a blue bird caught in a shaft of thick goopy sunlight,
winging above the jagged waves of a green sea. A
mermaid looked back at me.

'Feel better?' Rex asked. 'A little murder make
your morning?'

'You didn't protect the boy.'

'I didn't get there in time. Scotty was out of control.
Not like I did the rest.'

But maybe it tasted good. Maybe it was sweet. I
studied his eyes, the flicker of his aura, which was
a shallower shade of darkness than others of his kind.
The only evidence Grant had affected him.

'Scotty tried to kill Byron for a reason,' I said.
'And you know what it is.'

'Not true,' he replied, but something small
squirmed in his gaze, and I felt it click inside me
like a key, turning.

We were alone in the hall. I took off my gloves.
'Nothing gets past you, Rex. I bet you knew Edik
had a message for me, just waiting to be delivered.
Maybe you knew about Badelt, too. One human man,
looking for the Hunter. Seems like that would cause
some gossip. Gosh, I suppose you might even know
who ordered his death. Like . . . Edik? Blood Mama?'

Rex stared at my hands, the tattoos. 'You're
wrong.'

'Grant won't care if I get rid of you. Not now.
Not if you betrayed me.'

'Grant doesn't know what you are.'

165

'So you admit to holding out on me.'

'Fuck you,' he snapped. 'I've done *nothing*.'

'That's the point.' I placed my hand on his wound. His blood soaked into my skin, and he shuddered, fists digging into his upper thighs. He made no move to fight me. He knew better.

'Stop it,' he hissed.

'Give me what I want,' I told him quietly. 'Or sit there. The boys will bleed you out. You'll be dead in ten minutes.'

'And if I leave this body?' Rex drew in a shaky breath, looking at me with hate in his eyes. 'If I run? Would you still kill the host?'

'I'd kill you,' I replied. 'I'll kill you, either way. But only if you don't talk.'

'I did not betray Grant,' Rex snarled. 'Not him. Not his trust.'

'Touching. Answer my questions.'

'I don't know who killed the investigator,' he insisted.

'But you knew he was asking questions.'

'I'd heard rumors, but I didn't believe them. It made no sense.'

'And Edik? The *veil*? What game is Blood Mama playing?'

'Blood Mama does what she must to survive. But if you're asking if she made a deal, I can't tell you that. I don't know.'

'You know enough,' I retorted. 'You must have some idea.'

166

'I have an idea that all the inmates want to tear the prison down. Isn't that enough?' Rex closed his eyes, shaking his head. 'The only reason Blood Mama hasn't ordered my execution is that she thinks I'll be useful with Grant. She hasn't given up on him. She never will, Hunter.'

I took my hand off his leg. My palm was warm, dry. The boys felt cozy on my skin. They liked snacks. 'Blood Mama and I have an agreement. A bargain made by one of my ancestors. Grant is off-limits. Anyone I mark is safe.'

I felt like an idiot saying those words. It was a lie. No one was ever safe. Rex gave me a disdainful look. 'Old bargains. You and your kin, striking deals for descendents. Nickel-and-diming your souls.'

'You don't know anything.'

'I know more than you.' His mouth curled, grim. 'Don't be so righteous, Hunter. You'll do the same, eventually. They all do. Even your mother.'

I slammed my hand against his throat. 'Say that again.'

Rex wheezed, clawing at my arm. I heard voices at the end of the hall and released him just as some children appeared, accompanied by one of the day-care professionals, a retired teacher named Betty. Nice old woman. She made June Cleaver look like a hack job, though her husband was serving a thirty-year sentence for a string of bank robberies committed in the early nineties. The police had never recovered the money.

'Mrs Sansbury,' I said politely. Rex leaned over his knees, coughing.

Betty frowned at him, steering the children away. 'You should cover your mouth, Mr Mongabay.'

Rex grunted, still hunched over his stomach. Betty shook her head. I smiled and waved at the kids, who were sweet and smiled like angels should. When they passed out of sight, Rex muttered, 'Don't ruin this for me.'

'Ruin what?'

'This life.' He turned bloodshot eyes on me, his mouth crooked. 'My freedom, what little I have. It is *all* I have.'

'You're a demon, Rex. You are *not* a man.'

'I can be both,' he hissed. 'Just like you. I can change. I *have* changed.'

'Only because of Grant. He forced you.'

'He opened a door I didn't know existed,' Rex replied, with a fervor that had always unsettled me. 'He broke my link to the Queen.'

'She still controls you.'

'But not here.' The zombie pressed a fist against his chest. 'I am not just one of her mouths anymore, Hunter. I am not a feeding tube. I am *me*. I am this man.'

'Stolen skin.'

'He didn't want it.'

'Convenient.'

Rex leaned back, rubbing his throat. Hate in his eyes. 'You're no better than a serial killer, Maxine

Kiss. Dress it up all you like, but you can't live without the hunt. It's in your blood. All of you Hunters, feeding the addiction.'

'And your kind?'

'My kind are available. And all these years you've had the moral high ground. You gave yourself permission because we hurt the humans. Fed on their pain. But it's harder now, isn't it? What Grant does makes it impossible for you.'

'It's a puzzle,' I admitted. 'But I'm not losing any sleep.'

'Of course not.' The zombie leaned in, eyes glinting. 'But if not us, then who, Hunter? Who will you kill if you can't have us?'

I tilted my head, studying his eyes, the flicker of his aura. Steady, strong. 'Your morality is nothing but artifice. Illusion. Grant gives it to you. He could take it away.'

'Playing God,' whispered Rex. 'And yet, you don't question *him*.'

If only he knew. I yanked on my gloves. 'The boy. Explain that.'

Rex looked down at the hole in his leg. Bleeding had stopped. 'Leave it alone, Hunter. You've got bigger problems.'

More and more, every minute of the day. 'I want to know.'

He closed his eyes. 'You don't. Trust me.'

'Rex. I need information. The veil opened. Something came through.' Something small and nasty and full of piss. Wearing my face. A sour knot twisted in my gut. 'What escaped?'

'A scout.' Rex looked suddenly weary. 'More than a scout. Something that should never have been locked away.'

I hesitated. 'Is it not a demon?'

Rex looked me dead in the eye. 'What is a demon? You think you know? Is it everything that isn't human? Or is there a sign on our foreheads that marks us with a big red "D"?' He briefly closed his eyes, shaking his head. 'You, Hunter. You are so ignorant. Better ask yourself what *you* are, before you come after us.'

He had a point, which I was loath to admit. Or maybe I had been around Grant too long. I was beginning to think of zombies as individuals. Not just . . . meat.

I touched the spot just below my ear, which tingled. 'What do you know about a demon with knives for feet?'

Rex stared. 'What?'

'Toes like knives. Big cloak, black hat. Dances like a charmer.'

He flinched, and stood. I caught his shoulder, feeling the demon squirm beneath his human skin. I saw terror in his aura, stark and hot. 'What is it?'

Rex wrenched away. I grabbed him again, and he punched my stomach. It did not hurt, but it surprised me so much I let go. He staggered backward, staring at me as though he was seeing my face for the first horrifying time. Reminded me of Jack's reaction to seeing Oturu's mark on my face.

I lurched toward the zombie. 'What is it?'

He danced away, then stopped, frozen. Behind him, I heard the children, laughing and shouting.

'Rex,' I breathed.

'The Hunt,' he whispered. 'You're going to kill us all.'

CHAPTER 10

LATER, I understood why my mother ripped those pages from her diary.

There were things I could never confess. Not to my daughter, should I live long enough to have one – and not to Grant. Not the boys, though I suspected they could read my mind. Some thoughts, the ones that lingered, were better left as ghosts.

Some things should remain beneath the skin.

REX ran. I went after him, but he was fast, slippery, and I lost him once he got outside. Hell-bent for leather, pedal to the metal – like a man with his heels on fire – and if I had not been entirely certain of his need for Grant, I might have imagined him burning tracks out of town. Right now, never coming back.

I did not waste time searching. I had alternatives.

But I went back to the apartment first. There were some things I needed.

It was quiet upstairs. Grant was already gone. I looked inside the guest bedroom, thinking of Byron. My promises to him. How I had failed to keep even one boy safe. One boy, when there was an entire world that needed protection.

Talk about screwed.

In the living room, I gazed at the large windows, the deep couches, the guitars and piano, the Triumph motorcycle, polished to a loving red sheen. Masks and photographs covered the brick walls, along with stones and other knickknacks scattered on tiny tables. So many books, smiling from their shelves; mostly religious in nature, covering Christianity, Judaism, Islam, Buddhism; even Shamanic faiths; myths and legends. Archaic texts, some of which were in Latin, Italian, and French.

My mother's trunk sat against the wall, underneath a Tibetan tapestry that hugged the edge of the long table where Grant carved some of his flutes. Amongst his tools, different kinds of wood had been laid out: bamboo, walnut, cherry.

The sun was warm. I could see, through the window, the metal and glass of downtown, sparkling.

I knelt before the trunk and fumbled at the combination lock. I opened it. The journals were stacked on top. Leather-bound books, bundled sheaves of loose paper, folders with newspaper clippings. A Bible. An old cloth box full of photographs sitting beneath a stuffed bunny, loved and stitched and full of rambling patches. A battered leather jacket, a pair of gloves, also leather. Black, supple, small. Custom-made for my mother's hands. Looking at them made me light-headed.

At the bottom of the trunk, beneath a false panel, I found the weapons. Two pistols and the old twelve-gauge, cradled on boxes of ammunition. I tried to ignore the guns. I remembered my mother cleaning them, sitting cross-legged on hotel beds with the news on, or Bugs Bunny and Elmer Fudd.

I remembered her body, too. On the floor. Blood, everywhere. My twenty-first birthday, candles still burning on the cake. The boys, weeping. All of us, orphans.

I took a deep breath. Reached for the bundle wrapped in black velvet. Held it in my lap, then on the floor, sitting back on my heels as I unrolled the rich, heavy cloth.

Inside were my mother's knives. I had not seen them since she died, had not thought about using them. I had promised myself I would not.

The blades were simple, noble. Custom-made. No hilt, just steel, folded and honed. Razor-sharp, double-edged, both ends pointed and serrated. Touching them was dangerous. Required thick skin, or gloves with iron embedded. My mother had inherited them from her mother, as had my grandmother from hers. Old, but still strong. Full of history.

I took off my gloves and pulled the turtleneck over

174

my head. Naked from the waist up, every inch of my skin up to my chin covered in the boys. I picked up the first knife, and the steel blended with the scales and spikes covering my palm and wrist, glinting like the silver embedded in my flesh. I remembered my mother also holding her knives, just so, and the memories grew stronger as I began to sharpen each blade – all twelve of them – against my arms.

Sparks flew. The boys loved knives. They loved my mother more. I wondered what kinds of secrets, if any, they had kept from her.

The leather brace fit like a shoulder holster. I slipped it on, and the fit was perfect. The knives rested against my ribs. I fingered my jacket, then pushed it aside for my mother's leather coat and gloves. Stupid. I was going too far. But it made me feel better, and the leather was soft, supple, every scratch like a scar.

I put everything back inside the trunk, except for the box of photographs. Those I left on the work-bench, for Grant. Just in case. He had never seen them. I had never brought them out, unwilling to make a production out of it, watching his reaction.

The stone circle was warm in my back pocket. I patted it, then stopped in front of the mirror on my way out.

Edik was right.

I did look like my mother.

THERE was always a cab or two around the Coop. I got a ride back to the university district to pick up the Mustang. Still morning, and Seattle was hopping. Good weather brought folks out in droves, all of them stripped down to shorts and T-shirts and those odd, clunky sandals that seemed to be a fad in this part of North America. The temperature was only fifty degrees, but it might have been Arizona in summer for all the skin I saw. Poor sun-starved bastards.

The Mustang was where I had left it. 'Bohemian Rhapsody' on the radio. I cranked the volume up and rolled the windows down, enjoying the crisp salty air in my lungs. The boys slept heavily against my skin: dreaming my life, dreaming others', women dead and gone. My only promise of immortality, lost in blood, memory.

The art gallery was open. No blood splattered on the walls. Only one person inside, a young pretty blonde dressed in jeans and a peasant blouse. She sat behind a small desk and stood when I walked in. I said, 'Sarai and Jack are expecting me.'

'Oh, yes,' she said. 'You can go on up.'

I paused before the painting of the unicorn trapped in battle. I did not see a name or date. 'Sarai painted this, right?'

The woman nodded. 'It's not for sale, though. None of her work is.'

'Then this art gallery is just a place for her to exhibit?' I found myself unable to look away from the painting. 'I'm surprised she isn't more famous.'

'And what is fame to a unicorn?' said Sarai, appearing from the side door. Two thick silver braids

176

framed her face, and her skin seemed to glow from within. I had as much trouble looking away from her as I did from the painting. Sarai glanced at the young woman. 'Linn, you can take the rest of the day off. I'll be closing early.'

No arguments, no hesitation. The blonde smiled at me, grabbed her purse, and almost ran out the door. Sarai locked it. A hush descended upon the room.

'Thank you for coming back,' she said. 'And for your understanding.'

'Don't thank me yet,' I replied. 'Things are getting out of hand. I had an encounter this morning with a creature . . . a *nonhuman* creature . . . who knows you and Jack. Called you old friends.'

Saying that much to a stranger felt like an invitation to be called crazy, but Sarai remained silently thoughtful, with little reaction to judge. She turned her head, just so, and stared out the gallery window at the street. We were near Pike Place Market. I saw brick and flowerpots. The sky was blue, and the sun shot bars of white across the clean wood floor. I looked behind me and met the gaze of a unicorn in the sea, fighting for shore, against bullets and blood.

I waited for Sarai to say something, anything, but she never did. So I took a moment to get my bearings, rest my mind. Sarai was a hard woman to read, but there was enough steel in her eyes, in the way she moved, to erase any doubt that this was a woman who needed watching. Like a hawk.

177

'You're talented,' I said. *You are hiding some-thing.*

'I'm patient,' she replied. 'I've had years to hone my craft.'

'Why unicorns?' *Why do you know me?*

'Do you find them childish?'

'Not the way you depict them.'

'Good,' she said. 'Let's go find Jack.'

Compared to the bright sunlit interior of the gallery, Jack's office felt like the cave of some mountain hermit, an intellectual scavenger hoarding words and paper and books as though preparing for the long starvation of an endless dreary winter. I loved it. Felt comfy, like having my mind and spirit cushioned by good strong things. I would have made an excellent recluse.

Jack was seated in the middle of the path, perched precariously on a wobbly stool far too small for a man his size. His knees pressed against stacks of books. He had books open in his lap. A book in his hands. He looked up when Sarai and I walked in, and his smile was warm. Despite all my questions – and fear – I felt a small thrill seeing him.

'My dear girl,' he said. 'Good morning.'

'Morning,' I replied. 'But not good.'

I repeated again what I had told Sarai, though with more details. I was not entirely certain how much I could say without blowing their minds, but given the circumstances, I had a bad feeling that Jack Meddle and Sarai Soars knew a great deal more about the state of the supernatural than even I did.

178

Jack's subdued reaction did nothing to change that opinion, which sent an unexpected pang through me. My fantasy, stuck full of pins and needles. I had gone looking for a grandfather, an archaeologist, a regular man who loved books and clutter and digging in the dirt. And what I was getting instead, while perhaps all of those things still, was something . . . far more complicated. And, perhaps, not as pleasant.

Jack closed his book and laid it on the table. A cup of tea sat on the floor in front of his feet. He sipped it, slowly, eyes distant.

'Silence is overrated,' I finally said, after counting, quite literally, to one hundred.

'Silence is customary,' Sarai replied, 'when one is thinking.'

I shot her a look. 'Think faster. Or better yet, just tell me the truth. You shouldn't have to think about that.'

'Just like Jeannie,' Jack said, sighing. 'I miss her.'

'You miss them all,' Sarai muttered, but before I could question her, she said, 'Did you look at your mother's gift, Maxine? Did you understand its meaning?'

I could not believe what I was hearing. 'You are both on the radar of a *demon*. You understand what that means, don't you? A demon who, very likely, is coming to kill you. And you're worried about a piece of rock?'

Sarai frowned, which only seemed to enhance her beauty. 'Humor me.'

179

I wanted to keep arguing, but I had a feeling the older woman would win hands down, simply through being too stubborn to live. I pulled the stone disc free of my pocket and held it carefully. 'A labyrinth. The warrior in the maze. Faith.'

'Faith,' said Jack, 'is the cornerstone of all great endeavors.'

'Faith is fine,' I replied. 'But truth greases the wheels. Now please, what is this about? Why would a demon come looking for the both of you? And *why* was Badelt investigating me?'

'Those questions can wait,' Sarai said firmly. 'Your mother left her gift to you for a specific reason, one you should *not* ignore.'

I hated that crisp arrogance in her voice, as though she thought I was five years old, eager to please for a lollipop. I leaned in, bordering her personal space. 'My mother isn't here. My mother is *dead*. And I just watched a boy get his brains beaten in. A boy who knew Badelt. So don't you dare tell me what can, or cannot, wait. Because *other* people are getting hurt now. That kid? He was warned not to speak to me.'

Jack rubbed the bridge of his nose. 'Is he at the hospital?'

'Someone's watching him. Don't change the subject.'

'How could we?' Sarai asked bitterly. 'You have invaded us. We can hardly escape.'

I wanted to grab those braids and swing the woman around my head. 'Who *are* you people?'

Jack shared a long look with Sarai. 'Friends to your family, my dear. Trusted friends.'

'Trust,' I echoed. 'Isn't that a funny word to use.'

'It is the truth. You must believe that.'

I wanted to. I wanted to believe a lot of things. 'You want to know what I believe? I believe you knew where I was. Before I found you last night, you could have marched up to me *at any time* and said hello. But you didn't. You were afraid of something. So afraid, Sarai hired Badelt. She gave him my name. She asked him to look into me. And he *died* for it. He was shot. And for what?'

I leaned in, anger building in my throat, a terrible, awful fury. 'He was on the Ave the night he died. He was talking to the homeless. And the only reason he would have done that was if he hoped to find someone who had stayed at the Coop. Someone who might have met me.' I stabbed my finger at Sarai. 'You already knew *what* I was, and where. You wanted Badelt to discover the *who*.'

Dead silence. A cutting, morbid silence. Then, almost as an afterthought: 'Told you. Just like Jeannie.'

'Then you can tattoo *her* name on your chest, as well,' Sarai snapped, braids swinging. 'And as for you, Maxine . . . ' Her hands clenched like she wanted to hit something, maybe me, and her little knuckles turned so white I thought something was going to pop. 'We knew where you lived. But not the person you had grown into. And we needed to know. It was important. Brian was supposed to find tendrils,

181

rumors, distant enough that no one would have reported the inquiries . . . but within a close enough circle for the truth.'

I stared, incredulous. 'You could have just introduced yourself. I'm not that subtle.'

Jack began to sip his tea, but his hand trembled, sloshing dark liquid over the rim. 'We promised your mother. No contact. Not unless you found us on your own. Which . . . we would have arranged, if Brian's death had not . . . sped up the process.'

Sarai looked away. 'Brian was killed as a message to me. A notice to stay away from you. Or perhaps, like the boy, punishment for not.'

I searched her face, but what few emotions I had seen last night were hidden away so deep she might have been discussing the death of a stranger instead of her ex-husband.

'A demon killed him,' I said. 'A demonic parasite, possessing a human. I'm certain of it. And that . . . doesn't surprise you. None of this does.'

'I know Blood Mama's ways,' Sarai muttered, surprising *me*. 'She cares only for herself. Even her children, she sacrifices. Killing one human man is nothing to her. Less than an afterthought.'

I had to sit down. I nearly knocked over a pile of books, but I balanced precariously on the edge of the table and hung my head. The stone disc was warm in my hands. I gazed down at the concentric lines: the singular, faithful path. Endure to the end. One step at a time. Made me light-headed. Or maybe that was the cold fear throbbing through my gut; a surging, awful, drowning fear. My entire life, prepared in theory for the shit to hit the fan, and now that it had, all I wanted to do was wring my proverbial hands and start chanting *I don't know what to do* like a religious mantra. I had no clue.

Focus. Baby steps. One little nibble at a time. You can handle it. Eye on the prize. Whatever the hell that might be. I had a lot to choose from.

But first: Blood Mama. The old demon queen did nothing without a good reason. She was calculating to a fault. A little too in love with machinations. Bored little queen. Who did not want me talking to Jack and Sarai. Friends of the family.

'What,' I asked slowly, 'do you know that I shouldn't?'

Jack shifted slightly, his knees threatening to topple books. 'Things your mother could not tell you. Things she hoped you would never hear.'

Sarai's knuckles still strained white. 'She was afraid for you. Of what would happen if the veil opened.'

I thought of the missing pages in her journal. 'It opened last night. I encountered what came through. That demon I spoke of. The one who knows you.'

The old man teetered forward on his stool, knocking books from his lap. 'Tell us.'

I could not look at his face. It hurt too much. Here, the man I wanted to be my grandfather – and he had known where I was. He had known, and not found me. Kept secrets from me.

My *mother* had kept secrets. 'She – *it* – looked like a younger version of me. Even down to the outfit. Disappeared into smoke when I tried to stop it.' I met Jack's gaze. 'You knew last night, though . . . didn't you? You knew exactly what was here.'

A flush stained his cheeks. More tea sloshed, and I reached out, unable to help myself, and took the cup from him. His breath seemed to catch when our hands brushed, and his expression turned so very pained I wanted to get down and beg him to tell me whether he was mine. But his fingers dug into his knees, and he said, 'I suspected. It would not be the first such visitor I've had, but there was a . . . specific sensation about that particular presence. Familiar, you might say.'

'So you *do* know the demon who passed through the veil.' I set down the tea, afraid my own hands would start shaking. 'The prison was constructed almost ten thousand years ago.'

'Longer than that,' Sarai muttered, and Jack shushed her.

'Ten thousand,' I said again, firmly. 'And unless that demon has been popping in and out at will over the past sixty years or so, I'd say it's pretty darn unlikely that the three of you are *old* friends.'

'Unless we're also . . . that old,' Jack said, weakly.

Fuck it. I drank his hot tea, knocking back the drink in one hard swallow. I choked on it and started coughing, tears streaming from my eyes. Jack reached

184

out, tentatively, but his hand stopped just short of patting my knee.

Sarai looked mildly disgusted. 'We don't have time for this. You know what the little skinner wants, Old Wolf.'

'My only priority is Maxine,' he told her, an edge to his voice. His gaze flicked to my chcck. My hair was down, covering the tattooed skin beneath my ear, but I imagined he could see it anyway. 'Besides, there was another.'

Glass crunched. I looked down and found the teacup in my hand. In pieces. I exhaled, slowly. Jack stood, towering over me, and pointed at Sarai. 'Fetch a towel, if you would.'

Her jaw tightened, but she made her way down the narrow path between books, disappearing into the kitchen. As soon as she was out of sight, Jack leaned in and whispered, 'We *are* your friends, my dear. Whether you know it or not. Your mother trusted us with your well-being.'

'My mother should have told me.'

'She had her reasons. Good ones.'

'And?'

'And nothing, I'm afraid.' He looked away, cheeks still red. 'Some things are out of my control.'

'That demon who came through the veil called you a friend. Care to explain that?'

'The little skinner,' Jack said grimly, pronouncing each word with cold, crisp disgust. 'No friend of ours. Or demon. Certainly not like those she was

185

imprisoned with. Frankly, I'm surprised she's still alive. I thought for certain the others would have killed her by now.'

I stared. 'Is this supposed to be answering my questions?'

Sarai reappeared. I still held the stone disc in my other hand and set it down in time to catch the dish towel she tossed at my head. I dumped the glass into the cloth. As I was bundling it up, Jack shocked me by gently pushing my hair from my face – exposing the edge of my jaw, below my ear.

'Clever,' he murmured, and stood back so Sarai could see. 'The evidence has been obscured, but I saw it myself last night. He marked her.'

'Oturu,' I said.

Sarai faltered, gazing up at Jack. There was so much history in that brief stare, I felt like an interloper merely by breathing the same air.

'So,' she finally said. 'Again.'

'Again,' he said, just as carefully. 'Maybe.'

'She was marked. No maybes.'

'I was speaking of interpretation. Nothing is ever what it seems.'

I battled a chill. 'What are you talking about?'

'Everything,' Jack said heavily, and tapped the book by his elbow; the same text I had been looking at the night before. 'An old bargain coming to fruition. Always coinciding with a weakening in the veil. Which I suppose would explain why, in ancient times, it was seen as a portent of dark events. War, plague, famine.'

'It,' I echoed.

'The Hunt,' Jack said. 'The Wild Hunt.'

It was too random, too out of place. My head hurt. I glanced at the book beside him. 'That's just a story. Myth.'

'And where do myths come from, that live so deep in blood? They do not spring, magically, from thin air. There is always a root.' His voice dropped to a whisper, and his eyes grew distant. 'Always.'

'And Oturu?'

Sarai made a low sound. 'Oturu is the hand of the Hunt. And the hand . . . always serves the heart.'

I studied their faces, fighting the urge to back up and put space between our bodies. 'How do you know all this? My grandmother, my mother, couldn't have told you everything. Not enough to make you say these things.'

'You thought you were the only one who knew about the demons?' Sarai raised her brow, a hint of disdain in her voice. 'Or the veil?'

'Enough.' Jack waved his hand at her. 'Be gentle. We haven't made this easy on the girl.'

'So make it easy. I'm here. I found you. What was my mother hiding that she was so afraid to tell me?'

'That, my dear, we can't say.'

Swearing in front of old people and possible relatives limited my choice of responses. So I fumed, silently. Sarai said, 'It was her decision, Maxine. She felt words would be inadequate. She wanted you to be *shown*.'

'Shown *what*?'

'Shown *you*,' said the woman softly. 'Just you.'

'What you're made of,' added Jack. 'Beneath the skin.'

I pressed my knuckles against my brow and tried to keep my voice steady. 'Meddling Man. What are you hiding beneath *your* skin?'

Jack stilled, and for a moment I saw something ancient peer out from behind those blue eyes; something so old and tired and hard, I had to look away – only for a moment. But when I met his gaze again, seconds later, there was nothing to be afraid of, nothing but the eyes of an old human man, intelligent and warm.

Sarai said, very quietly, 'None of us are what we seem, Hunter. We walk as reflections, only.'

'That's riddle talk.'

'Sometimes riddles are the only way to tell the truth.'

'And your . . . skinner? Blood Mama?'

'Other riddles,' Sarai said. 'Yet more players in the game.'

Chills rode up my spine. 'You're not demon. But you're not human, either, are you?'

Sarai never answered. Zee tugged against my stomach; all the boys, stirring on my skin. A warning. I looked behind, at the open door. Listening hard. Jack began to say something. I held up my hand, silencing him.

I stepped toward the door. I heard nothing, but the

boys were pulsing against my body, struggling from their dreams, and the silence I strained to hear beyond was full and heavy, drawn upon itself as though cloaked, in hiding.

Something, hiding.

Dread filled me. Cold certainty. I thought about that little demon wearing my face, or Oturu, but this felt different. I tried to remember the layout of the stairs, and recalled they went up another flight; but that here, on the second floor, this was the only door.

I returned to Jack and Sarai, stepping quickly down the narrow path between books. I shoved the stone disc into my back pocket, and started waving my hands. 'Go, move. Is there another exit?'

Jack shook his head. I pushed Sarai's shoulder. She hesitated, then said, 'Brian gave me his gun. It's upstairs.'

No time. They took a couple steps, then looked back at me. Past me.

I turned. And got shot in the chest.

CHAPTER 11

MY mother was shot to death. I stopped carrying a gun after that. I had not touched one in five years.

It was a fast attack. A man and woman swept into the cluttered room, one after the other – so quick, little more than a blur in my eyes. I saw blond hair. Windbreakers and jeans. Familiar ruddy faces.

Edik's Wonder Twins. Blood Mama's long reach. Made no sense.

The piles of books and paper did not slow their trigger fingers. They started shooting as soon as they came into sight; precise hits, softened by silencers. I got slammed with the first round – felt the impact, no pain. The Wonder Twins seemed unbothered that I stayed on my feet. Their gazes never changed: sharp, intensely focused.

Bullets bounced off my body. One of them nicked the gun-woman in the arm, but she barely faltered. She kept her weapon trained on me, reaching inside her jacket for a second gun when the first ran out of bullets. Drowning me in metal.

It took me less than five seconds to realize I was not their target. Five seconds to get rained on and pounded. Five seconds before I gathered my wits and reached inside my jacket for the knives.

My mother had trained me to use her blades. I sparred with her every day, even when I was hardly as tall as her knees – but it had been five years and all those skills were gone to shit. I had played it easy. Let the boys do the dirty work. And now one day of crap had hammered it home.

Dumb. I was so damn dumb.

I threw the knives. My aim was better with my right hand and the blade skimmed the edge of the woman's gun arm, shaving off flesh, making her drop the weapon. The other man, victim of my left, was stabbed in the upper thigh. He got off a shot before I reached him. The bullet hit my collarbone. I planted my fist in his face. He fell hard and did not get up.

The woman already had her hand on another gun. I body-slammed her, and we fell down in a pile of books, rolling and grappling. She punched me and I let her; a flamethrower or bazooka would have felt the same. The boys absorbed everything.

I finally pinned her, books and paper cascading out of control. She tried to buck me off, but I dug

191

my fingers into her armpit, pinching a nerve, and she screamed in pain. The boys rumbled in their dreams.

I looked for Jack and Sarai. The old man was gone. No sign of him, though I did not discount the possibility that he was hiding under the table.

Sarai was on the ground, lost in a heap of books. Legs twitching. Covered in blood.

My focus narrowed, my heart thundering in my throat. The woman beneath me started fighting again. I punched her. I hit her so hard, bone crunched, leaving a dent in her cheek the size of my fist. Blood spurted from her nose. She blacked out. I checked her pulse. Still alive.

I clambered off her body and stumbled to Sarai, falling on my knees at her side. She was breathing, eyes fluttering. I thought of my mother, and wanted to be sick.

'Sarai,' I whispered, reaching into my pocket for the cell phone. 'Sarai, hold on.'

She grabbed my wrist. I did not know how. She looked too weak to breathe, but her grip was strong. 'Don't call anyone.'

'You'll die.'

'Yes.' She began to laugh; short-lived, painful. 'But one more time won't kill me.'

I gritted my teeth, still struggling for my cell phone. Sarai whispered, 'Listen, Hunter. You, Hunter. The first Hunter. Like Athena and Inanna, Kali and Badb. Queens of the blood and sword. Queens of war, born again.' Her fingers squeezed. 'You are born again.'

Chills raced through me. 'Sarai. Give me back my hand. You need help.'

'*You* need help,' she breathed, blood flecking her lips. 'You are feared, Hunter. In every way, you *should* be feared. For good reason. But times have come to hand. The veil is falling.'

I waited for her to say more, but she turned her head sharply, like she heard something. I looked, but the shooters were still unconscious. We were alone. Jack was still nowhere to be seen. I felt like a kid in a horror movie, trapped in a nightmare. 'Sarai. *Please*.'

'Please,' she echoed softly, and her face contorted. 'Oh, Brian. Brian, I'm so sorry.'

Her grip was still too strong. I tried reaching into my pocket with my other hand, but Sarai yanked me to her, so hard I almost fell across her wounds. I held myself just above her body, breathless and desperate, and looked into her eyes. Her endless eyes. Same ancient strength I had glimpsed in Jack's gaze; only deeper, more powerful. Inexorable.

'You are a good person,' she whispered harshly, trembling. 'Your mother wanted you to stay a good person. What she did was for that reason only. Nothing else.'

Sarai released me, holding my gaze – but her eyes dulled almost immediately, tension draining from her body. Blood dribbled from the corner of her mouth. She made a sound, breathless. I leaned in, tears burning.

'Labyrinth,' she murmured.

'Sarai,' I hissed, but it was too late. I watched her die.

I was still sitting there when I heard the sirens. It might have been a minute, or ten. My hearing was very good, and they were distant. I looked over my shoulder. The Wonder Twins were still on the floor, covered in books, sprawled and bleeding and broken. I stood and walked to their bodies, my boots rolling over bullet casings.

The air in the room tasted cold. I bent and yanked my knife out of the man's thigh. Except for the faint rise and fall of his chest, he did not move, or make a sound. I found my other knife on the floor, and sheathed both blades.

Got colder. Icy. I could not feel it on my skin, but when I breathed, the air held an arctic flavor in my lungs. My breath puffed into a delicate white cloud. The boys rumbled against my body, restless and dreaming.

I walked past Sarai's body, calling out Jack's name, and checked the adjoining room. I found only a rumpled bed and small bathroom. No sign of the old man. I was scared for him. When I turned around, I had company.

The little girl. Little me. Still dressed in denim and red cowboy boots, dark hair sliding past her shoulders. She crouched by Sarai's head. One tiny finger poked the center of her brow.

'The unicorn lost her horn,' murmured the child.

'Get away from her.'

'This is just a skin, Hunter. Nothing left to harm.' The child jabbed her index finger into Sarai's skull, right in the center of her brow. Bone cracked. Her finger sank to its joint inside her head. I cried out, lunging, but books got in my way, and I went down, sprawled just out of reach. I scrabbled forward, but not before the girl removed her finger. It was covered in brain matter. She stared, frowning. As though there were words in Sarai's flesh.

I did not care. I gripped a knife and threw it hard. The blade slid through her chest and thudded into the wall behind her. Beneath my ear, Oturu's mark burned.

'You cannot take my life,' said the girl distract-edly. 'Not even the demons in their prison could ruin me. Though they tried.'

I crouched, sickened. 'What are you, then?'

She finally looked at me. She had never met my eyes. Her gaze was black as a shark, black as a doll, black as oil rich from rock, slick and hot, and the ageless intelligence of her gaze coated me in a miasma filled with such forebodings I could hardly think straight.

'I am an Avatar,' she whispered. 'I am what rests beneath the skin.'

I heard sirens again, louder. I had shut them out, but I knew they were coming here. Any moment now, this place would be crawling with police. 'And Sarai? Jack?'

195

The little bud of her mouth hardened. She wiped her finger on Sarai's blood-spattered dress. 'They are dead. They will be dead. Here, or in the Labyrinth.' Her gaze flicked to the man and woman lying behind her, who were both finally beginning to stir.

I glimpsed a braid of hair in her right hand. She said, very quietly, 'This should not have been. Someone is interfering.'

Blood Mama. I struggled to stand, trying not to look at the gaping hole in Sarai's perfect face. 'She's *gone*. What more do you want?'

'Answers,' said the child absently, staring off to her left, as though listening. She stood and drifted toward the books. I saw my mother's gift in front of her. The stone disc, shimmering like a smooth dark pearl.

I ran. If I had not been invulnerable, I would have broken my bones leaping over those books, but I slipped and slid across jagged mounds of leather and cloth, fighting to reach the disc before the girl.

I was too slow, and she was too close. Her hand closed over the stone, and her expression turned cold, so vicious that the entire room – the air itself, the books and paper – seemed to stiffen in shock. A tremble washed through me, a prescient flutter of horror. Zee tugged against my chest so hard I stumbled.

I saw things in my mind: buried memories, flashes, strokes of lightning. My mother, standing on the edge of the Grand Canyon with the sun blazing on her tattooed skin, jumping into the abyss with her arms outstretched like a bird – her descent bleeding into the eyes of wolves – a pack of wolves, racing at my mother's back toward a purple sunset striking golden against the crowns of evergreens. And in front of her, standing on a rocky outcrop, tanned and strong and smiling—

—Jack.

I lost him. I lost it all. Pain stabbed, and I slammed my palm against my eyes. Found myself on all fours, tumbled in books. I sensed movement, and looked up in time to see the girl – whatever she was – drop the stone disc as though burned. Her face was a mess, contorted as though caught in the reflection of a fun-house mirror, her eyes and nose scrunched so tight in her brow she resembled a Cyclops. She threw back her head, shuddering, and swiveled around to stare at me with that awful gaze.

'Where?' she breathed. 'Where did you get this?'

I snarled at her, lurching to my feet. Her features smoothed, but this time she did not take my face; another woman instead, small and dark, hardly a wisp. Sharp teeth glinted in her mouth.

'I will kill you,' she whispered. 'Tell me.'

I did not remember stripping off my gloves, but my fingers flexed free and hot, and the boys raged. I lunged, tearing books beneath my boots, and slammed my hands into the cloud of her body.

The boys tried to latch on, but as before, she was slippery like water, utterly different from holding the essence of a parasite. She spread out, across the man and woman beside us – who were sitting up, staring. I could not stop her.

And then, just like that, they were all gone. The Wonder Twins. The girl – demon or not. I stood alone with a dead woman and a roomful of books, and the sirens of the police wailing inside my head.

I had no time. I swiped the stone disc from the floor – startled at the heat that poured through into the boys – and shoved it deep into my pocket. The knife I had thrown was nearby. I grabbed it up, then scrabbled across the books to kneel by Sarai. I brushed the back of my hand against her cheek. Her skin was still warm, but I told myself it was just casing, empty. A shell. All skin.

All skin. I felt a tickle in my brain, but I was dense as a brick, too sick to think. I wiped my hand over my burning eyes, grief swelling in my throat. I did not know why. I had hardly known the woman. I hardly knew anything at all. I closed my eyes, darkness fluttering behind my ribs. 'Trust me,' I breathed to the dead woman. 'Trust me to take care of this.'

I left fast. On the landing, I called out Jack's name again but got no response. The sirens were loud through the walls. No time to leave through the front door. I turned and ran up the stairs. I found a studio. Empty, clean floors, empty walls, large windows that flooded the space with sunlight. One neatly made bed in the corner, and a tiny uncluttered bathroom. No Jack.

On my left I saw a table covered in a careful

arrangement of paints and brushes, and one canvas that was at least twelve feet square. Sarai had been working on a painting. Nothing but dark space on the canvas, painted a rich black full of blue undertones. An abyss, or some starless sky. A hungry dark. I thought of Oturu. His smile. The girl and her rage.

Sarai dead. Shot.

I needed to find Jack.

Sirens arrived. I wondered who had called the police. Maybe it was a setup. I had already been linked to Badelt. Placing me here, at the murder of his ex-wife, would make Suwanai and McCowan delirious.

I ran to the windows. There was a fire escape outside, over the alley. No police there yet. I scrambled outside. Closed the window behind me, and started climbing. The fire escape was old and rusty, and the hinges squealed beneath my weight. Made me cringe.

But no one shouted at me. No one told me to stop.

I climbed faster, and had to scale a narrow ladder the last ten feet to the roof. I hit the top hard, at a run. I still had to get down again, but this was no trap. The buildings on this particular street were old and connected, the joined rooftops constructed at the same height. I ran over gravel and exposed tar paper, splashing through puddles. When I hit the end of the block, I heard more sirens and peered over the edge of the roof. Counted three squad cars, and one ambulance. I took another moment to scan the street for

Jack, but saw nothing. Just gawkers, any one of whom, I supposed, could be working for Edik. And Blood Mama.

There was an access door that led down into the building I stood on. No lock. I walked into the stair-well and warm air flowed over me. Smelled like old tennis shoes. Below, silence.

I ran down the stairs as quickly and carefully as I could. I thought it might be an office building. I heard telephones ringing through the walls, and near the bottom, a voice: young, silly, some girl having a one-sided conversation about another person in her class.

I nudged open the stairwell door, just a fraction, and saw her standing in a lobby. There was a small candy shop and a New Age bookstore on her left, and just beyond, a glass door that led onto the street. I almost walked out, but remembered my appear-ance. I buttoned my mother's jacket to hide the holes in the sweater. Checked out my jeans and stripped off a glove to touch my face with my bare fingers. No blood.

The girl barely looked at me as I exited the stair-well. I walked fast into the crisp, sunny day. Just down the street were the police and a growing crowd. It had been hard finding parking near the gallery. My car was one street over. I walked to it, keeping my head up, trying to look relaxed. I managed to maintain the façade just long enough to reach the Mustang, but once inside, doors locked, my entire body began to shake. I had trouble sticking the key in the ignition. I had to sit for ten minutes and just breathe.

I kept remembering Sarai. Flashing back to my mother. Thinking about veils and demons and teenage boys.

I fumbled for my cell phone and called Grant. He answered on the third ring. He sounded tense.

'Byron has two broken ribs, a concussion, and one busted nose. Could be some internal bleeding. Might be other injuries we don't know about yet. Convincing him to sit tight hasn't been easy. He's scared to death of the police and the welfare people.'

'Have any of them shown up?'

Grant hesitated. 'I'm handling it.'

Handling it. That could mean anything. I had to take a moment to collect my thoughts. I smelled like blood. 'Something happened. Sarai is dead. Jack is missing. We were attacked. Shot at. Edik's people were responsible. I'm afraid Byron is going to be another target.'

'And you?'

'I'm fine,' I muttered, which was a blatant, screaming lie. 'You need to be careful. I'll try to be at the hospital in less than an hour, but if I don't show up, call Suwanai and McCowan. Tell them you think Byron witnessed Badelt's murder and that someone came after him. They might give you protection.'

'It'll lead back to you, Maxine. And Byron won't take it.'

'Doesn't matter. Do whatever you have to. These people are fast, Grant. They're professional.'

'Maxine.'

'Promise me.'

His silence was hard, uncompromising. I said his name again and heard, in the background, someone else do the same. 'Mr Cooperon,' a woman said, and tension flowed through me; a terrible, awful dread.

'They're moving him,' he said. 'I have to go.'

'Grant—'

'I'll do whatever it takes,' he interrupted quietly. 'Love you.'

He hung up on me. I stared at the phone, then slipped it into my coat pocket. I thought about going to the hospital – right then, right there – but my knuckles turned white around the wheel, and I kept driving in the opposite direction. One more thing to do. One more.

I parked the Mustang in the garage below Pike Place Market. I smelled fish. Elliot Bay was one good leap away, waters sparkling like diamonds kicking the waves. The boys stirred in their dreams.

I used the skybridge to walk over Western Avenue to the Main Arcade of Pike Place. It was dark inside the market, a rambling maze, walls cream-colored and cracking, the far edges of the floor caked with layers of fine debris. The air smelled ripe, and there was a buzz in my ears – voices, cars, the odd slide of roller skates – along with a hum, a soft throb that was not human, or of this world.

I did not like coming to Pike Place Market. It held only one good memory – that I had met Grant here, saved his life – but there was nothing else that comforted me. The veil was thin between land and sea, where so many humans gathered. The prison walls were weak, so sheer I could hear another kind of ocean, dark and red as blood. Made of blood. I could almost imagine Blood Mama's children gathered on the edge of the wall, spying on the humans who passed through these tangled halls. Looking for souls, someone broken. Temptation enough to squirm and squeeze through the cracks in the veil and fight for a good possession.

I felt those eyes watching me. I felt them through the veil, and beyond them, Blood Mama herself – bearing down on the other side, making her babies, listening to them clamor for a quick rush to feed.

I wandered. Waiting for a message to get passed on through the veil. I ambled through the Main Arcade, past the artisans and their jewelry and leatherworks; soap stalls, jam, T-shirts. I smelled flowers. Cars honked. People everywhere; kids with their mothers, and some out-of-towners laughing with coffee cups in one hand and cameras in the other.

I felt naked, exposed. I kept thinking someone was going to look at my face and point out blood or bullet holes; as if death were contagious; or witnessing brutal violence created a mask over the eyes, so that everywhere I looked, I saw Sarai, so still, with that awful finger-sized hole in her head.

Your mother wanted you to stay a good person. What she did was for that reason only. Her last words, whispered inside my mind. Which only begged more questions. First and foremost, why something so seemingly innocuous would be worth killing over.

I dragged out the stone disc, the little labyrinth. Nothing looked different. But I remembered. I remembered that vision of my mother. And Jack.

Not a fantasy. Not my memories. Something else.

Oturu's mark began to burn.

'Raspberry?' asked a silken voice, close on my right. I glanced sideways, and found a statuesque woman dressed in a red leather jacket and matching leather pants. Long red hair had been teased into loose curls that cascaded around a face that was beautifully groomed – plucked and polished and tight. Her mouth was striking – a cruel red slash of lips – and her eyes were dark as polished river stone, cold and hard. She had an aura like a hurricane, spitting shadows and thunder. Aura big as the sky, crammed into a space the size of a watermelon.

She held a container of raspberries, plump and out-of-season. She plucked one up and took a slow bite between perfect white teeth. 'Delicious. Honestly, Hunter. I do not know how you stand it, living amongst such a wealth of sensation.'

'Blood Mama,' I replied, 'I was expecting someone else.'

'Edik,' she said, smiling coyly. 'Oh, my little pet is around.'

'Killing people.'

'This and that.'

'You're trying to hide something from me.'

'Am I?' Blood Mama ate another raspberry. 'Let us walk, Hunter. I have a desire to travel amongst mortals and lower myself to their ignoble existence.'

'You faker. You wish you were one of them.'

'Never,' she protested. 'I am a traveler, only. A nomad of souls. To be bound in one body, from squalling babe to wrinkled incontinent prune, with no reward but death . . . oh, Hunter. *That* is a prison. I do not envy you. Not now, not ever.'

'But you come and go as you please.' I stared out of the market at the ocean, imagining all those prison rings folded upon one another, rubbing borders with this dimension. An army of demons, hidden from sight. No telescopes, no eyes keen enough to discern their beating hearts. If they had hearts. 'The veil is weak.'

'The veil has always been weak.' Blood Mama smiled lushly at a gawky young man in glasses who openly stared at her as she swayed past. 'But the difference is that the veil is *coming down* entirely, and when it does, this world will have no one to protect it. Save you.'

'Right,' I said, fingering the tingling skin below my ear. 'And you care because you're afraid of the others.'

Her smile slipped. 'I risk a great deal by meeting with you. If Ahsen sees me—'

'Ahsen,' I interrupted her. 'The one who came through the veil?'

'Ahsen. Avatar.' Blood Mama glanced sideways. 'Wayward Prison Builder.'

I stopped walking. She said, 'Don't pretend. I know you're not surprised.'

Blood Mama did not know me that well. I *was* surprised. But not as much as I could have been. I rarely thought about the builders of the prison veil. They were a force unknown, briefly mentioned in the family histories but never with details. All I knew was that they had fought alongside humans against the demons. All I was certain of was that they had created the prison veil.

After that, nothing. Never another mention. Sometimes I thought they might never have existed.

Until today. Jack and Sarai had changed everything.

Blood Mama was still eating her raspberries, savoring each bite like it was some long kiss goodbye. Men were watching her. *Good luck*, I thought. *She'll eat you alive.*

'Why,' I said slowly, 'are you here?'

She smiled. 'I have an interest in keeping you alive.'

'Because you want me to save your babies from the big bad demons. Even though I take them from you.'

'I am willing to sacrifice a few lambs to keep your hunger satisfied.' Her aura crackled, like her smile. 'A Hunter must be fed.'

'And distracted. Tamed into complacency.' I also smiled, grim. 'How many angles do you play, Blood Mama? What did you promise this Ahsen? What did she *make* you promise?'

Blood Mama's aura danced. She tossed the rest of her raspberries on the ground, container with them – even though a garbage can was nearby. No one complained, but I noticed dirty, even incredulous, looks.

She wiped her hands together. Her nails flashed crimson. 'I promised nothing but a temporary door. And, perhaps, some aid. If required.'

'You ordered Badelt's death. Jack and Sarai. The boy.'

Blood Mama said nothing. I looked around. There were very few places to stand that were out of the way. Ahead of us was the fish market. I saw men in orange overalls lobbing a salmon at one another like a football, laughing and shouting. Tourists everywhere. Cameras flashing, children squealing. Disneyland for seafood lovers, and all the other fish sellers were looking at those jokers like they wanted to stab red-hot pokers in their backs.

'A good world,' murmured Blood Mama. 'And I am queen of it.'

'One day I'll kill you. Or someone else will.'

She gave me a sharp look. 'You are not permitted to harm me. I made a bargain with your ancestors. On your blood.'

'Maybe. But I don't have to *save* you.' I smiled,

cold, hard; savoring the calculation in her eyes, the reevaluation. I thought of my mother, my grand-mother . . . hundreds of women murdered by the demonic parasite inhabiting the body in front of me. I could act civil because I had to. Because Blood Mama might be useful. But it was shallow as a dry riverbed, and just as cracked.

I hated her. I hated her so bad I could taste it.

'Why?' I said again. 'Why hurt them?'

'Because it served a purpose.' Blood Mama stepped out from under the market awning, into the sun. She raised her hand, and a black sedan rolled into sight. 'Ahsen is dangerous. Hunter. She is old and powerful – but her anger makes her weak, easily manipulated.'

The sedan parked beside us, and the back door opened from inside. I glimpsed Edik in the shadows. Blood Mama balanced a red patent-leather stiletto against the edge of the interior and looked back at me. 'If you know what Ahsen wants, Hunter, you can use it against her. You can *stall*. Keep her so hungry, she will not *want* to return to the veil.'

Her face showed nothing, but I heard the hint of urgency in her voice, perhaps fear. I swayed close. 'You haven't told the other demons in the veil, have you?'

Blood Mama looked at me with disdain. 'Told them what? That the Wardens are dead? That the Avatars, the creatures who built the veil, have aban-doned this world? Or perhaps I should explain how my children have managed to roam free all these

208

millennia, while *they* stay locked within their cells. Oh, they would take that well, indeed.'

'You've played them.'

'I have avoided them, when I can.' Blood Mama leaned against the open car door, staring hard into my eyes. 'Understand your enemy, Hunter.'

I also leaned on the door. I removed my glove, and rested my naked hand against hers. Blood Mama did not flinch. Her aura remained steady. Raw hummed against her skin. Hungry, but holding steady.

'There is nothing more intimate than death,' said Blood Mama, tilting closer, voice husky. 'I have taught that lesson to more than one of your ancestors.'

'And did you tell them what *you're* afraid of? You, Blood Mama?' I also lowered my voice, but only because tourists were walking particularly close to the car, staring. 'Maybe you could share with *me* what is so particularly worrisome about the secret my mother left? Because I think you know.'

Blood Mama's gaze faltered, and she withdrew her hand – sliding into the sedan with careless grace. Edik sat in the shadows beside her – a spare, silent figure, still pushing his glasses up his nose. He could not look me in the eyes, but Blood Mama held my gaze, the cold, sleek beauty of her host body fading beneath the storm of her immense aura.

'The truth is simple,' she said quietly. 'There is a fine line between salvation and damnation, Hunter. And you, I am afraid, are it.'

She shut the door. The sedan pulled away. I stood at the side of the cobblestone street, watching her go, and pulled the stone disc from my back pocket.

In the sunlight, nestled in the black leather of my mother's gloves, the engraved lines glowed like smashed pearls inlaid with veins of silver fire, flickering over the surface as though the aurora borealis were skimming stone.

Labyrinth, Sarai had whispered.

Some mysteries. I was in so much trouble.

I heard the roar of a large engine. I turned, and the sun blinded my eyes. Hands touched my back.

Someone pushed.

And a bus hit me.

CHAPTER 12

I had never been hit by anything larger than a dune buggy – and that was under extenuating circumstances involving a runaway donkey, a one-legged zombie with a shotgun, and the unfortunate arrival of a freak sandstorm. All of which contributed to my sudden and intimate connection with the wheels of a fast-moving vehicle.

A bus was infinitely larger.

I went down hard. Felt the boys move in the split second before impact, shifting their sleeping bodies across my face. My nose and jaw slammed into the cobblestones with enough force to crush bone, but I felt no pain.

I must have dropped the stone disc. I saw it in front of me, and my hand closed over it just as a bumper slammed into my shoulder and head. I flew;

I spun; wheels rolled over my legs – and the sun disappeared beneath a steel chassis that was long and dark, and choked me with exhaust.

Bad day. Very bad day.

Everything stopped. My body. The bus. All I could hear was the engine dripping and my blood thundering. My hands clutched the stone to my chest, my fingers digging into the engraved lines, and for a moment an odd sensation passed over me, as though I was fading away. I saw my mother inside my head – and beyond her, other women, all of them wearing my face. All of them afraid.

Afraid of themselves.

The vision faded, but was replaced: I saw the demon in his cloak – Oturu – and in front of him a woman with my face – wearing tattoos and little else. They stood together, close, leaning in with such comfort, such ease, it was clear they had done so often, for a long time. Behind them I saw a purple sky, two moons. Big moons. Moons totally unlike the single moon I enjoyed staring at when the sun went down.

I snapped out of it. The world poured back in. I sucked in a deep breath. Still under the bus, staring at an engine. Stone clutched tightly in my hand.

But for a moment, all I could see was that vision. Oturu, one of my ancestors – *not me, not me* – standing beneath an alien sky.

Sounds intruded: some woman, screaming so violently she might have been the one under the bus. My hands started to shake. I returned the disc to my pocket, then took a deep breath and rolled carefully on my stomach. Men were scooting under the bus to help me. I let them, trying to ignore their stares as they saw my face. Took me a moment to realize why they seemed so taken aback.

The boys. The boys had covered my face. And they had not shifted away. My face was covered in tattoos.

I took another deep breath. My rescuers were talking, saying my spine might be broken, my legs crushed. I could have brain damage. They told me not to move.

Like hell. I started crawling. People dragged me free. I heard a collective hiss from the crowd as soon as they saw me – whether from my miraculous survival or my face, I had no idea. A camera flash went off, though. Cell phones pointed in my direction. I was spectacle.

'We've called an ambulance,' said one of the men, crouching beside me. His gaze could not seem to fix on any one part of my face. 'Don't move.'

'Thank you,' I told him, standing. I pretended to wobble. Hands caught me and people stared. There were so many people. I tried to look through the crowd, but all I could see were eyes, countless eyes, watching my face, my every move. Mouths hanging open.

Something ugly crawled into my gut, and I remembered a hand on my back just before I spilled into the road. I needed to find out what that was about.

I lurched forward, pushing past men and women who tried to stop me. I heard words like *miracle* and *careful*, then turned around, just once, to look at the bus that had hit me. A tourist caravan, not public transport; the driver in the road, on his hands and knees, puking up his guts. I felt bad for him. He could not help that someone had tried to murder me.

In the distance, sirens wailed. Too many of those today. The boys were restless on my skin. I reached the spot where I had been pushed.

And found a man. Tall, broad. Skin the color of a cat's eye, golden and tawny, his hair black and long, wild around his angular face. I normally did not notice men's noses, but his was large, hooked, close to being ugly, closer still to handsome. Black eyes. Aggressive stare.

He wore jeans, a black turtleneck, and gloves, and a belt buckle the size of my hand, silver and inlaid with enough lapis to make it appear, at first glance, that he carried a solid sheet of precious stone on his belt. Hard to look away, but I did, and glimpsed a band of iron beneath his chin, peeking from the edge of his collar.

I had never seen the man before in my life, but I knew those eyes. I knew that face. I knew him as though he were part of a dream I could not quite recall, but even that much was enough. This was not a coincidence.

'You pushed me,' I said.

'You survived.' He smiled coldly. 'But then, your kind always does.'

His voice was craggy and hard, effortlessly masculine. I thought of my mother's knives. 'How do you know who I am?'

'The world is full of mysteries.' He started walking. I stared after him, torn, then followed without looking back. I had little choice. The sirens were louder, and people still watched me. Might as well leave in the same direction. Pushing me under a bus was not the best way to get my attention, but knowing I was invulnerable certainly was. And it seemed to me that too many individuals were well aware of that rather important personal fact. I had kept secrets all my life. For nothing.

I caught my reflection in a car window, and saw a mask of scales shaped like wings flaring across my cheeks. Above my eyebrows, Zee, staring with a gaze like rubies, the tips of his long fingers curled around my jaw. Not a glimpse of my own skin remained, not even on my eyelids. I could have been in the circus. *National Geographic* maybe. I hardly recognized myself.

But I was alive. Unbroken. I caught up to the stranger and felt sharp, tangled. My mother's coat had new scars. I watched for dark auras, and thought about time, slipping away. My hour to Grant.

'Who are you?' I asked.

His smile was cold. 'I'm hurt you don't remember.'

It was not Ahsen, no matter how well she could shift her shape. 'We've never met.'

'You're all the same. That look in your eye. It never changes.'

His aura was clean, but that meant nothing. 'Who *are* you?'

215

The man looked at me, his gaze blistering. 'I am your fool, Hunter.'

He grabbed my arm. The world disappeared.

I did not lose consciousness. Merely, sight and sound. I was in a place of absolute darkness; unremitting, hollow, until I felt a shift inside my body, my innards sloshing into bone; and though I found myself still in darkness, there was a moon in the sky, illuminating an endless field of snow and ice; and the air was bitter, and it was night.

Night. The boys woke up.

The pain was worse than usual, but I did not flinch or make a sound. I watched the man, who stood upon the snow with a look of cruel amusement on his face. And when the boys pulled free, swirling around my body like quicksilver ghosts, his expression never changed; only the corner of his mouth hitched higher, and I felt in him a satisfaction that cut me with fury.

No time to act, though. The moment the boys peeled off my skin, I was hit with a cold that stabbed me as surely as if I had slammed myself onto a bed of nails. The bitter chill stole my breath, and I wheezed, folding my arms over my stomach, fighting the urge to drop to my knees. The cold was unbelievable, horrifying; like being swallowed by winter and slowly digested by ice.

Then, Zee. A glimpse of red eyes, the bars of his sharp teeth, just before he wrapped himself around me, arms tight. Dek and Mal wound across my throat and head, while Raw took my back. My legs were harder to protect, but Aaz did his best, all of them clinging like monkeys. Heat seeped through my clothing into the core of my body. Hearts thundered. I could think again.

'The flesh is weak,' said the man, seemingly unconcerned by the cold. 'Even yours, Hunter.'

'Where are we?' My voice was hoarse, broken.

'North Pole.' The man stepped closer, and the boys snarled. He laughed, quietly. 'Zee. You haven't aged a bit, I see.'

Zee snapped at the air, hissing, then rattled off a stream of words that were as melodic and wild as the stiff wind cutting across the ice. Until, finally, his tirade slowed, and he rasped, 'Enkidu. You cutter slut.'

The man's smile faded. The moon cast daggers upon his black hair until he was nothing more than a block of darkness, striated with moonlight. His body, so still. His voice rough. 'Never use that name, Zee. Never again. You owe me that much.'

Zee spat, his saliva burning through the snow like acid. The man took another step. I tensed, ready to fight. He stopped, though, and looked up. I saw a shadow slice stars, and a demon fell from the sky.

Oturu. He slammed into the ice like an arrow made of night, and the crack of his impact made me shake. I forgot to breathe. His cloak suffocated light.

217

The lower half of his pale face shone like diamond dust glittering across the snow.

I reached inside my jacket, fingers grazing my mother's knives. My heart thudded against my ribs. 'Zee.'

'Yes, Maxine,' he whispered.

'Are you going to help me this time?'

He said nothing. The demon laughed, husky and warm. His feet, those dagger toes, perched on the surface of the snow as though he were lighter than air.

'Zee can do nothing to break his binding word,' said the demon. A tendril of hair snaked from beneath his hat, reaching for the man standing quiet as death beside him. I could not look away as the demon's hair stroked the human's cheek, and I glimpsed in those dark eyes a moment of pure hate.

'Tracker,' said the demon. 'You did well.'

'It was my honor,' replied the man, with a deference I knew was a lie. The demon seemed to know it, too. That tendril of hair, delicate as a long finger, snaked beneath the man's collar. I saw the band of iron around his throat; a protruding link. A hook. The demon's hair knotted itself through the small opening and jerked, once. The man fell to his knees.

'Tracker,' murmured the demon, again. 'Learn to kneel before our Lady.'

The man said nothing. He tried to stand, and the leash snapped tight, making him fall, legs encased in snow. His breath puffed, lips turning blue. Cold. He could feel the cold now.

The demon's cloak flared, snapping at stars. 'Kneel. In your heart, kneel.'

'No,' I rasped. 'Stop.'

The demon turned, and though his eyes were hidden behind the brim of his hat, I knew he looked straight into my eyes. Stark against the ice, standing on his toes with that wicked, living cloak breathing against the direction of the wind. Graceful. Dangerous.

The hard mouth curved. 'You admire us.'

'I admire your grace,' I admitted, hoarsely. 'But I'll kill you anyway.'

'You will kill us all,' said the demon. 'But not today.'

Not if I stayed out here much longer. The boys could only do so much in these temperatures. I supposed that was the point. Strip me of my armor, make me vulnerable. Easy to scare.

My teeth were close to chattering. 'What do you want?'

'You,' he said, and against my body, the boys stirred, red eyes blinking, hearts pounding. I glanced at the man in the snow. He watched me, shoulders shuddering, hands hidden in the broken icy drift.

'To kill me,' I replied.

The demon smiled. 'To *follow* you.'

I stared, and he danced toward me, floating upon the flat drifts, pricking the ice and snow with the toes of his feet. He dragged the man behind me, his long tendrils of hair still knotted in the iron collar – and though he had pushed me under a bus, I felt a moment of pity as the man tried to stand, again, and fell.

The demon loomed, blending with the night sky, his mouth a hard, dark line, straight and cold as the distant moonlit horizon. I could not see his eyes beneath the hat, but his cloak flared like wings, and I glimpsed movement, deep within: faces and hands, bodies roiling in the abyss. Eating moonlight, starlight, the cold reflection of snow. The boys tightened their hands around my body. I shook, but not from the cold.

'You are frightened of us,' whispered the demon. 'Your heart is lost, but we are here now. All of us, born again, for each other.'

'Then tell me,' I croaked, my voice frozen in my throat. 'Tell me what I should know.'

'What you should know,' he murmured. 'What you should know is the world at your feet. You, Mistress, with your hounds and the Hunt at hand. Goddess, eternal. But you have forgotten. You have become a mystery.' The demon hesitated. 'What has been done to you, Hunter?'

I thought of my mother. A tendril of hair snapped toward my head. Zee grabbed it, holding tight, but not before the very tip grazed my brow. Incredible heat washed through my bones. Golden as sunrise, blinding. Through my jeans, against my skin, the stone circle burned.

The demon went perfectly still. All of us, staring, caught in the dark arctic hush, in a river of stars and moonlight. I would have been breathless with its beauty if I was not breathless with fear and dying.

'You have been tampered with,' said the demon.

'Oturu, no,' rasped Zee. 'No bargain broken. Just shifts. Been a long time. Old mothers had new ways.'

'And new alliances,' he said ominously. 'I smell the wolf. I can taste the unicorn.'

My knees buckled. I fell into the snow and could not pick myself up. My muscles were too cold. Aaz crawled down to my numb feet, curling himself around them. The demon flowed into a crouch, his cloak spreading across the snow like a splash of ink. The man was behind him, lost from sight. I stared at the brim of that black hat, trembling.

'We forget time,' he whispered. 'We forget, always, that you are a mortal creature. You, Hunter, who should bear eternity upon your shoulders. We see you, we see them all, and we remember *her*. Always her.'

'Her,' I breathed, shuddering from the cold. 'One of my ancestors.'

'The greatest of them. The most terrible.' The demon made a hissing sound, a quiet draw of breath. 'You are like her, Hunter. We can taste her inside you. It is why we gave you the mark of our clan. Our mark, that we have given no other since her death. It is a prophecy of wonder.'

My hand shook, but I managed to touch my face. Just below my ear, I felt those lines. I could see them inside my head. The demon leaned in, the brim of

221

his hat close enough to touch. 'You think we are so different, but we are the same, Hunter. We are the raging hosts and the masters of the dead, and when we command men to follow, they obey. And so it is the men of the earth who kill and maim, like a flock of birds copper red with blood, while we dance upon this world as great and mighty shadows. But we are merely the sword, Hunter, and only the sword. We must have a heart to wield us. Those are the terms, and we keep our bargains.'

'What bargain?' I watched his hair dip into the snow and begin carving designs, knots and tangles that reminded me of the stone engraving, the labyrinth.

'The terms of our survival,' he whispered. 'Our dispensation for a favor done. Allowed to survive and hunt, but only at the command of your blood-line, or one of your choosing. It was her last request. She feared. She grieved.' A tendril of hair tapped Zee's shoulder. 'Your Hunter should have been told.'

Zee shook his head. 'Made a promise.'

'Your oath conflicts.'

'No,' he rasped. 'It saves.'

I shook my head, shuddering. 'I don't believe it. I don't. N-not with you.'

'Because we are demon. And you hate us.'

'You'll d-destroy the humans.'

'Or will you?' He smiled, faintly. 'We are forbidden to take the first blow, unless offered. But we are *always* offered, Hunter. The temptation is too great.'

222

Chills wracked me, shaking my teeth. The boys held me more tightly. Zee pressed his mouth to my ear, whispering, 'No lies, Maxine. Believe.'

My vision blurred; so did my thoughts. The demon murmured, 'We are summoned by your heart, when your heart has need. Can you not trust yourself, Hunter?'

'The v-veil,' I chattered. 'You c-came b-because it opened.'

'Because it opened, and you felt it, and what you felt, we felt.'

'Why? W-why w-would my ancestor m-make this b-bargain?'

'Your bloodline needed help. We needed you.' The demon's cloak flared, and warmth poured over me, melting through my muscles into bone. Delicious and smooth, sinking from the tips of my toes to the crown of my head. My teeth stopped chattering; my mind felt clearer. I wanted to tell the demon to stop, but I could not. I wanted to survive more than I wanted my pride.

But the rest . . . that was wrong. I was missing something. A catch. There was always a catch, and my mother . . . my mother would not have gone to so much trouble to keep things secret from me without good reason.

She was afraid for you, Sarai had said. *Of what would happen if the veil opened.*

'My mother knew about this,' I said to Zee. 'She knew about *him*.'

Zee held me tighter, pressing his face against my neck. All the boys refused to look me in the eyes. The demon leaned in, hair still weaving designs in the snow – more tangles locked in circles, bound in chains.

'My mother,' I snapped. 'Why would she hide this from me?'

'There have been many Hunters,' said the demon, as though it was only us, together, in all the world. 'Many of your blood. We have met them. We have helped them, as promised. But you are different from the others. In your heart. We can taste it. We can see it. You are like *her*. Closer to the darkness. And the Hunt is . . . dark. In the past, it . . . roused things.'

I looked down at the boys, who stared at the demon like they wanted to stick a sock in his mouth. 'What kinds of things?'

'Things,' he said slowly, 'that make a mother fear her child.'

Zee said a sharp word. He sounded angry. Behind, the man in the snow finally climbed to his feet. He took a step toward us. His lips were no longer blue, and the ice crystals had melted from his face. The leash of hair was gone, but his movements were rough, as though compelled.

Zee continued to rattle off a vicious litany, chittering with all the ire of some demonic squirrel. Raw and the others were silent, but quivering; eyes blazing, low-throated growls rumbling. The demon's words burned.

He rose to his feet, balanced effortlessly on the pointed tips of his long sharp toes. 'We hurt you.'

'Yes,' I said.

'Ah,' he breathed, then, softly: 'The Hunt has begun. Our promise fulfilled, again. You must lead us.'

'No,' I said. 'I'm not doing anything just because you say so.'

'You do not trust us.'

'Never.'

The demon went very still. 'We have a bargain made in blood, Hunter. Your blood. My blood. The blood of your wards.'

'I don't understand any of this, least of all some bargain.'

His mouth twisted with displeasure. 'And if you never understand? Will you break your word with us? The word of your ancestor?'

I felt the boys tense. 'No. But I need more.'

The demon turned away. I struggled for my voice. 'You can give me answers.'

He looked back, the brim of his hat sharp, like a scythe. 'The answers you want are in your blood, and those we cannot give you. All we can do is leave you with time. A little time.' His head tilted sharply toward the man. 'Protect her, Tracker.'

'No,' said the man, and a thread of darkness lashed from the demon's cloak, striking the man's face. He stumbled, holding his cheek. Blood seeped between his fingers.

'Protect her,' hissed the demon. 'Whatever it takes.'

I stepped toward the demon, the boys still clinging, bodies warm as coals, old fires in an old hearth, seeping into my body. I held a hand toward him, not meaning to touch, but desperate, determined.

A hush fell over the demon, stillness heavy and rich as the weight of the starry sky bearing down upon our heads. He swayed, slow and delicate, and inside my heart I felt a dark squirm, a shadow behind my ribs, fluttering. Memory, déjà vu, something old, cold, and hard; and I thought of wolves and swords, bells ringing and women dying. I heard my blood. I heard my heart. Music, in my veins.

The demon leaned near, hair and cloak fanning around me – not touching, but embracing the air above my body. Swallowed by the abyss, close to death. Kissed by death.

Coarse fingers grabbed my hand. The man. Tracker. A dark, bleeding cut in his face. I looked back at Oturu, the hard line of his mouth. 'We're not done.'

'Never,' he murmured, and with a flourish that had more in common with Errol Flynn than Freddy Krueger, leapt into the air. I craned my neck, startled, and watched him fly into the light of the moon, gone like a whistle shot. Embraced by night. Dek and Mal whispered in my ears. Zee and the others closed their eyes, shoulders sagging.

My heart felt strange. Tracker squeezed my hand. I looked up into his hard gaze and felt stones gather in my chest, in the pit of my stomach. I was suddenly so damned cold I could die, but I would not blink first. I refused.

His jaw tightened. 'This should be interesting.'

He yanked hard. I slipped into darkness.

And reemerged into the light.

CHAPTER 13

SUNLIGHT. Home. Four familiar walls, bricks and books; and windows the size of my car. I had no idea how I had gotten here, but the boys were soft against my skin. I was warm.

I rolled over. Tracker stood by the motorcycle, a large sinewy hand poised over the cherry red finish. His long, dark hair shimmered against his hawkish features. He was a difficult man to place, with an exotic sophistication that defied ethnicity. He could have fit in anywhere – and at the same time, no place at all. Like Grant, like me. Outsiders.

He glanced at me, and his gaze was dark, furious. I saw iron around his throat. I expected him to say something, but he seemed content to murder me with his eyes, in grim silence. I rubbed my hand over my face and turned away, staggering to the kitchen to grab a bottle of water from the refrigerator. I hesitated, then tossed one at him. He let it fall and hit the floor.

I ignored that, opened another, and took a long drink. My lips were cracked and bleeding. My tongue stuck to the roof of my mouth. Tracker watched me, unmoving. I finished the bottle, threw it in the garbage, then checked my watch. Almost two hours late. My life, this treasured life, just might be over.

I fumbled for my cell phone and tried calling Grant. I was transferred directly to his voice mail. I did not leave a message. I tried calling again, but the same thing happened. I was already on edge. I walked fast to the apartment door. No car. I was going to have to catch a cab.

Tracker appeared in front of me. Literally. I heard a puff of displaced air as he manifested, and it was like watching the boys pour from shadows, except it was broad daylight and there was not a shred of darkness in the apartment. 'Where are you going, Hunter?'

'None of your business.'

Tracker stabbed the band of iron around his throat. 'You *are* my business.'

I could not look away from that collar. I hated it with an intensity that startled me; hated, too, the memory of this man on his knees. Felt familiar, like déjà vu, but that was impossible, wrong – and not my fault.

I hardened my heart. 'You go tell Oturu that he

can take his *protection* and shove it where the sun don't shine. I don't want you here. I don't *need* you.'

Tracker grabbed my arm and I broke his grip, punching his gut. I could shatter brick with my fist – I should have been able to make him wheeze, at the very least. But he did not budge. Just stood there, looking down at me, like my fist was light as air. 'Had enough?'

'Haven't gotten started,' I muttered, then: 'I couldn't have hurt you. I don't *know* you.'

'You're all the same. All of you.'

'Last I checked, there's just one of me.'

'Just one,' he said coldly. 'But the culmination of countless ones. And your blood, your *nature*, never changes, Hunter.'

He was full of shit. Men with grudges were like men with rocks for brains: knock, hit, scream all you wanted. Nothing but a wasted effort, and I had no energy to argue. I felt like pieces of my heart were flopping around my chest, bleeding and useless, and if Tracker had not been standing in front of me, I might have been able to convince myself that it had never happened, that I had imagined sitting in the snows of the North Pole, faced by a demon who wanted to be my hand, my deadly sword.

'Fine,' I said. 'Stick around. But you start being a little less angry, then *maybe* I'll cooperate. Maybe I'll give a damn.'

'You want to bargain.' He said it like I was asking him to clean dog poo with his bare hands.

'I'm willing to *talk*. But not here. I have to go.'

He was a handsome man, but there was nothing attractive about rage – and it hurt more than it should. I almost expected him to make another move against me – he seemed to be one big raw nerve – but I watched a shift of light pass through his eyes, a moment of calculation, and he inclined his head, just so.

I turned, let out my breath, and left the apartment at a run. Outside, I headed down the garden path to the front of the Coop. No cab parked out front. I started dialing through my cell-phone contacts for the number of the taxi company. Tracker matched my pace. 'What are you doing?'

'Trying to get to the hospital.'

'Which one?'

His curiosity, however acerbic, made me suspicious. 'University Medical Center.'

He grabbed my arm and the world disappeared – as though swallowed, lost deep in the dark thunder of the sea. I could not struggle, could not move. My heart screamed.

And then I found myself free, returned to the world. Concrete. Cars. Voices nearby. I staggered, blinking hard, jamming my palm against my eye. Tracker stood beside me, a look of cold amusement on his face.

'You're an asshole,' I rasped. An effective asshole. We were at the hospital. Standing in a landscaped alcove of gravel and bushes just off the small drive

231

leading up to the emergency room. An ambulance was parked in front of the glass doors. No one seemed to have noticed our appearing act.

Ten miles covered in a heartbeat. Up to the North Pole and back in the blink of an eye. Never dreamed, never imagined. Not human. Not demon.

Something else. Something like magic.

I took a deep breath and started walking. Tracker followed. He moved with a particular grace that reminded me of a dancer – rolling, light, almost like Oturu. As though he could spin on his toes at a moment's notice; spin and kill, with just one touch.

Dangerous man. The boys rumbled in their sleep. Dek, resting on my right arm, kept pulling toward Tracker. He was stubborn about it. I had to concentrate not to brush against the man.

I tried calling Grant again. No answer. I started running. My heart felt very small and hard. I passed through the sliding doors and entered a waiting room paneled in dark wood, lighting turned down just enough to create an atmosphere of shadowed calm, helped in part by large windows that bordered a small garden. Several flat-screen televisions hung from the walls. A major news network was on. Images of crying children and collapsed buildings flashed. Massive earthquake. Iran.

The woman behind the admitting desk glanced from me to Tracker, and her gaze stayed there, staring, open-mouthed.

'Hey,' I said, then snapped my fingers. 'Ma'am.'

She blinked, a flush staining her cheeks. Flustered. I did not dare look at Tracker. Wolf in wolf's clothing, that was him. He stayed silent as I spoke to the woman and got Byron's room number. Grant had registered the boy under his own last name, Cooperon.

Byron had been assigned a room on the fifth floor. No one else stood in the elevator with us. I leaned against a metal bar, looked at Tracker, and said, 'Why did you push me in front of the bus?'

His mouth crooked. 'Because I felt like it. Because I wanted to watch.'

'You're crazy.'

'Maybe,' he replied. 'After all these years, yes, I think so.'

I pushed away from the wall. 'You listen. I don't know what kind of history you think we've got, but right here, right now, *it doesn't matter*. Bad things are happening, and I might find another in this hospital. You get in my way, you try to hurt the people I love, and I'll bury you.'

'Hunter,' said Tracker, as the elevator stopped, 'I would expect nothing less.'

We walked into a waiting room. Grant was not there. Neither were the police, nor an army of Russian gunmen waiting to assassinate one teenage boy. The only occupant was an old woman huddled on a chair in the corner. She was watching the news. The focus was still on Iran. Big red letters that spelled QUAKE! scrolled across the bottom of the screen, cutting into

233

disturbing video of a screaming man shaking his fists at the night sky.

The doors were locked. I picked up a phone hanging from the wall and dialed zero. Listened to two rings, then a woman answered. Crisp, no-nonsense. I asked for Byron Cooperon, and she said, 'Yes, some family is already here. Room Two. Are you his uncle's wife?'

'Yes,' I lied.

'Come on in,' she replied, and the door clicked.

The air smelled cold on the other side. Cold and thick with disinfectant, so much that the air almost felt dirty instead of clean, raw with chemical. I hated it. I had hardly ever been in a hospital, and never for myself. Only hunting. Medical professionals made frightening zombies.

Ahead, at the nurses' station, several women stood together, leaning on the counter with charts spread in front of them.

'—it's awful,' I heard one of the nurses say. 'There were earthquakes early this morning all *over* the Middle East. And those people dead? You *know* the Red Cross is going to start asking for volunteers.'

'I did my tour with Katrina,' said another woman. 'But that was in the States. I'm *not* going overseas, not with my kids still in school.'

'Mount St Helens will blow next,' replied the third woman, with a hint of grim amusement. 'Seattle is due for the big one.'

'Or perhaps locusts will fall from the sky,' Tracker whispered in my ear. 'Or water turn to blood?'

234

I gave him a hard look, trying to understand what kind of man I was dealing with. 'You don't mean to say that earthquake can be blamed on demons?'

His mouth turned down. 'Use your imagination.'

I stared. Behind me I heard a familiar clicking sound, faint and careful. I turned. Grant stood in the doorway of a room just down the long hall. Everything in me stilled, hungry. He was wearing jeans and a faded navy sweatshirt. His hair was rumpled. He leaned hard on his cane and stared from me to Tracker.

Everything about him went sharp when he looked at the man – sharp as teeth – and he studied the crown of Tracker's head with an intensity that felt like a wolf before some hard kill. Both men, wolves. The nurses stopped talking and were watching us.

I walked toward Grant, fast, and his gaze flickered to the crown of my head; my aura, my heart, exposed. By the time I reached him my knees were wobbly. His arm slid around my waist, and he hauled me so tight against his chest I could not breathe. I closed my eyes, heart pounding. His lips pressed against my hair.

I only let him hold me a moment. No time, no place, not the right people watching. I met his gaze, briefly, long enough to see new lines around his eyes; and he backed up to let me into the hospital room. I entered, then turned to watch as Tracker followed. He glided like a shadow, passing close to Grant. I felt a moment of fear, seeing them so close together. But neither man made a move. Just stared at each other, unblinking – and the energy that poured from them made the boys stir in their sleep.

It was a private room, lights dimmed, curtains half-closed. Byron lay in the bed, seemingly asleep. His cuts had been cleaned, but the swelling was worse. I could hardly recognize his face.

Grant limped into the room and shut the door softly behind him.

'Maxine,' he rumbled, not taking his gaze off the other man. 'Are you all right?'

'Fine,' I lied.

'And if she wasn't?' Tracker's gaze was hooded, almost lost behind his long hair and nose. 'Think you could fight me? With just one leg?'

The corner of Grant's mouth curled. 'I would make you sorry you were ever born.'

Tracker smiled – bitter, ugly – dazzling and awful – and gave me a look so filled with disgust, loathing, my skin crawled. Grant took a step toward him. I reached out, grabbing his arm.

'Not worth it,' I said, staring at Tracker. 'Not even worth the thought.'

I saw it only because I was looking in his eyes – a flicker, a moment so brief I thought I might have imagined it.

Hurt. I had hurt him.

And then a mask fell over his face, that same old anger, and I looked away from him, to Byron. I moved close to the bed and took off my glove. Touched the boy's hand. Raw stirred, restless. Grant moved close to my shoulder, solid and warm. His flute case hung from his shoulder, a long, narrow padded pouch of midnight velvet, a hint of his twenty-four-karat gold Muramatsu peeking from beneath the flap. His most prized instrument, custom-made. He rarely used it in public, especially at the Coop. Too flashy; too much temptation for thieves.

'They did an MRI,' Grant said. 'Finished about thirty minutes ago. You just missed the doctor. No swelling. His brain looks fine. They gave him a sedative, though. He refused to sit still. Started fighting to get out of here before they cleaned even one cut.'

I leaned into his shoulder. 'You didn't answer your cell phone. I was worried.'

'Doctor made me turn my phone off.'

'And the police? You should have called them.'

A faint, wry smile touched his mouth. 'I knew you would come. Even if the police were here, you would still have come. And you did.'

'If I hadn't?'

'The thought didn't cross my mind. I know you, Maxine Kiss. I know what you're made of.'

His words echoed too closely what Sarai had said to make me entirely comfortable. I did not feel like a good person. I had never felt good. Not even right-eous. Just . . . dedicated. Girl with a job to do. Girl on a mission. My mother had discouraged thoughts of anything else. She said it would lead to mixed priorities. A big head. Glory over the right thing.

237

And the right thing, she said, always took precedence. No matter what.

'There's something you need to know,' Grant said.

'About Byron?'

He hesitated. 'No. Maybe.'

I looked at him. Behind us, the room door rattled. I expected to see a nurse, but what I got instead made me wobbly, insane.

It was Jack. His clothes were rumpled, his white hair wild. His arms were full of sandwiches and drinks. He did not seem entirely surprised to see me, but his gaze slid to Tracker and stayed there.

'Old Wolf,' said the man. 'Still causing trouble?'

'Oh, dear,' said Jack.

'MR Meddle showed up twenty minutes after you called,' Grant told me grimly. 'I tried *your* cell phone, too. Couldn't even get voice mail.'

I had no record of a missed call. I gave Tracker a dirty look. Then, to Jack: 'What happened? Why are you here?'

The old man set down the food he carried. 'Some things require personal attention. And I knew you would come. Eventually.'

'Personal attention? *Eventually?* You *ran*. Sarai is dead.' *And I was worried about you. I was so afraid.*

Jack made a small sound, arranging plastic-wrapped sandwiches into a heaping pile. He would not look at me. His hands shook, slightly. 'Sarai would have run, too, had our positions been reversed.

I can assure you of that. One of us needed to survive. The alternative would have been . . . unfortunate.'

Unfortunate did not cut it. I could still smell Sarai's blood, feel the force of her grip on my wrist. Her pain and determination. Fighting to help me, even in the end. Anger rocked. 'You don't sound too broken up.'

Tracker folded his arms over his chest. 'Why would he? He's a skin, Hunter. An Avatar. Mortality doesn't rattle his kind.'

Hearing those words sent heat through me, made my stomach feel weak. Again, like I was drowning. I glanced between both men, then at Grant. I expected to find confusion on his face, and there was some – but mostly, a pained resignation that made me think he had already heard this story.

He met my gaze, shoulders tilting in a mild shrug. I gritted my teeth. 'Someone. Explain. Now.'

Silence was heavy. I touched Byron's hand, again. Jack said, 'The child is resilient. He will recover.'

I gave him a hard look. 'I want to know what you are.'

Jack picked at the plastic on the sandwiches. He seemed normal as an old man could be – dapper in slacks and tweed, his once-handsome face still rugged and deep. If I had not seen, or heard, or known what I did, I would have thought myself insane for asking these questions, imagining this man could be anything but what he appeared: sweet, brilliant, bumbling, and shy; a man I would delight in calling my grandfather; a man I still wanted to be mine, in blood. Grandfather. Family.

But appearances deceived. Zombies did it all the time. Now I was the one being duped. On the receiving end.

Jack studied his hands as Sarai had, as though they were new and unfamiliar, a burden or wonder. 'I am human. In this life, human. I have been human many times, over many years. I have been other creatures, too. But right now, here, I am Jack Meddle. I am this skin.'

My heart skipped a beat. 'And beneath the skin?'

His jaw tightened. 'I am . . . something else.'

Grant bowed his head close to mine. 'His aura is multitonal. Two layers, one over the other. I thought I was seeing things.'

Jack made a small sound of protest. 'Lad, you shouldn't have been able to see that much. Your eyes are too open.'

'My eyes are just fine. Nothing wrong with seeing the truth.'

'That depends,' said the old man, giving him a speculative look that made me uneasy. But he glanced away, meeting my gaze square and true. 'This body is my avatar. My shell. Just as every human on this planet, or any other, is nothing but a shell. A home for the soul.'

'The soul,' I echoed.

'The soul, which is energy with a purpose. Energy

with a mind. And my kind, long ago, learned to live as nothing *but* that energy.'

His words bounced. I struggled to focus, my thoughts skittish, wild; as though Jack had become fire, and I was some horse trapped in a barn, smelling smoke. No way out. I wanted to tell him he was full of shit but could not. Too much truth in his eyes. Too much in my gut that said, *Yes, I know this.*

It terrified me. I felt like I was being swallowed by the world, and I scrunched my toes in my boots, wiggling them until they hurt. Reminding myself that my feet were on the ground. Solid. Here. Now.

I exhaled, slowly. 'Where did you get the body?'

Jack blinked owlishly. Tracker laughed, but it was ugly. 'Where do those demon parasites get theirs, Hunter?'

Grant's hand brushed against my back. I did not look at him. Chills settled in my gut. 'You possessed that man?'

'No.' Jack gave Tracker a hard look. 'I was born into him.'

'Born.'

'In the womb. I entered his body months before birth. To preclude a conflict of personality.'

I wanted to sit down. I squeezed Byron's warm, limp hand, then let go and squeezed the bars of his bed instead. My head ached. It had been sore since yesterday, when I felt the veil open. A quiet pain, simmering behind my eyes. As though my brain wanted me to see something – straining so hard it hurt.

I closed my eyes. 'Sarai?'

'Alive. Somewhere.'

Somewhere. I did not know whether to laugh or cry. 'And Byron? The zombie who beat the boy called him a skin.'

Jack hesitated. 'He was mistaken. The boy was a candidate, briefly, but was abandoned. The demon would have tasted the echo of that contact.'

'Some coincidence. Byron, friends with Sarai's ex-husband?' I leaned in, anger swelling in my throat. 'What games are you playing, Meddling Man?'

'None,' he said heavily. 'I promise you.'

'And Ahsen?'

He flinched. 'Where did you hear that name?'

'Is she one of you?'

'The *name*. Tell me.'

'Blood Mama.'

Jack looked ill. 'Yes, my dear. The little *skinner* is one of us.'

'She wants you dead.'

'Does she now? How civil.'

I stepped toward him. 'Don't. Don't be flippant. People have died. People are *going* to die. And you . . . you're no better than the demons. Stealing bodies.' My voice was low, harsh – sour disappointment tying knots in my gut. 'What do I do, Jack?'

I did not mean to ask that question. What I meant to say was *How do I stop her?* or *What are her weaknesses?* but the words came out hard and plaintive, and I felt like a kid at the foot of the proverbial rocking chair, seeking advice from the village elder. Made my cheeks flush in shame, but I could not take it back. I could not hide how weak that one question made me feel. Or how lonely.

Jack regarded me silently, shadows gathering around his eyes. 'You must take care, my dear. Tread lightly. Our *skinner* was formidable once, and that has not changed.'

'Why didn't she kill you last night? When we first felt her in the gallery?'

The old man hesitated. 'Flesh holds no dominion. Kill this body, and I will simply retreat and be born again. Extinguishing *me*, what rests beneath, is a great deal more difficult.'

If you know what Ahsen wants, Blood Mama had said, *you can use it against her*.

Like killing Sarai. Her death nothing but a distraction. A means of keeping Ahsen hungry, here, hunting. Buying time so I could figure out what to do.

'How would she kill you?' I asked Jack. 'If it's so difficult?'

The old man said nothing. Tracker laughed, quietly. 'He doesn't trust you, Hunter.'

'Or maybe it's you,' I snapped, though I still felt the sting. 'Jack. I need to know how to keep you safe.'

'Don't worry yourself,' he muttered, glancing at

243

Byron. 'I have the ability to hide from the *skinner*. Now that I know she's looking for me.'

'Why didn't you do that earlier?' I asked him. 'When Sarai was still alive?'

'Arrogance,' he replied. 'Nor did we expect outside . . . interference.'

Which was all well and good, but if Ahsen could not find Jack, then I would likely become her next focus – and splitting town and running was not an attractive option. I had no way of knowing how much of my life Ahsen had seen. She might try to use the others against me.

Beside me, Grant made an odd small movement. I found him looking between Byron and Jack with a faint frown. Tracker was also studying the boy – surreptitiously – as though something bothered him.

'Jack,' I said slowly, 'you put Ahsen in the prison. Locked her up with the demons. You did that to one of your own.'

Tracker tore his gaze from the teen. 'Old Wolf. You *are* cold.'

I ignored him, focusing on Jack. 'I want to know why. What did she do?'

The old man looked away, a faint flush staining his cheeks. 'What she did to deserve imprisonment doesn't matter anymore. You cannot fight her. She has no body to harm, no physical link in this world to tether her.'

'You must be wrong.'

'My dear,' he said slowly, 'I wish.'

I steadied myself and looked at Tracker. 'Could Oturu do it?'

His dark eyebrow twitched. 'You should ask him yourself.'

'I'm asking you. You're one of them, aren't you? An Avatar?'

'Never,' Tracker said coldly. 'As for Oturu, it takes a killer to know one. You don't need my help to figure it out.'

I stared at him, cold anger settling hard in my gut. Tracker met my stare – bold, defiant – but there was never a question in my mind, not a doubt. No way in hell I was going to back down.

Tracker could not hold my gaze. He blinked first and looked away. I did not feel particularly triumphant. Just tired. Grant sidled close enough that his shoulder rubbed against mine. Subtle, brief, but solid. I was grateful. He was my only real friend here. The only person I knew I could count on.

'Jack,' I said. 'I can't let Ahsen return to the veil. And she can't be allowed to roam free. That leaves only one option.'

'You have no means to capture her, my dear.'

'Prison builders. That's what your kind are.'

'A long time ago. That power is gone.'

Grant leaned hard on his cane. 'Sounds as though you want to give up.'

Jack shot him a chilling look. 'Lad, if surrender was in my nature, I would have abandoned this world ten thousand years ago.'

Grant did not appear impressed. He glanced down at me, and I knew in a heartbeat what he was thinking.

'Too dangerous,' I said.

'Is there another option?' His mouth tilted into a grim smile. 'Blood Mama was scared enough to try to possess me. And if this Ahsen is structured like Jack, then the same principles should apply. Energy is energy, Maxine.'

The idea of his being anywhere near Ahsen terrified me. I had seen little of her capabilities, but a taste was enough. She was lethal, merciless. She might kill Grant before he got the flute to his mouth. I shook my head. 'Last option.'

'No,' he said. 'I'll take the opportunity if I can get it. We might be able to get through this without more violence.'

I doubted it, but this was not the place to argue. We had witnesses – two men who were suddenly staring at Grant as though he were some foreign beast, replete with horns, tail, and an army of singing lady-bugs perched like a crown atop his head. I did not like it. Not one bit.

Byron stirred. Maybe we were talking too loud. I held my breath as his right eye, which had escaped swelling, cracked open. He looked at me – made a sound, low in his throat – and then his eye closed again. His breathing settled. I exhaled, slowly.

'We need to get him out of here,' I murmured to Grant. 'It's not safe.'

Not safe. And not simply because Byron had

proven himself a target, temporary or not. The need to spirit the boy away went deeper, a primitive urgency that felt the same as my need to breathe.

Grant's gaze was dark, knowing. 'I already asked. They won't discharge Byron until they're certain the danger from his concussion has passed. In this case, I have to agree with the doctors.'

Jack softly cleared his throat. 'The circumstances have changed. When I . . . first arrived here, I took the liberty of healing the physical injury to the boy's brain. He *can* be moved . . . if that's what you wish.'

Grant and I stared at the old man. Tracker smiled dourly, studying his boots as though black leather held some infinite fascination for him, perhaps lessons in how to hold a grudge.

I bit the inside of my cheek. I had questions, but they could wait. 'Grant, can you handle the doctor? Convince him that Byron should be discharged?'

He hesitated, still staring at Jack. 'Give me ten minutes.'

Grant limped from the room. I waited for him, caught in awkward, uncomfortable silence, surreal as a bad dream, in the company of strangers, and strangeness. Jack stared at the wall, a furrow between his eyes; his lips moved in silent conversation.

Tracker managed to make sitting in a chair seem like an act of aggression; and when he looked at me, there was too much in his eyes, a heaviness that felt like a scar. I had no sense of the man, and I felt trapped by that ignorance – and his hate. It hurt me, in ways I could not explain. No words. No courage.

The boys helped, dreaming on my skin. My little friends.

But inside my heart I was alone. I had never felt so alone.

I held Byron's hand, and with my other, reached into my back pocket and pulled out the stone disc. It was warm against my hand. Shimmers of pearl seemed to push up through the soft dark surface, those veins of silver glittering inside the engraved concentric lines. I placed the stone in my lap and traced my finger through the lines. Felt light-headed.

A large, wrinkled hand engulfed my wrist. Jack. I had not heard him move. He held my gaze, a hint of urgency in his eyes. 'Not here, my dear.'

I blinked. 'Not here, what?'

'Exploring that.' He inclined his head toward the stone. 'Your mother's gift is more than it appears to be.'

'Ahsen certainly thought so,' I mumbled.

Jack flinched. 'She saw it?'

'She touched it.'

I thought my words were going to kill him. A great and terrible strain filled his face, as though he were struggling with all his might not to shatter. My mouth went dry. I sensed Tracker standing, staring, but I did not dare look at him. I could not. I thought if I did, Jack might disappear. Fall to pieces, like glass.

'Oh, dear,' he breathed. 'How unfortunate.'

'Jack,' I whispered, and felt the boys stirring against my skin. I held up the stone disc, staring hard. Thinking of my mother. I traced the lines with my gaze, searching deep into the silver veins – pretending I was on the path, enduring. The warrior and the maze. A message after death. I felt dizzy again, but refused to look away. I kept seeing my mother's face. Jack said something. So did Tracker.

And then, quite suddenly, I was no longer at the hospital.

I was standing on an empty street. It was night. Cool breeze on my skin.

My mother stood beside me.

CHAPTER 14

M Y mother.

I called out to her, but she did not hear me. Her gaze was fixed on some distant point, sharp, focused. I tried to touch her shoulder, and my hand passed through her body. I tried again, feeling like some bird throwing herself against a window, breaking bones on glass. Dumb as dirt. Desperate to get through.

Nothing. I did not exist. I was a ghost. Or maybe she was. Not that it mattered.

We were together.

She was younger than I remembered, with a glow in her face that was exhilarating and vital, full of a raw vigor that I had never seen in my own reflection. She was beautiful. I could not imagine a person who would not love her. I could not imagine a power on earth or in the prison veil that could stand against her. She was a force of nature. Bigger than life.

She was also pregnant.

Huge, ready to burst. Dressed in a thick sweater, a shapeless muumuu and cowboy boots. Dek and Mal were coiled low over her shoulders, with Zee and the others ranged around her like demon wolves. She held a twelve-gauge across her stomach as though it were a holy relic.

'Come any closer and I'll blow your brains out,' she said to the shadows.

'Hunter,' said a softly chiding female voice. 'You know better.'

My mother narrowed her eyes. 'I know you wouldn't be here unless you wanted to deal.'

'Merely to pass along a message. Personally, as I like you so.' A figure emerged from the shadows; a redheaded woman dressed in a long, crimson coat. Surrounded by an aura so thunderous I could hardly see the possessed human beneath the miasma of demonic energy.

The face was different, but I knew that aura.

'Blood Mama,' said my mother. 'Get to the point.'

'Your baby is the point,' replied the zombie queen. 'The veil is falling, Hunter. She will be the last.'

'Old story. You told my mother the same thing.'

'But you can feel it now. In your bones, in your heart. Your daughter will herald the final breath of this world.'

A cool smile touched my mother's mouth. 'Is that fear I see in your eyes?'

'You know it is,' admitted the zombie queen. 'The same fear in your eyes. We are both mothers, Hunter. No matter how incompatible our interests.'

My mother's hands tightened around the gun. 'And?'

'And this world will survive or die based on the strength of your daughter. It is as simple as that.'

'No pressure, right?'

'How you raise her—'

'—will be *my* business and not yours.'

'And if she's not strong enough? If her heart cannot contain the beast?'

'Then you're fucked,' said my mother, 'and I'll be laughing my ass off in Heaven.'

Blood Mama's mouth tightened. 'You cannot afford to make a mistake. She will *not* be like the others.'

'Thank God,' shot back my mother, but I knew that look on her face. She was hiding something. Blood Mama narrowed her eyes, swaying forward – her host body almost completely devoured by her aura.

'Jolene,' she whispered. 'We have danced too long for secrets. What are you keeping from me?'

'Something you already know,' said my mother quietly. 'Something you can't ever tell the others in the veil because you know what will happen. You know what they'll do.'

Blood Mama went perfectly still; even her aura, like ice. 'Who told you?'

'Doesn't matter. But I get it now.' My mother leaned forward, her mouth tilting into a smile that was more like a snarl. 'And *she'll* get it. She'll find out what she is, and when she does, you start running. You pack your bags, and you get the fuck off this world. Because it won't be yours anymore. It'll be *hers*.'

Blood Mama reared back her head. Quivering. 'And you, Zee? What do *you* have to say about that?'

My mother tensed. But Zee wrapped one arm around her legs and laid his other, ever so gently, across her swollen belly. Raw and Aaz also hugged my mother's knees, while Dek's and Mal's purrs threatened to drown thunder.

'She is ours,' Zee said, defiantly. 'And we are hers. No matter what. No matter who.'

The zombie queen looked as though she wanted to puke. 'Sentiment does not become you, little man. It makes you weak.'

'Ah,' said my mother cheerfully, 'then let's see who's standing when the walls come down, shall we? Because, honey, you'll be dead . . . and my baby, my sweet beautiful baby, will still be fighting.'

Then she cocked the twelve-gauge – and shot Blood Mama's host dead.

I lost her. Unable to say good-bye. Just like when she died.

The night bled into darkness, then light. I opened my eyes.

I was on a couch, my feet dangling, head lolling. Drool dribbled from the corner of my mouth. I had a good view of a ceiling, and the upper row of some bookshelves. I recognized the sight. I was back in the apartment.

I was not alone. The television was on. Tracker sat on the edge of the ottoman, elbows braced on his knees, watching the news.

It was such an unexpected sight – and I was already so addled – all I could do was stare. I doubt he noticed I was awake. Like the nurses at the hospital, he appeared intensely preoccupied by reports that southeastern Iran had been devastated. Thousands dead, thousands more thought to be under the rubble. Rescue operations were overwhelmed. It was night there, which was hindering efforts to find people.

'This is your fault,' Tracker said suddenly, and turned his head just enough to fix me with a glare so harsh a shock of fear thrilled through me.

I did not know how I had gotten here, or what, exactly, had just transpired, but I was still full with my mother, lost on a dark road with her at my side, and I looked Tracker dead in the eyes, and said, 'Stop speaking to me in fucking riddles.'

He stared for one long moment, then rose slowly to his feet. I did not move. I held his gaze, watching as he glided across the floor, each step full of cold grace. He stopped, so suddenly it was almost as though he balanced on the edge of a cliff. The cut on his face, from Oturu's hair, was still livid.

'Are you thirsty?' he asked.

'Where are Grant and Byron?' I replied. 'Jack?'

'I don't know,' he said. 'Coming, I suppose.'

There was nothing dismissive about his answer, which was the only reason I kept my mouth shut. I sat up, wiping spit off my face with the back of my hand. 'Why did you bring me here?'

'You passed out. Old Wolf wanted you out of there.'

'Something happened to me.' Both statement and question. I waited for him to decide which it would be. He was a man who cared about control. I understood why. Demanding answers would not get me any.

His gaze flicked down. I looked, and saw the stone disc on the floor by the couch; the little labyrinth, coiled and gleaming as though infused with black pearl. Tracker crouched, and stretched his hand just over it, palm flat, as though soaking in heat. 'Here is your answer.'

'It's a rock.'

'A rock,' he echoed disdainfully. 'This is a seed ring, Hunter. Or call it what you will. It has too many names to count.'

I slid off the edge of the couch to sit on the floor beside him. 'What does it do?'

Tracker leaned over the disc, almost protectively; his entire focus, now that it was off me, very nearly soft with reverence. A startling thing to witness. I was afraid to breathe, that I would break the spell.

'A seed ring stores memories,' he said gravely. 'Yours, or someone else's. Size determines how much can be retained. A large seed ring, something the size of that wall, could hold the entirety of a person's life. An imprint of her soul. This here . . . perhaps a year at most. Or enough memories, chosen from a lifetime, to fill a year.'

I had to take a moment – lost, still, with my mother. 'How is that possible? To retain a person's memories in stone?'

'Thought is energy,' Tracker said, as though it was the simplest thing in the world. 'And this isn't stone. It's a fragment from the Labyrinth.'

I stared, blankly. Tracker raised his brow. 'It's physics, Hunter. Quantum mechanics. Multiple-worlds theory. Except, it's not a theory, and the Labyrinth is not some hedgerow. It's a place *between*, outside of time, outside of space. A crossroads that connects every world, every dimension.' His gaze turned dark, mocking. 'You realize, don't you, that Old Wolf and his kind made the prison veil after the war with the demons? Folding reality is their game. So is the Labyrinth.'

I searched his face, wondering if he was lying to me. 'That can't be real.'

He leaned back, bitter amusement touching his mouth. 'A woman covered in living tattoos that peel off her body when the sun goes down? How real is that? How real is a creature with knives for feet, who dances when he kills? Or old men who wear human skins like some comfortable coats?' Bitterness touched his mouth. 'You live in a world of wonder, Hunter, but you see none of it. Your life is as small as this seed ring.'

'Don't,' I said softly. 'My mother is in there. Don't belittle that.'

He looked away, jaw tight. Behind him, images of wreck and ruin scrolled across the television screen: flashlights, children crying, haggard, sweating faces filled with horror. Southeastern Iran had suffered another earthquake several years before. Fifteen thousand had died, maybe more. Even now, here, with everything gone wrong, I could not ignore that.

'You said that was my fault.' I tore my gaze from the television to look at Tracker. 'What did you mean?'

'You wouldn't understand.' He rose to his feet and pointed at the seed ring. 'Guard that with your life, Hunter. Not just for your mother, but for the stone itself. Pieces of the Labyrinth are fragments of possibility. And there is nothing more dangerous than *maybe*.'

I picked up the seed ring and found it warm, with a pulse. I held it to my heart, thinking of my mother – wanting to see more. Desperate for it.

Nothing happened. Tracker turned away and walked back to the television. Stared at the screen.

I pressed my cheek to the stone, and then slid it into my pocket. Took out my cell phone and dialed Grant. He answered on the second ring, breathless. 'Maxine.'

'I'm fine,' I said, aware of Tracker listening. 'You?'

'We're in the car. Byron, me, Jack. Coming home.'

I exhaled slowly. 'Any trouble?'

'Just you. Are you safe?'

'As much as I ever am. Just get here.'

'Hang tight,' he said, and I heard a low voice in the background, groggy and young. 'I'm with you.'

We hung up. I found Tracker watching me instead of the television.

'What?' I asked, when he did not look away.

A faint line formed in his brow. 'Your man. Who is he?'

'Don't.'

'It's a simple question.'

'No.' I leaned in, holding his gaze. 'You hurt him, you even look at him funny, and I'll rip every limb off your body.'

His mouth tilted. 'And beat me to death with them?'

'I'll let the boys do that.'

Tracker's smile widened – just a fraction. 'Who is he?'

I reached inside my jacket. My mother's knives were still there. Tracker turned his back on me and studied the television, a wall of sleek hair hiding his strong features. I did not relax. I stood, then joined him, glimpsing, just before his expression hardened, sorrow: profound and heavy, a helplessness that turned to ash every hateful word and look, every preconception. Tracker, born again inside my mind – but I still did not know what to make of him.

'You want to help those people,' I said. 'You want to be there.'

'If I did?' He glanced down at me, so proud. 'Would you, if you could?'

'Go there?' I hesitated, thinking of Grant and Jack. Byron. Ahsen, loose and hunting. Tracker shook his head in disgust.

'It's not so easy,' I protested. 'There are people who need me. Right now. Here.'

'And they don't?' His gaze searched mine. 'How do you judge, Hunter? How many deaths are required before one reaches the end of the world? Just one? A thousand? Or does it ever end, only when the last heart is dead?'

'No,' I said, grim. 'But I'm just one person.'

'Ah,' he replied. 'And I suppose just one person never did any good at all. Hunter. Last Warden of this lonely, caged world.'

I stared, torn. Tracker, after a moment, held out his hand.

I thought of Grant and Byron. Jack. Coming here. Expecting to find me. They would be worried. If it were me, I would be terrified.

Tracker's expression hardened. He began to pull

back his hand. I grabbed his wrist, fingers squeezing tight. Holding his gaze.

I did not let go. I found my cell phone, and called Grant.

'Change of plans,' I said.

IT was night on the other side of the world. I heard screams. I saw flashlights and smelled smoke, listened to children crying. Made out the slide and broken stone of rubble. The air choked me with dust, the acrid scent of blood and bowels loosened in death. The boys peeled off my body, tumbling to the ground, nearly taking me with them, in pain.

Tracker stood beside me. I did not waste time asking questions, and neither did the boys. I heard a woman groaning and followed the sound to a pile of stone and wires. I had excellent night vision – better than human – and saw an ankle, a twitching hand.

I snapped my fingers. Zee and Raw began digging into the rubble. Aaz prowled past them, like a small dragon, sniffing the air. I followed him, stumbling, and when he started to dig, I followed without question. Dek and Mal slithered off my shoulders, disappearing inside crevices too small for my hands. Rock crunched, their jaws chewing and grinding. Within moments they made a hole big enough to reach into, and I did, blindly, patting the ground. I felt something soft – a stuffed toy – and then a small hand.

I pulled gently, and Aaz disappeared into the shadows to wriggle the child free, from beneath.

It was a little girl. I tugged her into my arms, and she began to cough, crying. I rocked her in my lap, and Mal dragged a rag doll from the hole, one little patchy arm between his sharp teeth. I placed the toy in the girl's arms, and stood. Found Tracker staring, his expression utterly unreadable.

I found a safe place for the little girl, and left her curled around her rag doll. I did not want to leave her, but I could hear cries beneath the stone, young voices, and I ran to them, the boys at my back. It was so dark, and there were so few people searching the rubble, I did not worry about them being seen. Only once did someone lock eyes with Zee. An old man, bleeding from a head wound and half-delirious. He looked into Zee's face as the little demon chewed through the crude metal beam pinning his legs, and said a word I did not understand.

'It's Persian for *djinn*,' Tracker muttered, near my shoulder. 'He thinks Zee is a spirit, something that can possess a human.'

I grunted, wiping sweat from my brow. 'Close enough to the truth.'

'You'll find a lot of zombies here,' Tracker said.

'Zombies everywhere,' I replied carefully.

'Only one of you,' he said, a hard note creeping back into his voice.

I dug my knuckles into stone, then reached over Zee to help cushion the old man's head, which was lacerated with cuts. 'That's not my fault.'

Tracker's silence implied he disagreed. I was too

tired to argue. Instead, I said, 'Oturu. Are there others like him?'

'He's the last of his kind. A wanderer, before he was brought here.'

'Where is he now?'

'Somewhere between,' he said distantly, shoving rocks away. 'Beyond this world. His time on this earth is limited to fragments. Too long, and his hunger to hunt will overwhelm. He won't risk breaking his word.' He straightened, pushing back his hair, staring down his nose at me. 'I was sold to him. One of your ancestors needed a favor. I was the prize.'

I felt dizzy and tried to focus on the old man. I hardly dared to pull him free. His legs were crushed. 'Where was this?'

'Sumeria.'

I risked a quick glance. 'Sumeria hasn't existed in five thousand years.'

'Remarkable,' he replied. 'It thinks.'

I bit my tongue. The old man was no longer making any sounds. I checked his pulse, and it was still strong. He had fainted.

'Help me,' I said, as Zee finished clearing rubble from around his feet. I glimpsed Raw and Aaz carrying a small boy between them, their little bodies disjointed and hunched, like wolves trying to walk on two feet.

Tracker followed my gaze. 'How long did it take you to train them?'

I gave him a sharp look, as did Zee. 'They're not dogs.'

'They obey you, don't they?'

'They're my friends. Family.'

Zee flipped his middle claw at the man and melted into shadow. I saw him reappear some distance on my right, burrowing through stone. Sparks flew from his claws. I heard sirens, distantly, and voices shouting, screaming out names. More activity. If the boys were not careful, someone else would see them soon, even in the dark.

I said, 'Tell me about the woman.'

'Look in the mirror.'

'I think they're all cracked,' I muttered. 'You'll just have to settle for words.'

Tracker pushed me aside, poles in his hands. He grabbed wire from beneath some rubble and pulled hard until he had a decent amount coiled at his feet. He began binding the old man's crushed legs together to hold them steady. Quick, efficient. 'She went insane. Too much power. It changed her.'

'Changed her like Oturu thinks I'll be changed?'

Tracker's hands faltered, then resumed tying knots. 'He gave you his mark. Which means he sees something of her in you.'

'You must, too. Unless you hate all of my blood-line, just on principle.'

He turned from me before I could see his face. Dek appeared at my feet, dragging a bottle of water in his mouth. I had no clue where he had found it, but I was grateful. I tried pouring some into the old man's mouth. He did not wake up, but I was satisfied with the tiny dribble I got past his lips. I found Tracker watching me again.

I handed him the water. 'Whoever she was, I'm not her.'

He took a sip, his gaze never leaving my face. 'We'll see, Hunter.'

Before I could think of an appropriate response, the boys melted from the shadows, surrounding me. Oturu's mark began tingling. Tracker stiffened.

'Cutter,' Zee hissed. 'Hot slicer.'

I straightened. 'Where?'

'Coming from behind,' said the little demon. Raw and Aaz tore spikes from their spines, and the wet sounds of ripping flesh made my skin crawl. I glanced at Tracker. Noted the speculation in his eyes as he gazed into the shadows. I remembered what he had said to me at the hospital.

'You were serious,' I whispered. 'Demonic activity caused this earthquake?'

Tracker finished lashing the old man's legs. 'Not this one. But that doesn't mean they won't try and benefit from it. There are many demons hiding on this earth, Hunter. Feeling the veil open will make them bold.'

I thought of the rescued children resting nearby, and started scrabbling across the rubble. Tracker grabbed my arm. I tried pulling free, and felt the temperature drop like a bag of ice cubes was being poured down my spine.

I caught movement ahead of me, a flash of pale skin – a glimpse that reached down into that most primal place in my gut and screamed *not human*. Silver hair braided into ropes, flowing down a gaunt body dressed only in a leather belt. Fingers like the tines of pitchforks, impaled with chunks of red, dripping flesh. The demon moved like a leaf falling from a tree: graceful, with odd, sweeping movements that sent it low to the ground, up and down, over and over again.

Alien. So alien, part of me wanted to scream. Even Oturu had felt more familiar than this creature, which was so far removed from anything this world could offer that it crossed my mind, with terrible certainty, that whatever the demons were, they had not been here first. Interlopers. Invaders. Something beyond the pale of this world's horizon. Maybe, even, *demon* was inappropriate, a word so excessively steeped in religion it had ceased to apply. Because what I saw now did not feel supernatural, no matter how bizarre its appearance.

I glanced at Tracker and caught him analyzing the demon in a way that struck me hard – both with my own inadequacy and a terrible sense of familiarity. Déjà vu, even. As though I had done this before – crouched with this man, prepared to hunt. It made me uneasy. Frightened me, even.

'Mahati,' Tracker whispered. 'Second-ring prisoner.'

'How could anything like that hide on this planet?'

'Easily. But that isn't a real Mahati.'

Ahsen. The stone circle was hot in my pocket. I did not dare touch it. 'How did she find us?'

'Energy.' Tracker's lips pressed together in a hard line. 'Every living creature gives off a quantum signature, a vibration that is distinctly unique.'

'She could have come for me at the hospital,' I muttered, and tapped Zee's shoulder. 'Ready?'

'No,' Tracker said.

'Ready,' Zee told me, as Dek and Mal settled heavily on my shoulders. 'But we got a crowd, Maxine. More than one slicer. More coming for the blood.'

'Stop,' Tracker said, more firmly. 'Something is wrong. This doesn't feel right.'

'No choice,' I replied, thinking of the injured just behind us and all those approaching rescuers: people unprepared for another kind of disaster, for something that belonged only in nightmares. No invisible spirits, not some weak zombie parasite – instead a demon made of flesh and bone and blood, one that could feed easily in this wreckage, without leaving a trace of its existence behind. Dead bodies would be expected. Missing bodies anticipated. No one would think twice.

I stepped free of the rubble, the boys gathered close. Felt a charge beneath my skin, momentum, as though as I were driving one hundred miles per hour down a desert road at midnight, blasting through the world in a body of armor. Not invulnerable, but full

266

of something big and breathless – old-fashioned, even. Pure grit.

Ahsen's silver skin and sharp fingers frayed into smoke as I approached, enveloped in a shimmer that momentarily collapsed like a balloon with all its air sucked out; all that was alien fell away like a dream, until, moments later, a little girl stood before me. Still wearing my young face. A braid of hair in her hand.

The air was so cold I could see my breath. Ahsen gazed slightly to her left, like a doll stolen from a little girl, dropped, polished and shining, within a gruesome pit. Nothing sadder; nothing more chilling.

'You travel with dogs now,' she said.

I tilted my head, confused; then felt Tracker step close. A bitter smile touched his mouth. 'Skinner. I don't believe we've met.'

Ahsen swayed, her small body almost lost within the rubble, my young face smooth as virgin snow. 'You were but a germ in my mind before I was placed in the veil. Enkidu. Tracker.'

Tracker showed nothing on his face. Neither did I. But inside I wobbled. Ahsen took another step, light as air, her gaze drifting like two black beetles. 'I have had time to consider the situation, Hunter. My brothers and sisters were hypocrites. They despised my methods. They valued the results.' Her gaze floated across my body. 'I believe I could have done a better job with you, as well. The mistakes made with your bloodline . . . reprehensible, born of desperation.'

I had no idea what she was talking about. 'Care to elaborate?'

A faint cruel smile touched her mouth; she was amused, but in the way an executioner might be, as though savoring the final drop of a good hard kill. 'Hunter. You should ask yourself what is so different about your runts, that instead of being imprisoned in the veil, they were sentenced to an eternity upon human skin? The veil, I can assure you, would have been large enough to accommodate five extra bodies. But for some reason . . . not theirs.'

Zee snarled, his claws raking trenches in the concrete. Ahsen said, 'You, runt. Little king without your crown. Do you know what you are?'

I heard an uncomfortable echo in her words, too much like the memories I had seen in the seed ring. I thought of my mother. My hand slipped into my pocket. Ahsen's gaze dipped, as well, and the skin of her face pulled so taut it seemed there must be hooks in her scalp, yanking back. Tracker stepped even closer to me, as did the boys.

'Ahsen,' I said quietly. 'You were, you *are*, one of *them*. An Avatar. Why are you here? Even if you were imprisoned, why are you helping the demons? Is it just revenge?'

'Because I have no choice,' she whispered, her adult voice eerie and throbbing. 'But I have reevaluated my priorities. I have decided to reshape my destiny.'

She clicked her fingers. I felt a breath of air on

my face, caught a scent so raw, so vile, it was like someone made of sulfur and shit had just cut open a vein and bled on my feet. Bodies shuffled from the darkness, skeletons made of flesh and shadow. No eyes or mouths, but only dripping holes where noses should be; limbs long, knitted with rough sinew, thick veins that pulsed like ropes made of crude oil. I had never seen anything like them. There should not have been so many. Beyond, the world pressed – a surreal reality: low cries, sirens, the chop of helicopter rotors.

'I was first amongst my people,' said Ahsen quietly. 'First of the grafters, the spinners, the connivers; first to master the divine organic. And I will begin once more. I will make my own army. I will not be denied the Labyrinth. Never again.'

The creatures surrounding us swayed and snuffled. On one of them I glimpsed a whisper of blond hair peeking through the crude scalp, like the last threads of a quilt, not quite bound. Horror slit my heart. I stared harder, seeking anything recognizable, and wondered if those broad shoulders were familiar.

'They're not demons,' I said, sickened. 'They used to be human.'

Ahsen made a quiet humming sound. 'Humanity is such a tenuous classification, so easily rendered obsolete. Something you should know, Hunter. You, who are hardly as human as my shambling constructs.'

The creatures attacked.

It had been a long time. Expectation meant nothing.

They were fast, and I was out of practice, mortal, my hands full of knives and nothing else. I forced myself into a cold, hard place, trying not to think of the people they might have been. Made me sick. My heart pounded in my throat, and sweat stung my eyes as all those years of training bled into my muscles, taking over like I was another kind of zombie, slave to my mother's lessons.

I lost track of numbers. Too many. Too many to have hidden here, unseen, unless they could move like Tracker and the boys – through shadows, winking from dark to light. What she was doing made no sense, though. Throwing bodies at us, just throwing them away. Zee and the others tore through the human constructs like they were made of paper, ripping holes, tearing off limbs – while on my shoulders Dek and Mal lunged, hissing fire at those who got too close. Hot ash blew against my face. I saw charred stumps where hands should have been.

I looked for Tracker. Found him fighting at my back, a length of pipe in his hands, wielding it with impossible grace, as though it were a sword, the most perfect ever made. He met my gaze only once, and in it I felt a shock, a dreadful familiarity; again, that I had done this before. With him.

Ahsen never moved a muscle. Not for the entire fight. She simply watched me, just as I watched her, until I suddenly stopped fighting, facing her like a showdown in Tombstone. No guns, but an army at my back and knives in my hands. I trusted the boys to keep me safe. I trusted them so much I paid attention to nothing else but Ahsen as I stalked near, never once taking my eyes off her small body, that ghost of me.

'You want the seed ring,' I said to her.

'It is a trinket to you,' she replied. 'Give it to someone who understands its worth. Just one touch, Hunter . . . just one, and I became more. Powerful enough to make *them*.'

I shook my head. 'You didn't come here to ask.'

'No.' Her body began evaporating. 'But I enjoy our conversations.'

It was night, and I was mortal. Eminently killable. I already knew I could not harm her. I steadied myself, one hand holding a blade – the other hand in my pocket, gripping the seed ring like it was a lifeline. My mother's life.

Behind me, Tracker still fought. So did the boys. Her plan, I realized. Wait for the right moment. Then distract, occupy anyone who could help me, overwhelm them with numbers – while she overwhelmed me. I thought it might work. My heart was afraid – dearly, deathly afraid. I heard a small voice inside my head whisper, *Please*.

Oturu's mark tingled. I heard a low roar of wind, like the first riot of a winter storm. Suffered a pang in my chest, an eloquent calculation of need and knowing. I looked up. Just in time.

A sleek tall body slammed into the rubble like a hammered blade, the impact so violent I was lifted off the ground. A massive black cloak flared backward, just short of touching me, and I gazed – throat closed, heart pounding – into a breathing abyss that pulsed and writhed: a hard, pale jaw, the curve of a smile, the brim of a black hat, and hair that coiled, wild.

'You will not touch her,' Oturu whispered.

Ahsen stared, her pitiless eyes old and glassy. 'Not all the Queen's men can hold the Hunter together. Not again.'

She vanished. And reappeared around my body. That pulverizing strength, brought to bear on mortal flesh; squeezing inexorably as though I were inside the stomach of a python, being slowly digested. I felt tremendous pressure around the hand that held the seed ring, but I refused to let go. I refused, with all my heart.

I stopped breathing. Lights flickered in my eyes.

Something shifted inside me. A shadow behind my ribs. I remembered that sensation. Old and dogged, a childhood nightmare; a click, a key turning, and the seed ring suddenly grew so hot I was certain my hand was going to catch on fire.

Anywhere but here, I thought, as I began to die. *Anywhere she won't follow.*

And another voice, deep inside my mind, said, *Yes*.

The world disappeared from under me. I fell. The pressure eased, but I kept falling. There was no floor to catch me. I imagined Tracker's voice calling my

272

name, but the darkness swallowed him, swallowed night – and I had nothing, I was nothing, I was consumed.

I fell, without end.

I fell, and did not stop.

CHAPTER 15

THERE were things a person learned while falling in the dark.

Anticipation, for one, was a thing of terror. Every moment I thought, *This is it; next I will hit*, but the moment passed, and still I cringed – and it was the anticipation that made my heart thunder, my skin crawl. A body was never meant to fall forever.

There was something else, too.

Darkness made it worse.

I could not see. I felt air pass over my body, the plummet of gravity, but that was the only sensation, the only reason I knew I was still moving. I went on and on, and finally closed my eyes. Afraid of losing myself. Unable to do anything but endure.

I lost track of heartbeats. I forgot the world.

In my head, I heard Grant's flute. I saw his face, and clung to that.

I held tight.

FINALLY, rock.

Sprawled on rock. Air, cold in my lungs. I had no memory of impact, just that I had been moving, and now I was not. I saw only darkness, and lay quiet, listening hard. I heard my heart, the rasp of my breath; farther, a drip and faint splash. Water.

I pushed myself up and felt like an old woman: dizzy, thirsty, disoriented. I could not see. I waited for my vision to adjust – my eyes that had never failed me, no matter how dark. But I saw nothing. I was blind.

The boys were on my skin. Restless. Dreaming.

I was also naked. My clothes, knives, boots – gone as though made of air. Including the seed ring. I tried searching but encountered nothing. I was blind, my hands outstretched. My belongings could have been hanging from a hook only a heartbeat distant, but my sight was so nonexistent, I wished I could ask a stranger if I still had eyes inside my head. I could feel them, sure, but the possibility of losing one's mind tended to undermine even the most obvious of certainties.

I had lost everything.

Desperation rolled through me. Fear. I fought for calm. Took deep breaths. Nothing helped.

I was sitting in a narrow, rocky crater, a broken crack roughly the shape of my body. I could feel it with my hands. I stood slowly, teetering when my balance faltered, and forced myself to hold very still in the darkness. Listening, sensing. I rubbed my arms. The boys stirred against me. I heard the drip again and started walking. Reluctant. Slow and careful, shuffling along like a baby with my hands outstretched. I encountered nothing but air, and the stone beneath my feet.

Until, finally, I heard another drip, close.

I stepped in something wet. I knelt, and my fingers encountered a pool of water surprisingly deep. My hands lingered, allowing the boys a taste. When I felt no resistance from them, I leaned in to drink. The water tasted cold and sweet, which was some relief. I could live off the boys if I had to – share their metabolism – but it would do nothing to assuage my thirst or hunger.

When I had drunk all I could, I sat back, knees held to my chest, quiet and still. The darkness was heavy. I had never been afraid of the dark, of empty places, but this was the first time since my mother's death that I had felt so totally alone. I wished I had the seed ring. I hoped desperately it had not ended up in Ahsen's hands. Or that it was not lying here, somewhere, out of sight.

'Get up,' I told myself, just to hear my voice. It sounded tinny, small, but in my head, an endless litany: no time to feel sorry for myself, no time for fear, no time to dwell. Nothing I did was going to make me feel better. I might as well get going. The boys tugged at me. I whispered, 'Hey. I need some direction.'

After a moment, the right side of my body tingled. I took that as a sign.

I wandered for a very long time. The boys guided me, and I found myself turning, slowing, depending on tingling sensations in my limbs. I knocked my head once, but for the most part, the path was clear and silent. I stopped only when the boys found water again. Swift-moving, churning, and cold; a creek, perhaps. I heard it for quite some time before I reached its rocky shore, and considered resting. But I thought of Grant and Byron, even Tracker, Jack – the entire world – and I kept moving. I had to.

I was in the Labyrinth. I knew it. I could not explain how or why, or what it meant, but I had opened the door myself. I had fallen into the world *between*, but there were no doors here, and if this was a crossroads, then no one else was traveling. I had a feeling I had made a terrible mistake. I was not on a road. I was in a holding cell. A place to be forgotten, forever.

I stopped only for water. There was no food. The boys shared, metabolisms linking to mine, but that did nothing for the ache in my gut. After a while, too, the darkness hurt my eyes, the strain of trying to see.

I closed them. Imagined lights on the other side of my eyelids, but those were just tricks of the brain. So many tricks. I tried talking out loud again, but hearing my voice, small and lonely, just made the isolation worse.

Quiet was easier. Moving was easiest of all. I tried not to think about whether there was anything in the darkness, watching me. I did not know what would be worse – to be lost in a true void or to know that I was being hunted.

I thought about my mother. I forced myself to think about that day, almost twenty years past, standing in the snow. That bad. The zombie in his suit with his skin flaking off, telling my mother to have another – another child. The rattle of his screams inside the bar. Those zombies gathered, fighting to possess me.

Part of the game, I had read in my mother's journal, after she died. A game, an ancient bargain with Blood Mama. Chance or wits, played for the life of a child. To test that child and discover her strength. Strong enough to fight; more importantly, strong enough for the boys. Because if a future Hunter could not fend off a demonic possession as a child, then she had no business carrying the burden as an adult.

The concept, brutal as it was, made sense to me – but I had never understood why Blood Mama would care whether a Hunter was strong – or why she would have a vested interest in maintaining that strength. Never why my ancestors would have allowed such a test.

But I understood now. There were demons even Blood Mama did not want to face. Demons that were my responsibility to fight.

278

I thought of my mother, pregnant, standing in the street, facing down the zombie queen with a smile. Secrets in her heart, then and now. But I could live with that. Even if I never discovered what she had hidden – even if I did, and it was terrible – everything would be all right.

I might be falling down in secrets, but I knew something true:

My mother had loved me. No matter what.

I was loved.

I felt as though I walked for years. I measured time by the length of my nails and hair. No lies there. No distortion. My nails grew long. My hair, longer. Matted and wild.

My mind changed as well. I did not know how it began. I never guessed. But when I closed my eyes, as I walked, I dreamed.

Waking dreams. Walking dreams. Swift dreams, black and white like old scratchy movies tinted and blurred with age. I dreamed in sparks and moments, and saw women in moonlight, pale as snow, hair as black as a raven's wing – steel in their hands, always, sword bound, hair bound, in sunlight, tattoo bound – and I flew with them, I ran, and their bodies merged into one, a woman large as thunder, with eyes like the starry night, and wolves at her back.

I chased echoes in my dreams. I sprinted after flights of notion and fancy: dragons wet with ocean spray and men with bows and hooves and long, sleek tails; giants slumbering in mountain streams; or the sphinx, riddle-heavy, crouched with a whisper. I dreamed of moons; I dreamed of war, armies breathing down my back with armored princes begging; and I dreamed the boys unleashed as hounds of Hell, burning the earth beneath their claws, destroying it with a fury.

When I closed my eyes, I dreamed. But my eyes were always closed, and here, in the Labyrinth, dreams coated the walls, dreams painted my eyes, and as I walked, surrounded and nourished by the boys, aching with days or years of hunger, I lost myself in trails of blood, cast in the veins of paths I traveled, walking – then dancing, then running.

I ran. I ran so fast, fleet-footed as a shadow, and I did not stop, I learned to listen to the boys, I learned to become the dark and the stone, thick and coarse and rough with age, and I forgot what it was to walk, I forgot, and when I stopped to drink at streams, my skin screamed to move, and I screamed, and I screamed.

I screamed.

I, Hunter, in the ground, Hunter, do not die, Hunter, keep moving, Hunter, run, Hunter, do not, do not, do not give up, Hunter. Dream, Hunter. Fight, Hunter. Do not forget yourself, Hunter.

Remember, Hunter.

I remembered my mother as I drank from a cold river, the waters crashing off the walls like thunder.

Something small. In a hotel in some city with all

the lights off except for the bathroom, door closed so that only a bar of gold slid into the room, my mother on a cot beside mine and the boys prowling, and her voice whispering, *In the dark there are things that will wake inside your heart, things you never knew were there, and you must be careful of what comes stirring; you must beware.*

I was careful, but all I had was the dark, all I had were the boys, and sometimes I heard them in my mind, so close that should the sun ever set, I wondered if they would leave me, if I would survive the cut. It had been a long time. We were closer now. We were one.

At the river's edge the stones were round and soft, and the water was deep. I waded into the current simply to feel the texture, to savor the difference between water and air. The river was swift, the roar of it deafening. I had a whim, and lay down. The water carried me like a child in a cradle, swept away. I did not think about consequences. I did not worry about losing the shore. The river stole me, and I laughed.

Stop, said a voice inside my mind. *Maxine*.

But I ignored the voice. I closed my eyes. I lost myself in dreams. I lived in another place and time, away from the darkness, and I saw Grant, the boys. My mother was there, and it was more real than the water and my skin – my heart, beating; my soul, caged. I dreamed of swords, and in my dream I tasted the blade, cold on my tongue. Found it made of tears.

My tears. I was crying.

I opened my eyes and did not close them again.

The waters became choppy. I hit a rough patch and went under. My lungs ached, and I broke the surface, gasping. Started kicking, paddling, but the current was rough. I hated swimming. I hated boats. I remembered these things, distantly, and I did not know what I had been thinking, jumping in the river. I did not know how I could forget.

You lost your mind, whispered that little voice. *Maxine*.

I went under again, as though hands were holding my ankles, but when I tried to come back up, my head hit stone. Terror shot through me. I grappled, swept along, fingernails dragging across the rock above my face. My lungs screamed. I screamed. The boys yanked on my skin, and I felt them shift, pulling and spreading, but with a violence I had never felt. I jerked once, thinking I was going to drown, but the ache eased in my lungs.

I breathed. Underwater, I breathed. It tasted like stone and ash, perhaps like blood. I was too relieved to care. I touched my face, trying to understand. But when I did, I wished I had not.

My nostrils were gone. So was my mouth. My eyes and ears, covered in skin. I had no face.

Horror pummeled me. Revulsion, dismay. I felt sick. I wanted to vomit, I wanted to cry out, but I could not. I clawed at my own skin. I tore at my face. I screamed soundlessly at the boys, slamming my fists into the stone above my head. I tried to swim, but could not go back. I found no bottom, no sand.

The stone pressed me under the water for a very long time. Longer than days and weeks. Longer, still. It felt like forever. I was dragged by the current like a rag doll, faceless, voiceless, and though I breathed through the boys, all I felt was fear. I was so afraid. I was so alone. I had been buried alive and this was a water-coffin, a tomb of flesh, swift moving.

I was immortal now. I would be like this forever. Lost forever. Buried in water, raging with thirst.

All of me, raging.

But as I raged, something woke up.

I felt when it happened, like a prick inside my heart, and it snapped me back to sanity as though my brain were a rubber band pulled to the breaking point until – in a flash – pressure eased.

I was still trapped inside my body, but as I floated down the underground river, the water and the darkness became a nest rather than a coffin: a shift in perception, so sweet. My flesh, a cocoon. Spinning me into something new. I listened to myself. Heartbeats, the click of my bound jaw, the swell of my chest as I went through the motions of breathing. Deeper, too, past thoughts and memory; deeper yet, into blood.

It is of us, this hunt, this wild raging hunt that takes upon itself the nature of an Age, and destroys

283

so that others may be reborn. Words, swift words, accompanied by a face I could hardly recall: white hair, blue eyes, power hiding beneath wrinkled skin.

Power beneath my skin. Sleeping in darkness. Resting against my bones, sunk into muscle, sharing blood. Another body dreaming inside my own, sleek as moonlight on dark water, or the edge of a blade.

I felt like a blade.

You are *the blade*, whispered a voice inside my head, and the darkness turned inside my skin, reaching out, just so. I felt it, a delicate touch, as though spirit arms were stretching like coarse silk threads, spun and woven, searching. I did not engage, nor did I think; merely, I drifted in my cocoon, waiting, waiting, to see what would return.

But nothing did except an impulse – sudden crazy desire – to buck down deep and writhe my way through the water like an eel, shot by the current.

I obeyed. I had not worked my legs and arms in a long time, but I kicked, and my body turned, and I kicked again harder, cupping my hands against the water. The boys worked, too, helping me gather strength as I followed instinct and swam deep, searching for the river's bottom.

I had not found it before – and I almost did not, again. But the darkness surged inside my chest, goading me, and I pushed harder – until, to my shock, my hand touched sand – and then, a moment later, metal.

I clung. I gripped. I held on with all my strength

284

as the current raged around me. My fingers tightened, cutting into a hard, curving sheet of armor, and my other hand grappled with rocks, turning them aside. I touched chain link, small and delicate, and beneath, the long hard surface of bone. I did not let go. I kept searching, driven, following that arm until I reached a hand.

And in that hand, a sword.

The metal was serrated, engraved, and very sharp. The hand holding it, however long dead it might have been, did not want to let go. I broke finger bones in the process, but felt as little guilt as if I were stealing from myself.

The darkness inside me approved. The moment I held the weapon in my hands, I felt no more need to stay at the bottom of the river. I let go of the armor, and though I held a sword against my chest, I floated upward, the current chasing me.

I ran my hands down the blade. The weapon was slender, but long, the guard delicately wrought; resembling, in my imagination, stiff, extended claws. The grip was smooth, and fit my hand as though made for it.

As though *I* had been made for it.

Home, whispered the voice in my head.

The world fell away from me. Water, gone. Walls, gone. No floor to catch me. I fell. And I continued to fall.

Anticipation was a thing of terror.

But this time, I pretended I was flying.

CHAPTER 16

FROM the Labyrinth to city lights, dazzling as a heart full of stars.

I hit concrete, and even though I had recaptured my sight through memory and dream – such astounding dreams – the use of my physical eyes was shocking, stupefying.

I was in my own skin. I had a mouth and nose. I could see.

I also had no time to accustom myself. It was night. The boys woke – Zee and the others, peeling off my body – and every inch, from my toenails to my eyelids, felt as though it left with them: like I was being pulled apart, inch by quick inch; or bathed in fire, acid; rubbed in salt, my body some skinned raw nerve.

I thought the separation would kill me. I did not

think I could live without the boys on my body. It had been too long. We were part of each other. They were me.

'Maxine,' Zee rasped. Raw and Aaz gathered near, Dek and Mal curling warm over my shoulders. They stared, eyes huge, but I could not answer. The pain was too much.

Zee winked out. I heard voices nearby, and coarse laughter. I was suddenly terrified of being seen and bit my hand, trying not to cry out. I did not know if I was on a sidewalk or in an alley. I smelled trash.

Zee reappeared. Behind him a large shadow blocked out the city lights. Arms folded around my body. I screamed, too much in agony to fight for silence.

'Hush.' I recognized Jack's voice. 'Hush now, sweet girl.'

I could not breathe. My body shook. I was having a seizure. Dying.

Jack touched my neck.

I passed out.

I woke up in Hell. There was a sign above my head that said so, which meant it must be true. I was in a narrow bed, sunk deep into a thick mattress beneath heavy covers that smelled like pipe smoke. I was naked. I saw a mirror in the ceiling. Written on the glass in red ink: YOU ARE IN HELL.

Story of my life. I lay very still, hardly able to breathe. Afraid. Desperately afraid. Full of memory,

287

full of terrible things, building and burning. I wanted to scream, but bottled it in. If I started, I would not stop. I would make myself sick on tears, and it would never be enough.

I exhaled slowly, and little bodies uncurled around my throat. Dek and Mal peered into my face, red eyes wide, little jaws slack as their black tongues tasted the air. I wanted to scratch behind their ears, but when I tried to lift my arm, my muscles were too weak. Paralyzed, all over again.

'You're awake.' Jack stepped near, peering at me. He was as I remembered, wearing tweed and slacks. Trickster. Avatar. Whatever that was.

'Old Wolf,' I murmured, feeling faint at the crusty sound of my voice. 'I had a wild ride.'

Tears bristled his eyes. 'Just like my Jeannie.'

It was too much. I started crying. I cried like a baby, but quietly, shaking – so weak I could hardly afford to shake, but the sobs were involuntary, and my body burned with them. Jack wrung his hands, then ran out of sight. I heard objects falling, then he reappeared with a wad of tissues in his hand. He dabbed at my nose, then held a tissue over my nostrils, and said, 'Blow.'

I did, feeling ridiculous – grimacing as I watched Jack try in vain to be gallant about the snot that got on his fingers.

'Thank you,' I mumbled, hardly able to breathe. Jack wiped his hands on his trousers, leaned forward, and planted a heavy kiss on my brow. Dek and Mal licked my face. I wondered where Zee and the others were, but Jack left the room before I could ask.

His face was red and mottled when he returned, holding a porcelain cup so tiny it looked like a thimble in his hand. He sat on the edge of the bed. Very carefully, he slid his hand under my head and lifted me. He pressed the tiny cup to my lips. I smelled chicken broth.

I took a sip. The broth tasted hot and salty, and each swallow seemed to bypass my stomach for the bloodstream. It tasted so good. Best meal of my life. My heart pounded harder.

I murmured, 'Smile, Meddling Man.'

Jack remained impossibly grim. 'When I was told what happened, I tried to track you. But I couldn't. Not even Enkidu – Tracker – could follow you. Or Oturu. And we tried, my dear. We tried so hard.' His eyes were very red. 'You entered the Wasteland. Do you have any idea what that place is?'

I simply looked at him. I had lived through it. I probably knew better than he. Jack flushed, ducking his head, waving an apologetic hand. 'Of course. But you shouldn't have escaped. No one does. There are no doors. We thought . . . we thought we had lost you.'

I tried sitting up, but nausea surged in my throat and my vision blurred. Jack placed a strong hand on my ankle. For a moment, he seemed to transform. His appearance, his body . . . less *him*. His eyes did not match his skin. I saw a wolf in sheep's clothing.

I needed to say something. Anything, to fill the silence. I fumbled for words. 'Where's the seed ring? Did Ahsen get it?'

'Oturu managed to retrieve it. He is keeping it for you.'

'You trust him?'

'I had no choice. But it *is* safe. She will not be able to fetch it from him.'

'You call her *skinner* or *she*, but never her name. Never Ahsen. Why is that?'

Jack looked down, at his hands. 'It is . . . painful. She was the greatest of our minds, our most adept at organic divination. But she went too far. She had . . . no conscience.'

'She hurt humans.'

'No,' he said. 'She brokered deals for demon flesh. And it was those . . . transactions . . . that led the Reaper army to earth.'

'She caused the war?'

'The war had already begun. We were simply trying to escape fighting it.' The old man met my gaze, a bitter smile touching his mouth. 'You must understand, we had never encountered anything like the creatures you call demons. They were . . . scavengers, hunters, creatures made only for death. My kind would retreat, again and again. We left millions to die. Humans, and others. We brought some survivors to this world, thinking it was too distant, that the demons would not be able to follow. But then *she* took matters into her own hands. Justified herself by saying that if we could only develop more powerful skins, we would be able to defend ourselves more easily.'

'You tossed her in jail for that.'

'Not in the beginning. Some defended her decision. It was not until the war began to go badly that she was . . . turned against.'

'You and Sarai?'

'We always opposed her. And we locked her into the prison veil when it was time.'

'And now she's loose.' I closed my eyes, briefly. 'Will your kind help us?'

Jack sighed, rising to his feet. 'Enough, enough. You need to rest.'

'Why don't you want to answer the question?'

'Why must you ask so many?'

'Because I'm like my grandmother,' I replied. 'I'm like my mother.'

'That,' he said, 'is a dirty tactic.'

'Old Wolf,' I said. 'Will they help us?'

'No,' he replied solemnly. 'The war destroyed the backbone of my kind. You cannot imagine. We, who were supposed to be immortal, *dying* in battle. After the war, only a handful remained on this world. Most left through the Labyrinth to heal, and forget.'

'They aren't concerned about retribution? Or that everything they sacrificed for will be destroyed?'

Disgust twisted his face. 'They think the demons will have learned their lesson, that they will avoid our worlds. It is the great bluff, with their heads in the sand. Once the demons are loose, once they have taken this world, they will enter the Labyrinth, *again*, and no one will be safe.'

'That's why you're fighting so hard. That's why you stayed.'

Jack hesitated. 'This world is not the most beautiful, my dear, nor is it the kindest. But it wears its flaws with depth, and hard beauty, and even I, at my great age, find myself constantly surprised.'

'Ah,' I said gently. 'I know why my grandmother liked you.'

'She was a lovely woman,' he replied, with reverence. 'She would be proud of you.'

A flush touched my cheeks. I swallowed hard, casting about, and saw a dirty clock on the wall. Another kind of fear filled me. 'How long was I in the Labyrinth?'

Jack followed my gaze. 'Time passes differently there. To you, perhaps months. Out here, only one day.'

Months. Felt like years. I was going to tell him that, but when I looked back at him, he was staring at my right hand, utterly preoccupied. For the first time, I noticed something heavy on my finger, and looked down.

I was wearing a ring – a thick, heavy band that could have been made from iron or dull silver, but that stretched from the base of my finger to the joint at the center, entirely covering the skin. Runes had been engraved, etchings that resembled odd roses; elegant, even deadly. When my finger twitched, I felt an undercurrent, an electric burn between my skin and the ring.

The sword.

I knew they werc the same. I knew it in an instant. Just not how. I kept my mouth shut, though – as if to speak that knowledge out loud would be a violation of some trust: not a secret, but not something to throw around.

Crazy, maybe. But I had a sense. I had a feeling between my hand and the hilt, my hand and the ring, like it had been waiting for me. Patient. In the dark. I was afraid to abuse that.

Jack still stared. I cleared my throat. 'What about the others?'

'Fine,' he said shortly. 'You'll see them soon.'

I started to feel tired, my eyelids heavy. I looked past Jack for Zee, but all I saw were dusty plastic curtains, a cheap plastic card table piled with newspapers, and a golden shag carpet that looked like a roach motel. Jack reached down by the bed and picked up a water bottle.

'Forgive the accommodations,' he said, holding it to my mouth. 'I had to make do with breaking into a stranger's flat.'

'Never pegged you for a criminal,' I replied, drowsy.

'You learn things by the time you're old,' Jack said gently.

The water tasted good but not as sweet as what I had drunk in the Labyrinth. I shut my eyes, needing

293

the darkness. I missed being blind. I thought about Zee again, but it was too difficult to ask. My brain stopped working.

I fell asleep.

I fell upon paths of stone and night, hunting dreams along the Labyrinth walls. I dreamed I held the sword. I dreamed I was blind and had to stop along my journey. Sword in my lap, the flat of the blade pressed against my thighs. Rocking, pressing a fist against my throat to stifle some grief I could not name. I dreamed a slither, silent, beneath my heart. Darkness, whispering.

Monsters, in the deep. Monsters, in the blood.

I dreamed my way into a forest, winding blind through a grove of trees, trunks smooth beneath my searching fingers. A scent of snow and ice came upon me. My foot caught something large and soft. I fell hard, my leg hooked. Sword still in hand.

My leg pressed against warm, smooth fur, a slender flank. Ribs expanded and contracted, and my fingers touched a coarse mane twined with leaves and small, round stones.

'Greetings,' whispered a familiar voice. 'Greetings again, Hunter.'

I went still, breathless, and the voice said, 'Take your time. I know what it is to be lost in the darkness.'

So I sat and dreamed, and my hand remained tangled in long hair. After a while, I scooted closer. A broad nose brushed my arm, and the tip of something hard and cold pressed against my brow. I touched it and found a horn, long and spiraled.

'Do you know me?' asked the voice, quiet as winter.

'Yes, Sarai,' I breathed, heart thundering. 'You're the unicorn.'

She remained silent; until, in a whisper: 'It is good to hear that name.'

'Good,' I echoed. 'You died. So I'm dreaming. Or insane.'

'Insane people,' said Sarai, 'do not have polite conversations with unicorns.'

'Maybe not in your world. Whatever that is.'

'My world . . .' Her voice drifted, thoughtful. 'My kind, we have many worlds. We are . . . travelers of them. Wayfarers, if you will. The Labyrinth is the crossroads, the old tree with its branches in the stars. From the Labyrinth, you may see every world, you may walk through the dreams of worlds and find rare islands adrift in the dark.'

'Jack explained a little,' I told her. 'Nothing about unicorns. But then, this isn't your body, is it?'

'What you feel is only flesh,' she replied simply. 'And in the Labyrinth, my kind can exist as we desire, no matter how odd the shape or form. Though I admit a particular fondness for this skin. My last echo of a race that perished eons ago.'

I dreamed her spiral horn touched my brow. I said, 'I can't stay here. I need to wake up.'

'Then wake,' Sarai said softly from the darkness.

'But you are of the Labyrinth now, Hunter. It is in your blood.'

My body felt heavy. For a dream, far too heavy. I struggled to stand, blind. My palm was sweaty around the sword hilt.

'Good-bye,' I heard Sarai whisper. 'Thank you for sitting with me, in the end. Thank you for caring about Brian.'

I tried to say something to her – anything, everything – but I felt a great sucking sensation upon my brain, as though a vacuum had been shoved inside a hole in my skull, and quite suddenly my eyes fluttered open.

Awake. I saw Jack standing near my bed. Another man was with him.

'Grant,' I whispered. My skin felt prickly, hot.

'No,' said the man, leaning in. It was Tracker. Cuts covered his throat, above the iron collar. His eyes were sharp and hot. Dek and Mal raised their heads.

'We need to move you,' Tracker said, his voice low, hoarse. 'It's almost dawn here. We can't let the boys sleep on your body. It's too soon. You almost went into shock from the first separation.'

I tried to shake my head. Tracker placed his palm against my cheek – just for one moment, before flinching away as though burned. 'I will take care of you. You have my word, Hunter.'

My word. Once, I could trust his word. Once, he could trust mine. I remembered that. Maybe.

Something came over me. Delirium. I wanted to hold Tracker's hand, I wanted to touch him, so badly it felt like I had been waiting five thousand years for that one gesture. Like it would fix something. Make things better.

I struggled to pull my arm from under the covers, but my body seemed to be made of concrete, and something as simple as freeing myself from a comforter felt like having that block of stone over my head in the Wasteland river. Drowning, again.

I struggled harder, swallowing a whimper that made my cheeks flush hot with shame. My heart pounded, out of control. I needed to move. I needed to be free. I needed to scream.

Maybe it showed on my face. Tracker leaned in, pulling back the blankets. The pressure eased. I could breathe. But the moment was gone, and my hand stayed glued to my side. I looked at the cuts on his face. 'Did Oturu hurt you?'

He kept silent. Jack said, 'Quick. The sun will be up in less than a minute.'

Tracker pulled back the remainder of the covers, leaving one sheet over my body. He scooped me into his arms. My head lolled. I had no strength to hold it up. Dek and Mal curled down my chest between my breasts.

We blinked out of the world into utter darkness. It was a relief on my eyes.

It did not last. A room appeared around us. Hardwood floors, brick walls, large windows. A big, soft white bed with the covers pulled back. And a pacing man, leaning hard on a cane, a gold flute held white-knuckled in his other hand.

Grant. He reached for my face as Tracker settled me on the bed, soothing back my hair, the palm of his trembling hand lingering on my brow. There were new wrinkles around his eyes, his jaw thick with stubble, and though he was still in his thirties, I swore I saw glints of gray. His gaze was impossibly grave. Zee, Raw, and Aaz appeared on the bed, pressing close, crawling under the covers to lie against my skin.

Grant did the same. I was dimly aware of Tracker backing out of the room. Jack, as well, though I had no sense of how he had gotten there. The old man turned off the lights. The door clicked shut behind him.

'Okay,' Grant breathed, kissing my cheek, holding me. 'It's okay, Maxine. It's just me now.'

I closed my eyes. I had already cried with Jack, but this was Grant.

I've been waiting a long time for this, I thought, and found enough strength in my finger to scratch Zee's head.

I talked to Grant. I talked to him like my life depended on it, even when I was too groggy to pronounce my words. I told him what happened to me in the Wasteland. I told him everything. All the dirt and ugliness and terror that still clawed up my throat with panic. Buried alive. Running to stay sane. Losing sanity. The sword and ring.

Grant listened. He gave me water when my throat ran dry. He helped me when I had to use the bathroom. He dressed me in soft clothes and did not leave me alone. He held me in the dark.

He held me tight.

AN hour before dawn, Zee said, 'Can't stay, Maxine. Gotta go where the sun don't shine.'

'I'll be fine here,' I told him. 'I'm better already.'

Grant made a low rumbling sound and brushed his lips against the back of my neck. 'Turn over and kiss me.'

I gave it my best shot. I managed to roll all the way to my back before I ran out of steam. The covers, all two of them, felt like they weighed a hundred pounds. I stared at the ceiling, heart pounding, dizzy. Grant was very still beside me. Dek and Mal began humming Elton John's 'I'm Still Standing.'

'Right,' Grant said, turning on the light by the bed. 'I've got a sumo wrestler out in the living room you can tackle after breakfast.'

I tried to bat his arm, but my hand flopped uselessly on the covers. Aaz picked up my wrist for me and smacked my palm against Grant's shoulder.

'Ow,' he said.

'Thank you,' I muttered, and the little demon gave me a toothy grin.

Across the room, someone knocked on the door. Jack peered inside, his hair rumpled, clothes wrinkled, silver bristles covering his face. He looked like a frazzled professor who had become obsessed over some obscure text and spent the night making coffee rings on student papers and library pages. I wanted to imagine him surrounded by cups of chewed-down pencils and stale muffins, and a framed picture of my grandmother, hidden away behind stacks of books – except for those special moments when he uncovered her, like a magic treasure. I wanted to see him look at her with a smile on his face. I wanted it so badly, and I realized, with a startled pang, that I was one messed-up girl.

'I have tea,' Jack said, blushing when he saw us still in bed together – clothed, no less.

Grant pushed back the covers and sat up, running his hands through his hair. Jack pushed deeper into the room, a cutting board in his hands doubling as a tray. I tried to sit up, and did a little better though Zee and Raw had to help me. Aaz stuffed pillows behind my back. Dek and Mal gave my neck support.

Grant bit back a smile. 'How do you think they'd look in little white nursing outfits?'

'Hot,' Zee said, and the others snickered.

I glimpsed a shadow in the bedroom doorway – Tracker, hovering, staring at the boys like he had just seen a rock sprout legs and do a pole dance. He caught me watching and backed away, out of sight.

Jack set down the cutting board, and perched on the edge of the bed. He held the cup to my lips. The tea was hot and sweet. I tried to hold it myself, but my arm would not lift that high. Jack caught my hand and pressed it against his wrinkled shirt, above his heart. He set down the teacup.

'Lad,' he said to Grant. 'Watch this and learn something.'

I frowned. So did Grant. Jack closed his eyes. The ring tingled against my finger, glinting in the shadows of the bedroom; heavy, but comfortable; pressed so close to my skin I imagined silver roots spreading from the metal into flesh, binding with bone: quicksilver for marrow.

I did not notice anything different at first – nothing except the expression on Grant's face as he sat on the bed, staring between me and Jack, a deep line furrowed between his eyes, his fingers dancing a melody in the air above his stomach. Like taking music lessons for the soul.

Until, suddenly, I noticed incredible heat in my hand. A pulsing warmth that spread from Jack's touch, into my skin. Sweat broke out over my back, against my neck, and the boys gathered close, sniffing the air. Zee licked his claw, then ran a line through the air above Jack's body.

'Meddling Man,' he said, and Jack cracked open one eye.

'What are you doing?' I asked him.

His smile was strained. 'Try lifting your arm, my dear.'

I did. And I could. I was stronger.

'Lad,' Jack said, faint lines forming around his eyes, 'go fetch your flute.'

The instrument was on the nightstand. Grant reached back with his long arm and, in one smooth motion, picked up the golden flute, brought it to his mouth, and released a lilting trill of notes. I felt the music pass through me; I felt the power of it – but even as I remembered that Grant's music had never affected me or the boys, I realized he was playing for Jack. Bolstering *him*. And I could see it in the old man as his spine straightened, and the strain faded from his face. I could feel it, too, as the heat between us intensified, as though a baby sun were bouncing between our hands.

'Oh, dear,' Jack murmured, as Grant's playing intensified. 'You *are* strong.'

And so was I. I leaned forward, testing myself, and found that I could move easily, without feeling tired. Zee tugged on my hand and pointed at Grant. I looked at him, a smile bubbling up my throat. I had never heard him play so wildly, his fingers moving so fast it seemed he hardly needed to breathe. Notes rippled through the air. I could taste them in my mouth. I could almost see the light. He caught me looking, and his eyes crinkled, warm and sweet.

But even though Jack had asked him to play, there was suddenly very little amusement on the old man's face. He turned quite pale as he stared at Grant. I heard movement at the door and found Tracker again, also staring. But not at Grant. At me. A look in his eyes that was somber and grave.

Somewhere distant, I thought I heard pounding. Fists.

Jack let go of my hands. It was difficult; our skins seemed to stick together, peeling apart with a pop. A bang came from the other room, a low shout. Tracker disappeared for a moment, and I heard him grunt. Grant stopped playing, and the silence was so profound it felt almost like death.

Mary appeared in the doorway. White hair blazing, sticking out like a helmet full of static electricity. She wore a shift covered in flying pink dragons, and an old navy cardigan, dotted with tattered little holes, some of which had been mended with red yarn.

Her eyes were wild, her hands full of Grant's mail; one of the little jobs he had given her, which she took very seriously. She stared at him, chest heaving. Her gaze slid sideways, to Jack.

And everything changed.

The mail slid from her hands. A hard, sharp fury pricked her face.

'Wolf,' she said.

CHAPTER 17

*W*OLF.
Tracker appeared behind Mary. Bent slightly over his stomach. Hard for me to imagine one old woman being able to hurt him – when I had hardly made a dent – but there was a look on his face that made me think she had done just that.

Mary glided into the room with surprising grace and speed, staring at Jack as though he were nothing but a piece of bad news. Mail lay scattered on the floor, but in her right hand she held a tinfoil block that smelled suspiciously like brownies. Zee and the others sat beside me on the bed, very still – dolls with razor blades for skin. Mary studied them, too, but only for a moment. Her focus was Jack.

'Wolf,' she whispered again, withered lips hardly moving. 'Sinner.'

She might have been a bullet instead of a woman. Jack stared, muscles ticking spasmodically in his cheek.

'Marritine,' he finally choked out. 'Such a surprise to see you.'

Oh. God. I stared at the old man, incredulous. Grant made a small, choked sound. We shared a quick glance. He looked just as confused – and concerned.

Mary began to shudder. Slowly at first, hardly a tremor, but the shakes got worse until her teeth began to chatter. It was eerie, watching the old woman's body fall apart while her unblinking eyes, hollow and cold, stared holes into Jack's head.

Grant struggled to stand from the bed. I fumbled for his cane, and he took it in grim silence, heaving himself up on his feet. He shot Jack another quick look, then limped swiftly across the room until he stood between Mary and the old man. He did not say a word. Just bundled her up with his free arm, cradling her against his chest. Mary buried her face against his sweatshirt.

I grabbed Jack's shoulder. He blinked, tearing his gaze from Mary to stare at me, past me, far away.

'It makes no sense,' he murmured. 'Fate does *not* conspire.'

I squeezed his bony shoulder. 'Jack. What is going on?'

'Marritine,' he said again, vision clearing. 'Oh, dear.'

Grant made a low, rumbling sound that could have been a growl. 'She's scared of you.'

Jack shook himself, regaining some semblance of composure. 'Nonsense. Bad memories, yes . . . but if Marritine is scared, it is because of where I found her. That woman . . . she was not born on earth.'

I gave up. I buried my head in my hands. Tracker stepped into the room. He had been standing so still, I had almost forgotten him. Shadows from the lamp made his face appear even more menacing. Hard man to read, but he was looking at Jack with brutal intensity. Like something needed to be done. And he wanted to be the one who did it.

Grant's eyes narrowed. 'Mary is human.'

'I don't disagree,' muttered the old man, giving Tracker a fleeting look. 'But she's not from this world.'

'What?' I snapped. 'She got here on a spaceship?'

Jack shot me a scathing look. 'The Labyrinth, Hunter. Lost in the quantum rose.'

Mary clutched Grant's sweatshirt, face buried, peering at the old man with one blazing eye. I leaned close, also trying to divine the emotions passing across his aged handsome face. 'What did you do to Mary?'

He rubbed his face, cheeks blazing red. 'I found her in the Labyrinth. Years ago. She could not tell me how long she had been wandering, but it was clear she had gone insane. I brought her to this world.'

'You put her on the street,' Grant said, his voice hard. 'I found her in an alley, freezing, almost dead from a drug overdose.'

306

'I left her in the care of someone I trusted,' Jack replied mildly. 'In Hawaii.'

Grant still looked angry. He ran a soothing hand down Mary's back. 'How did she even end up in this . . . Labyrinth?'

'In fairy tales,' Jack said, 'men and women are always falling through holes into other worlds.'

'A lot of things happen in those stories. Doesn't mean they're real.'

'Aren't they?' Tracker said – his voice low, strong. 'Hunter. Just as the prison veil has cracks, so does the Labyrinth. People can step wrong, anywhere, and . . . lose themselves.'

'And there are . . . humans, elsewhere?' Grant's voice was strained.

'Everywhere,' Jack said. 'The Labyrinth is a place of infinite doorways.'

'Wolf,' Mary muttered again. 'Offender.'

'Marritine,' he said, and she hurled her foil-wrapped brownies at his head. Jack ducked.

'Stay away from Grant,' she said, bristling. 'Light-eater.'

Jack flinched. Tracker tensed. Grant hugged Mary tighter and turned her so that she did not have to look at Jack. I stood before it occurred to me that I might still be weak.

My legs held. My head felt fine. My heart did not pound. Not from overexertion, anyway.

Grant had that farseeing manner about him; a preternatural unrelenting awareness: truth seeker, music man, my dangerous Pied Piper. His voice was soft as thunder, his tone lyrical, rolling with power. 'You're wrong, Jack. Mary isn't *just* scared of the Labyrinth.'

His words echoed inside my head, relentless. My heart sank. *Of course*, I thought, staring at that old baffling man.

'Meddling man,' I whispered. 'Jack.'

Maybe it showed on my face. The old man paled and started shaking his head. I held up my hand, a sharp gesture that made his mouth clamp shut.

'I keep forgetting the way it is,' I said to him, softly. 'I push it away, because I like you so much. But your kind . . . they treat humans like cattle, same as the demons, same as any zombie. You just . . . dress it up nicer. No teeth.' I closed my eyes, steadying myself. 'So why *did* the demons chase your kind, Jack? Was it because they didn't like you? Or were you . . . competing . . . for the same resources?'

He looked stricken. 'My dear girl. No.'

'No?' I held his gaze. 'Really, Jack?'

He said nothing, the flush in his cheeks spreading down his throat. My skin felt hot, too. I was burning up. Burning. Tracker took a step toward me. Grant gave him a sharp look, and the men stared at each other – wolves, both, a hunt in their dark gazes.

Tiny hands grabbed mine. Zee. Raw. Aaz. Dek and Mal quiet on my shoulders.

I turned and left the bedroom.

*   *   *

MY mother once asked me to choose truth over lies.

An iron room, she described, with no windows or doors. A room I could not leave. People sound asleep, inside. All of us, suffocating. All of *them*, falling into an easy, painless death.

Would you wake them? she had asked. *Would you prefer they go to death fully conscious? Would you be that cruel?*

Lu Xun. My mother loved his writing. And I was a punk at the time, told her that yes, I would be that cruel. Because truth was better than ignorance, and people should have the choice to reconcile their end. Make those last moments mean something. Or try to find a way out.

I was not so certain of myself anymore.

The television was flickering in the living room, sound turned down. News on. Still talking about the earthquake in Iran. Thousands dead, thousands more thought to be under the rubble. Concerns growing elsewhere: Volcanic activity in Hawaii, snow and ice storms all across the Midwest and upper East Coast. A school shooting in Maryland. More gunfire in an office building in Vegas. Serial rapists in Florida, missing girls in Idaho. Might not be demonically related – any of it – but it hardly mattered. This was the iron room, the iron house. An iron world, suffocating, dying in its sleep. Me, one of a handful who knew the truth.

And even that was nothing. I knew nothing.

I left the bedroom. I was almost halfway across the living room before I realized I was wearing a tank top and sweatpants, and that if anyone saw me without my tattoos, I would have some explaining to do. Careless. Or maybe living for months and years in the Wasteland darkness had cured me of caring how others saw my body, or whether anyone questioned the peculiarities of my skin.

I kept walking. I could not go back into the bedroom and face Jack again. Or even Tracker. Conflict made me feel like a kid again, and not in a good way.

Zee and the others loped into the shadows, swallowed up like wraiths, or drops of water, soft and quiet. The door to the guest room was closed. I hoped Byron was asleep and not listening to us.

I walked upstairs to the roof garden. I needed air. The wind smelled wet and was cold enough to make me shiver. I stuck with it, though. Stood against the baby gale, matted hair bobbing like a soft helmet from my face. The sky was lightening. Purple velvet clouds streaked the sky east, humming with a wink of gold. Dawn soon, punched by the sun. Singeing my skin with demons.

Oturu's mark tingled. Heat washed over my skin, as though I stood within the bubble of a sauna.

I did not look. I did not turn. Not even when Dek hissed softly, or when I felt a delicate scrape against my elbow, a probing, ethereal touch.

'We heard your heart,' Oturu whispered. 'Between

the eternities. But we could not reach you, not for all our fury.'

I looked back. All I saw was a writhing cloak, dancing against the wind. He stood so near he could have swallowed me into the abyss of his body. Simply leaned forward, just a fraction, and taken me.

Zee, Raw, and Aaz blinked from the shadows around my legs, pressing close. I scratched behind their ears, and their purrs cracked and popped like ice. I sensed Oturu gazing at each of them, a surprising softness to his mouth that might have been affection. It made my heart feel odd. His cloak brushed against my arms, soft and cold as frozen silk.

'Friend,' Oturu breathed. 'We feared for you. We fear still.'

'No,' I said. 'Not you.'

He leaned in, so close we could have kissed, and still I could not see his eyes. But I felt him, the weight of the abyss, the touch of his hair as it wound through my own. I should have been disgusted, but I searched my heart and found nothing but a déjà vu that bordered on memory.

'The first time we met,' he murmured, 'you let us live in return for a favor. And that would have been the end, except you did more, beyond our bargain, beyond promises. We were alone, Hunter. You became our friend. You . . . were kind.'

'I was not,' I told him. 'That was not me.'

'Even so,' he breathed. 'It is life.'

311

'You tried to kill me when we first met.'

His mouth curled into a smile. 'To prove ourselves. We choose to keep you safe, Hunter – but it is in our power to take your life. *She* gave us that right. *She* trusted us not to abuse her faith. A trust no other has shown us, or will again.'

I could not believe such a bargain. I could not fathom it. I stared, helpless. 'Did my mother know?'

At my side, Zee tensed. Oturu said, 'She also had a need, once.'

I turned from him. I remembered my vision under the bus – Oturu with a woman who looked like me, standing beneath an alien sky full of moons – and for a moment was not certain if it was fantasy or reality, past or future. The sky was getting lighter, a golden shade of pale, chasing violets and cumulous roses made of fleeing night. I walked to the edge of the roof, staring at the city. Oturu joined me.

'You have the seed ring,' I said.

Oturu remained silent, but his cloak opened, and his hair dipped into the writhing abyss. Faces pressed against the darkness, the outline of cheeks and hollow eyes, then the demon turned, just slightly, and his hair pulled free of his cloak, coiled around a bundle.

My mother's jacket. Her gloves. Her knives. And on top, the seed ring, gleaming like a dark pearl.

'You saved it all,' I said quietly.

'You shed your belongings like a wraith,' he murmured. 'Ahsen could not grasp them fast enough.'

I ran my hand over the soft leather of my mother's

jacket. My eyes burned, my throat thick. I nodded once, trying to speak, but all I could whisper was, 'Thank you.'

'Your heart lives in them,' he said softly. 'A danger, Hunter, to care so much for small things.'

'Small things, small moments.' I picked up the seed ring and cradled it in my palm. 'Haven't you ever loved, Oturu?'

'I have loved,' he said. 'If love is the desire to see others survive. If love is the desire never to hunt alone.'

My hand closed around the seed ring. 'What was my mother hiding from me?'

'Only she can tell you that. But take care. As soon as you use the seed ring, Ahsen will feel it. She will come to the source.'

I hesitated. 'Will you stay with me?'

'I cannot protect you from her.'

'I know.' I stared at the brim of his hat, pretending I could see his eyes. 'I don't want to be alone.'

'Ah.' He sighed. 'Ah, Hunter. You have others.'

'You're here,' I said, but it was more than that, more than I could face, or name. It was hard for me. The longer I was around him, the more I suffered an unsettling comfort, as though his presence was an old glove, a familiar knife, the weight of my mother's coat.

It was wrong. He was a demon. I was sick.

Oturu danced away, the daggers of his feet cutting the roof as he spun into a crouch. His cloak spread across tar paper and steel. I knelt, just on the edge of the abyss. It began to rain. Zee, Raw, and Aaz gathered close, while Dek and Mal rested their chins on my ears. I held the seed ring, staring hard, fingers tracing the engraved Labyrinth lines. I felt dizzy.

Oturu whispered, 'Take care where you fall, Hunter. It is a long way down into your heart.'

Long way down. But not to my heart. I thought about my mother. Stared hard at the seed ring, those veins of silver and pearl. Against my finger the engraved iron, the sword, burned.

Zee grabbed my wrist. Oturu flinched, a tendril of his hair snaking out to touch the metal.

'Wait,' he breathed. 'Hunter—'

But it was too late. The seed ring swallowed up my mind.

And spat me out.

I opened my eyes somewhere else. The sun was up in a sky as big as the world, casting a golden haze. Grassland, far as I could see, though against the horizon I glimpsed jagged peaks, snow-riddled, haunted by clouds. I smelled horses. I heard rough male laughter. Bells chiming.

I was still dressed in my tank and sweats, but the boys were on my skin. I turned slowly and saw I was on top of a small hill. Below me, quite near, squat round tents had been erected near a snaking silver river. Sheep grazed. Four men sat on horse-back. One of them held a golden eagle on his arm, which rested inside a padded brace that rose from the side of his saddle.

The men stared at me. I stared back – lost, for a moment, in the intensity of their clear honest gazes, and the sudden wonder of standing barefoot in the grass of another time.

It occurred to me, too, that I should be invisible. At least that was the way the seed ring seemed to work.

'Well,' said a gravelly voice. 'This *is* different.'

I flinched, hopping back on one foot. Sun cast daggers in my eyes, but I blinked, holding up my hand—

—and found myself face-to-face with my grandmother.

Jean Kiss.

I knew her only from old photographs, but those eyes were the same: dark, intelligent, crisp with scrutiny. A woman who missed nothing. She was young, too. In her late thirties, at most. Dressed like the men on horseback, a combination of loose blue slacks that bunched into tall fur boots, as well as a lightweight navy coat that clung to her slender frame. A fur hat framed her face, enhancing the cream of her skin. She stood tall and regal. A brace of knives hung across her chest. She was beautiful, noble. Naturally daunting.

'Oh,' I said, heart racing. 'Oh, boy.'

It was a shock to see her. A raw blow to my heart. I did not expect her to attack me. My grandmother

315

was incredibly fast, like a viper: darting, furious, without mercy. Her blade was already skidding off my neck, racing sparks across my skin, before I realized what she was doing. I fell, and she traveled with me, riding me into the grass with her knee in my chest. Her eyes were terrifying. Full of murder.

She pinned me, pressing her blade against my throat. My heart hammered. It was hard to breathe. I was too shocked to protest when she tried stabbing me – again. The knife bounced off my skin.

Her mouth twisted. 'What are you?'

'Maxine,' I stammered. 'Your granddaughter.'

She frowned, every line and angle of her face hard as rock. 'Impossible. You're a demon.'

'Look at me,' I pleaded. 'Listen to the boys.'

My grandmother recoiled, searching my face. My finger tingled. The iron ring.

Finally, *finally*, she very carefully eased off my body. Slumped in the grass at my feet. Rage gone from her eyes. Replaced by something haunted. I heard bells, close, it seemed, and felt the men on horseback drawing near. My grandmother never looked away from me; only barked out one sharp word. A moment later I heard the horses move again – in the opposite direction. The grass hissed with the wind. An eagle screamed.

'How?' asked my grandmother, hoarsely.

'I don't know.' My voice weak, breathless; my heart, still stunned. 'I was . . . trying to do something. But you shouldn't be able to see me. I shouldn't . . .' I stopped, licking my lips. 'Where am I? *When* am I?'

Her frown deepened. 'Mongolia – 1972.'

I exhaled, sharply. 'I was in Seattle – 2008.'

My grandmother closed her eyes. Off to my left I heard a girl call out. Everything in me stopped. I could not move. I could not breathe. I sat, frozen, listening to that voice. My grandmother seemed petrified as well, but at the last moment she leapt to her feet, turning, her hands outstretched.

Too late. My mother appeared.

She was only fourteen, already tall, but skinny as a rail. Hair in braids. Glowing skin, shining eyes, a healthy flush to her cheeks that would have made a rose jealous. Her arms were bare. No tattoos. Not yet. I felt a sob rise in my throat. I wanted to melt into the grass.

She went utterly still when she saw me. Dead stop. I did not know whether to laugh or cry – or scream. It was too much. Three of us, together. Like this. I was going crazy. The seed ring had twisted me up.

'Jolene,' said my grandmother. 'Sit down.'

My mother gaped at me, taking in the tattoos on my arms. But she finally sat, dropping into the grass as though her knees had stopped working. She was gangly, awkward. I knew she would grow out of it. I was still learning how to do that.

My grandmother tapped my mother's knee with her finger. 'This is Maxine, baby.'

'Hello,' said my mother uneasily.

317

'Hi,' I breathed, and looked again at my grandmother. She was staring at me, rubbing her cheek in that same way my mother had when I was growing up. I felt like a butterfly with its wings pinned.

My grandmother reached into her jacket and pulled out a small tin. Inside were thin papers, loose tobacco. She rolled herself a cigarette. Found a match, leaned forward, and struck it against my arm. Flame burst. She lit up, took a long drag, then put the match out on her tongue. She showed no pain. I was reasonably impressed.

'Well,' said my grandmother, exhaling smoke in my face, 'you pose a pretty problem, my dear.'

The smoke smelled acrid and good. 'I don't know what to tell you. I don't even know if this is real.'

She grunted, leaning back on her elbow, relaxed as a leopard, claws sheathed. 'A man once told me that nothing is real. Just is. And right now you seem to think you're in the past, while I . . . I seem to think I'm right where I belong. So let's pretend we're all sane here and get you figured out.'

'The man who told you that,' I said slowly. 'Don't suppose his name was Jack?'

Jean Kiss went very still. 'How do you know that name?'

I tried not to look at my mother. 'I found him. Things are happening.'

The older woman sat up and looked at her daughter. 'Baby. Walk away.'

'Mom—'

'Now . . . please.'

'No.' I clambered to my feet, throwing my grandmother a look that felt raw, desperate. 'Give me a minute.'

Bitter comprehension filled her eyes. I hesitated, then walked to Jolene. My mother. She was on her feet, watching me warily. Ready to bolt. I swallowed hard. I could see the woman I knew in her face: younger, softer, but still her. A shadow of grit and fire.

'It was nice to meet you,' I said lamely. 'Take care of yourself.'

'Sure,' said my mother, looking past me at Jean Kiss. Searching for an escape, answers to the riddle of the weird woman standing in front of her – tattooed to the gills in Zee and the boys. Tattoos no one else was supposed to have. Made me smile, made my eyes burn with tears.

I flung my arms around the girl. Holding tight.

'I love you,' I breathed in her ear. 'Remember that when you meet me again. I'll always love you.'

She shoved me away. Eyes huge. I felt like a fool, standing there. Bereft. But I did not regret a word. Not one.

'Go,' said my grandmother, hoarse. 'Jolene, baby. Run along.'

My mother hesitated, then took off like a little mustang, racing across the grass toward the men on horseback. One of them kicked his mount to meet her, and midgallop, reached down with one long arm to sweep her up into the saddle behind him. She

319

hugged his waist, but turned to stare back at us as he carried her toward the others. I could not look away.

My grandmother stepped close. Smoke leaked from her nostrils. She looked like a hard-living woman. Her gloves were off. I had not noticed her removing them.

'Seeing you means she's dead,' said Jean Kiss. 'Do you know how that makes me feel?'

'At least you won't watch it happen.'

'Fair enough.' She stabbed the cigarette into her palm. 'Let's walk, Maxine.'

Grass sang beneath the wind. My grandmother removed her knife brace and handed it to me while she unbuttoned her jacket. She wore a sleeveless linen sheath beneath, and slung her jacket over one shoulder, along with her knives. Tattoos covered her arms. Red eyes glinted in her skin. The boys tugged. Straining hard.

My grandmother smiled briefly. 'Feel that?'

'They always did love themselves.'

'Cheeky brats. More so now than before. Time was, the other Hunters treated them as mindless, like dogs with teeth. Stupid bitches.'

I stared. 'Never heard that.'

'Didn't you?' My grandmother made a small sound. 'Well. I guess every mother shares something different.'

I rubbed my arms, trying to calm Aaz and Raw. Zee shifted against my sternum, restless. 'Why am I here?'

320

'I have no idea,' she muttered. 'What were you doing?'

'Holding a seed ring. My mot – your daughter—' I stopped, unsure how to explain. How much to say.

My grandmother stared up at the sky. 'I know about seed rings. Jack gave you one, didn't he?'

'You worked together.'

'He told you that, too?'

'Is he my grandfather?'

A slip of the tongue. I could not stop myself. Jean Kiss paused in midstep and gave me a long, inscrutable look. 'Do you have a man?'

I hesitated. 'Yes.'

'Do you love him?'

'More than anything.'

'Poor girl,' she replied immediately.

I shook my head. 'You loved Jack. I saw a picture.'

'I still love him,' admitted my grandmother, surprising me. 'Hard man not to. But there's a reason we don't stick around.'

'It's not safe. I know.'

'No. You don't.' Jean Kiss turned in a full circle and looked back at the encampment behind us. I saw very distant figures on horseback. I imagined a fourteen-year-old girl, watching us. Wondered if this was real.

My grandmother said, 'I was only ever with one man. Never had another since.'

'Jack,' I said.

'Old Wolf,' she muttered, and gave me a sharp look. 'You know what he is, don't you?'

'Avatar.' I paused, trying to find the right words, and settled for being blunt. 'They're like demons. Possessors. Manipulators.'

'So are some humans. Don't fool yourself.' Jean Kiss stepped close, searching my face. 'Lines are always blurry, my dear. You *know* what people will do to each other, simply to satisfy a need. They will justify it, they will praise it, they will sanctify the worst of crimes as a means to whatever outcome they desire. How can you fault demons for doing the same? Or the Avatars?'

'Whose side are you on?'

'Mine. Ours. We are the Wardens, Maxine. We are the hammer and the heart, and there is no room for absolutes in this game. Just the right thing. And you know what that is, deep in your gut. You know.'

'I don't know anything.'

Jean Kiss grabbed my arm, and the contact was electrifying, chilling. 'Don't you dare feel sorry for yourself. What we do is a privilege. It is an honor.'

'And if we're not enough?' My cheeks were hot. 'The veil is falling.'

My grandmother's grip did not loosen. 'So it'll fall. Doesn't matter. So the world will get eaten up. Doesn't matter, either. What *does* matter is that you fight. You live. You keep breathing. You survive, and you get yourself a baby, and you make sure she does the same. You teach her how to fight. *You* fight.

You dig deep inside that heart of yours and push the cutters back. You take care of what you can, when you can, but you *don't* give up. Respect yourself. Do *not* belittle what you are.'

Her eyes blazed. Her touch was eerie. I was not entirely certain whether I should be inspired or ashamed, but I felt neither of those things when she suddenly enfolded me in her arms, and pressed her mouth to my ear. Her strength was immense, warm; she smelled like horses and grass and smoke.

'I know what you are,' she whispered, chilling me. 'Same thing as Jolene, but stronger. I can feel it. Veil gets weak, so do parts of us. Walls around our hearts that were never supposed to come down. But they're coming. Fast, now. Faster, in your time, I bet. So you remember something, Maxine Kiss. You stay true. Because *this*' – Jean Kiss laid her hand above my heart – 'this is what will break the world, or save it.'

She pressed her lips to my cheek, then pushed me back, just enough to stare into my eyes. I saw pain there, sadness deep as bone; and a determination that made me love her more than I ever imagined I could, this woman who had always been dead to me, until now.

My grandmother grabbed my wrist, her fingers slipping over the iron ring. She closed her eyes, lips moving. I stared, breathless, trying to pull away – then staggered, dizzy.

'What are you doing?' I mumbled. 'Stop.'

'I'm sending you home,' she whispered. 'Give my best to Jack. Tell him I miss his tea.'

'No. I'm not ready.'

'You're my granddaughter,' Jean Kiss said, her voice sounding more distant. 'You'll always be ready.'

And suddenly she was gone, and there was rain on my face, rain that tasted suspiciously salty, and the sky was golden with clouds. I was not alone. Zee and the others covered my body, staring into my eyes. Patting my cheeks. Oturu's hair was still wrapped around my wrist.

'Hunter,' he murmured.

I closed my eyes, still trying to hold on to my grandmother's face, her voice, the scent of her cigarettes. My mother, so effortlessly young, without the hard glint in her eyes that I remembered from my youth.

The seed ring lay on my stomach. It was hot, almost burning. Zee whispered, 'Maxine. We remember.'

Tears welled. 'It was real.'

'You traveled into time,' said Oturu. 'The ring you wear, the iron ring, is Labyrinth-born, hewn and crafted from ore mined in the heart of the maze. It is a key, Hunter. A key to any door, in any time or place. A key that reflects the desires of its bearer.'

I placed my hand on top of the seed ring. 'So when I looked at the memories . . .'

'It brought you to them, in body and soul.' Oturu's chin dipped against his chest. 'You must take care,

Hunter. The ring is bound to you now. You cannot remove it until death.'

I stared, then tried to tug the thick band off my hand. It would not budge, not in the slightest. I felt a moment of panic, took a breath, and fought to stay calm. 'How do you know so much about it?'

'Because it was *hers*. A gift, from the Labyrinth. Meant *only* for her. That it bound itself to you . . .' Oturu did not finish, nor did he need to. I held up my hand, gazing at the iron band, engraved with fine lines that curled like roses. I remembered the body in the Wasteland river, the sensation of the chain mail, the bones. I had stolen from a grave. I had stolen from family.

Zee and the others pushed close.

'You knew before,' I said to them. 'You knew I would travel back in time. You met me.'

Raw and Aaz stared at their feet. Zee chewed the tips of his claws. 'More secrets. Things we couldn't say.'

'Fate is fragile,' Oturu murmured. 'As I said, Hunter. You must take care. *She* had trouble controlling its power. You will, as well.'

He rose. I got a good look at his toes, which resembled steak knives the length of my forearm. He took the seed ring with him, and tucked it deep within the abyss.

'Hunter,' he whispered. 'Trouble is coming.'

CHAPTER 18

TEN minutes before dawn. Ten minutes to stay alive.

I careened down the stairs into the apartment – but halfway there, a strong arm reached out of thin air and grabbed me.

Tracker. He melted close, pinning me to the wall, and pressed his mouth against my ear. Dek purred. Zee and the others hugged my legs. Tracker smelled like the desert at sunset, hot and full of shadows.

'We have a situation downstairs,' he murmured. 'Grant took Mary away, but the boy woke up. Wasn't too happy to see strangers. He tried to leave. Opened up the door, and there was a zombie waiting for him. Russian. Old man.'

'Edik,' I breathed, as Mal's tail tightened around my neck. 'Son of a bitch.'

'He's got a gun. He's sitting with the boy. And Jack. I'm worried I won't be fast enough for the demon's trigger finger.'

Raw snarled. I tried to push myself past Tracker. He refused to budge. I peered into his eyes. His breath was warm on my face. I shoved him again, but he was immovable.

'What?' I asked him – but all I received was a contemplative stare that felt, unnervingly, like an attempt to memorize my face. As though a good-bye was coming soon. As though he might not see me again.

'I'm sorry,' Tracker said, finally.

'Sorry?' I echoed.

He sighed. 'For pushing you in front of the bus.'

I blinked, startled. 'Oh, that.'

'Yes, that,' Tracker rumbled, and leaned away. 'You distract; I'll extract.'

He winked out of sight, and the vacuum created by his disappearance washed cool air over my face. I felt it, too, in my heart. Just a little ache. A disturbing, little ache.

Raw grabbed my hand, tugging.

Zee said, 'The boy.'

Yes. Byron. Jack. I looked down, studying secrets in their ageless eyes. 'You've never shown interest in any child. Why him?'

Zee hesitated. 'No time.'

Never time. Such a fine excuse. I gave him a hard look and continued down the stairs – more careful now – though I made no secret of my approach. When I entered the living room, I tried to act appropriately surprised.

Which was not all that difficult.

I saw Byron first. He sat on the edge of the couch. He looked as if a horse had kicked his face, which was bandaged and swollen. His arms were folded over his ribs. His eyes widened when he saw me, but only for a moment – replaced instead by a dull, resigned fear that hit my heart with a panicked flutter.

Jack sat nearby on the piano stool, fidgeting. He was quite pale. I met his gaze briefly, and he gave me a faint nod that was old and canny like a wolf.

Grandfather. Mine. Those words meant so much to me. Music in my mind.

Grandfather.

Edik Bashmakov sat between them. He held a gun to Byron's head. His hand was steady, his finger tight on the trigger. I did not know how long they had been sitting like that, but I figured Edik would tire soon. Zombies were only as strong as their hosts, and Edik was an old man who looked like pushing pencils was the most exercise he ever got.

'Edik,' I rasped. 'Don't be an idiot. Get away from the boy.'

The zombie dipped his chin, his glasses sliding down his nose. 'I apologize, Hunter. But I am acting on my Queen's behalf, and this is what she has ordered.'

I raised my brow. 'She ordered you to hold a gun to a boy's head? She ordered you to act like bait?

This is a suicide mission, Edik. Coming here? Before dawn, while the boys are still awake? What were you thinking?'

The old zombie said nothing, but the strain of his silence was palpable and infinitely unhappy. He did not want to be here. He did not want to hold a gun to Byron's head. The agitation of his aura was immense, sparking so hot and bright I could have seen the zombie from a mile away. I glanced at Jack, but he was focused on the boy. Staring as if he were trying, through sheer force of will, to pour strength into the teen.

Byron looked like he needed it. He hardly seemed to breathe. Watching me. Holding me with those old eyes. I stepped sideways, turning just so to hide the right side of my body, and reached into my hair. Mal curled into my hand. Edik could not have seen the little demon, but his eyes darkened.

'One chance,' I whispered to the old zombie, noting the position of Byron's head in relation to the lamps in the room. 'Go now, or die.'

'Better now than later,' Edik replied unevenly. 'After the veil falls, there will be no quick death for any of us.'

'Ah,' I breathed. 'You coward.'

'Not by choice,' he replied, and I saw Jack close his eyes. Even Byron had a furrow in his brow. Not too frightened to listen. Not too afraid to be confused.

'Done, Edik,' I said, and squeezed Mal's tail. He chirped once, vanished between my fingers—

—and reappeared, partially embedded in the shadows of Byron's hair. The little demon emerged with his mouth over the gun muzzle. Edik flinched and pulled the trigger.

The blast roared through the room, but Mal swallowed the bullet, protecting Byron. The teen shouted, eyes closed, throwing himself off the couch and clapping his hands over his ears. Mal was left suspended in the air, hanging from the end of the gun as Edik pulled the trigger a second time. Mal jerked once, then bit down hard. He swallowed half the gun. Fell to the floor, chewing loudly.

Byron began to turn to look, but Tracker appeared just behind him and yanked the boy away. As soon as they were gone, Zee and the others melted from the shadows. Edik flinched. Jack stood from his stool, but I ignored him as I moved close to the old zombie, holding his hollow gaze. 'Why the boy? Why the focus on him? He's been a target from the start. Pushed, picked on.'

The old zombie said nothing. Raw ripped a spike from his back and rammed it into the floor, again and again – like a war drum or a heartbeat. Zee sidled forward, spitting acid at the zombie's feet. I would have done the same if I could have. I thought of my grandmother, my mother – Jack – and felt a shadow gather in my heart, heaviness like ten thousand hands pushing against my back.

Jack said, 'Leave it be, dear girl.'

'No,' I told him. 'And if *you* know the truth—'

330

I heard low, quiet laughter behind me. I knew that lush voice. I hardly needed to turn, but I did – and watched Blood Mama enter the apartment through the front door, which was already standing open. She wore a simple red suit and red heels, and her thin slash of a mouth was crimson. She posed for a moment, aura crackling like a hurricane in a beer bottle, and caressed Jack with a long look that chilled me to the bone.

'Old Wolf,' she said slowly. 'Been a long time.'

'Blood Mama,' he said, quietly. 'Queen of the rats and rabble.'

'And yet, you do not deny that I survive, ever so prettily, upon this prison world you lashed me to. You Avatar. Pretender.' Blood Mama's lips peeled back from her teeth in a grotesque smile. 'Hunter, because you ask, the boy is Old Wolf's Achilles' heel, the only way to give Ahsen *exactly* what she wants.'

Jack lurched forward. 'You leave him alone.'

'*You* should have left him alone. Dear old bastard.' Blood Mama gave me a piercing look. 'The boy is not what he seems, Hunter. He is the key to killing Jack Meddle's soul. Kill the boy, and you kill the Immortal.'

Her words skimmed over me. I shut them out. The temperature in the room dipped, throwing a wash of frigid air over my skin. Oturu's mark tingled, and a moment later I heard the scrape of knives against wood. I looked back and caught the edge of a black cloak floating down the stairs from the roof.

331

'Why did you arrange this?' I said to Blood Mama, hurried, desperate. 'Why now? Why here?'

'Part of the game,' Jack muttered. 'The ugly game.'

'And you play it so poorly,' she said. 'Ahsen thinks she is coming here to murder your soul, Old Wolf. Whether she does or not is hardly my concern. But you, Hunter . . . do not let your opportunity go to waste. You have so few, and so many, to kill.' She smiled and snapped her fingers. 'Edik, my child. Come along.'

Edik lurched to his feet, took a step – and without my leave or call, Raw fell on him, tearing into his body. I did not expect it. Not the suddenness, not the solitude. Zee and Aaz held back, leaving Raw to it. As if he deserved the kill.

The old zombie screamed, trying to fend off the little demon, but the assault was like setting fire to tissue paper – an effortless annihilation. Horrible to witness. I tried to stop Raw, but he was fast, efficient, and by the time I opened my mouth, it was too late. Most of Edik's stomach was gone, his arms ripped away and devoured in giant bites. Raw snarled, slamming his claws deep into Edik's skull – yanking the demon free of his possessed body. He tore into the parasite, ripping the wraith to shreds. The old man's blood was already absorbing into his skin.

Jack made a small sound, watching him. Tracker reappeared at my side, without Byron, and gave me a swift nod. Someplace safe. That was all I could ask for. Cold air washed over me, heavy with the scent of blood, a deep, arctic cold. A tendril of hair caressed my shoulder. Oturu, looming. I looked for Blood Mama. She was gone. Of course.

'It begins,' Oturu whispered.

'Maxine,' Jack rasped, 'I—'

He never finished. I wished he could have. In the center of the room, a tiny figure coalesced. Dark hair, dark eyes, roses in her cheeks. Red cowboy boots stood firm on the wood floor. My body. A living echo of my childhood.

'Hunter,' Ahsen said. 'How remarkable to see your face.'

I felt the sun break over the horizon like a long, hot drink of water. Zee and the others vanished, instantly reappearing on my skin, bound and hard. But though the sun must have broken open, none of that dawn light entered through the apartment windows. The lamps flickered.

Shadows shifted, stretching like mouths across the room, spreading and rising from the floor and walls in churning waves. Like oil running up walls, or the abyss of Oturu's cloak, full of pressed faces and twisted bodies. A breathing, aching darkness; a tsunami of soul cages; demons hurled and writhing. The interior of the apartment grew dark and closed, as suffocating as the Wasteland, and it was the wall of demons who made it so; entombing, consuming us.

Ahsen remained a small figure in the hovering darkness, shining like the morning star. I walked across the room. I stopped less than ten feet from her, demons spreading beneath my toes like spilled oil. Ahsen removed a narrow braid of hair from her pocket and wound it slowly around her small wrist. She searched my face, as I did hers, and glided forward, closing the distance between us – eyes glittering, her body frayed at the edges, becoming smoke.

'You didn't make these,' I said, gesturing at the demons.

'No,' she replied. 'But I gathered them. They could smell the Labyrinth upon me, just from that one touch of the seed ring, and it was enough. You cannot fathom the allure of the crossroads, Hunter. But you would know, I suppose.'

'I suppose,' I said dryly.

The skin around her mouth became unnaturally taut. 'How *ever* did you escape the Wasteland?'

'I just did.'

Her eyelid fluttered. 'Not even an Avatar could accomplish that.'

I smiled, grim. 'Perhaps that means I'm more powerful than you.'

'Doubtful.'

'Really. We could go there now. Find out.'

Her fingers stroked the braid. 'You are trying to goad me.'

'I'm trying to tell the truth. But that's worse, isn't it? Almost as bad as tossing up someone's reflection when you're about to kill them?' I shook my head, still smiling. 'I think you're afraid. I think you've been afraid for the past ten thousand years. All alone. Little lamb amongst the wolves.'

Her body flickered. Jack moved close to my side, brushing against my shoulder. Very gently, he said, 'I'm here. Let this end.'

Ahsen closed her eyes, as though she could not bear to look at him. 'You do not have the luxury of making requests. You, who condemned me. You, who trapped me with our enemy.'

'I did what I had to.'

'No,' she whispered. 'There were alternatives. You must have known what would happen. You must have. And even if you did not, you should have. Old Wolf, you cannot imagine. I was their *whore*. For millennia, I serviced an army. Reduced to filth.'

She finally looked at him, and her eyes were black with loathing, coarse with horror – horrific for me, to see those emotions painted on my own face, as though it were my body subject to her memories, my flesh that bore the burden. She held up the braid of pale, glossy hair, still wrapped around her wrist. 'Do you remember this, Old Wolf? This is all I have left of the body I wore the day you imprisoned me. All I have left of the *humanity* I had cultivated.'

Jack said nothing, but I felt a terrible strain pass through him. His hand quivered.

Ahsen gazed around the room, studying the inky bodies of breathless, waiting demons. 'I was promised a boy,' she said.

'He's gone,' Jack told her. 'Safe.'

335

'But still yours.' Her lips thinned. 'The eternal child. Your greatest mistake in the divine organic. Doomed to live as a boy for eternity, forever forgetting, forever wandering. You should have killed him, Jack. I would have. He is your weakness. Your failed experiment, who carries part of you inside him. If I murder the boy . . .'

I glanced at Tracker, but his expression was closed, hard. 'Byron is immortal?'

Jack gave me a heavy look. 'He is a special child. You were never supposed to meet. Fate conspired.'

Ahsen clicked her fingers. The old man staggered, falling to his knees. His breath rattled in his throat. He clutched his chest.

I spun around and slammed my fist into Ahsen's face. My hand passed through her, and she laughed, brief as a clap of thunder. Desperation made me sick. I tried hitting her again, and each time I did, something inside me broke a little – that shadow behind my ribs, fluttering wilder, harder. Jack groaned.

'You will never hurt me,' Ahsen whispered. 'And when I am done with Old Wolf's human shell, I will come for you, and I will come, and I will hunt you until you give me what I want. And then I will kill you. Or remake you, Hunter. Perhaps you will be my skin, and your boys my slaves.'

Anger poured through me. The iron band around my finger tingled.

A weapon, I thought. *Give me a weapon.*

The iron burned hotter. I remembered the river,

the living tomb, fighting the current and the sensation of the sword in my hand, cold and alive. The whispers that had led me there. I remembered. I could taste it.

Ahsen blinked, glancing down. I also looked.

My hand was glowing. White hot. Until, suddenly, the light died.

And in its place, I held a sword.

I could not have imagined such a weapon. It seemed better suited to artistry than warfare. A slender blade, polished and glittering as though fragments of starlight had been scattered into the steel – serrated and etched with runes shaped like roses. A thin chain ran from the hilt to my ring finger, which was still bound in iron.

Behind me, Jack started laughing. It was a coarse, ugly sound – and when he raised his head, his eyes were bloodshot. Foam flecked the corners of his mouth.

'No,' Ahsen whispered, and I could not tell if it was greed or horror that passed through her eyes. Nor did I care. My hand felt as though it were encased in a glove made of lightning – skin tingling, a cascading current surging from the sword and ring into my bones.

I had never wielded such a weapon – not unless fencing Zee with a stick counted – but I swung the sword like I was in an old movie and sank the blade into my eight-year-old body with a hoarse shout. The sword passed through Ahsen's stomach like she was made of air, but she cried out, twisting. For the first time, affected by a weapon. And with her cry, the demons attacked.

It was like being swallowed by the oubliette all over again. I struck blindly, the sword glowing against demon flesh, but there were too many. Tracker shouted. I tried to find Jack. Oturu's feet clicked in my ears though I could not see him.

Something, too. A flute.

Music cut like a knife, swelling through me, coursing over my skin like a hundred baby razors. The demons, the darkness, writhed and peeled, and I saw Grant – cane abandoned – sitting on the floor against the wall, just inside the front door. He held my gaze like a lifeline – my life, his life – roped together in his music.

Ahsen made a low sound, looking from the sword to Grant, and though I had thought her expression could not become more distraught, the stare she gave him went beyond alarm: a distress that ripped her small frame with a bone-shattering shudder.

'Lightbringer,' Ahsen whispered, her face screwed into an expression of such pure devastation it was like being kicked in the teeth. She evaporated, but I heard Tracker's low warning and found the rebel Avatar poised above Jack's prone body.

'You knew!' Ahsen screamed at him. 'If the others discover what this world is harboring—'

Jack snarled breathlessly, cutting her off. 'They will *never* know. You will not tell them.'

'I must,' she hissed. 'You stupid—'

I plunged the sword between her shoulders, power surging between the ring and the blade – and Ahsen arched her back, writhing.

Jack grabbed at her ankle, his fingers passing through her flesh like smoke. 'I *never* regretted what I did to you,' he growled. 'I was *glad* to put you away. Sarai was, too.'

Ahsen screamed, wrenching herself off the sword. Tracker tried to punch her, but his fist passed through her body exactly as mine had. Oturu did nothing. He watched only me, and I felt a question building in that flat line of his mouth, the quiet of his cloak.

Grant's melody changed. Ahsen cried out again, whipping around to stare at him – but not before she slammed her foot into Jack's head. The old man went still.

I reeled, all the breath in me gone, but I had no time to check him. Ahsen winked out of sight, then reappeared a heartbeat later, very nearly on top of Grant. His eyes were closed, his fingers flying with lightning speed. His music swept through the apartment, gathering the demons as though they were pieces of paper caught in some terrible wind. Grant's shoulders were hunched, spine curved, skin pale.

He was not alone. Rex stood in front of him, wielding a baseball bat. And behind them both, at the top of the stairs, I saw Mary with a frying pan, hate in her blistering eyes as she stared at Ahsen.

I ran. I ran as fast as I could. Ahsen was going to

kill Grant. I could feel it in her. All the anger was gone from her body, and in its place was a terrible desperation that was more frightening than rage.

My skin tingled, stretching. Power swelled through my veins. An abyss opened in my heart, deeper than any cloak or wasteland, and I sank deep as I stared at Ahsen. I heard Tracker call my name, but I did not let go of the rage that filled me. I could not. I had the taste of death in my mouth.

I did not make a sound. I charged Ahsen, swinging the sword. She turned at the last moment, eyes widening, and evaporated before I could touch her. I screamed her name, then Oturu was there, his hair and cloak winding around my body – and Tracker grabbed my hand.

We passed into darkness, dancing between voids, skipping from light to dark. And in my heart, something stirred. A cascade beneath my ribs, into my throat. A twining body turning, writhing beneath my skin. Jaws rising behind my mouth, the sensation so strong I fancied my own mouth might unhinge, stretching into a yawn that could swallow a sun. Hunger, such hunger, burning. I remembered. Obsidian and starlight.

In my hand, the sword glowed. Inside my body, another glow, hot and pulsing.

Tracker stole us out of the void. I did not know where we were. I saw water. I saw a city stormy with lights. It was night here, and the air was cool in my lungs, on my hot skin. I breathed deep.

Tracker stood on my left. Zee and the boys peeled off my body, but I felt no pain. Nothing but determination.

In front of us, Ahsen. Tall now, as immense as Oturu, with hands like pitchfork tines and that silver braid flowing over a bony shoulder. Built like a whip, with slits for eyes and a small, sharp hole for a mouth. The illusion of a Mahati, swaying into a crouch.

'Come,' she whispered. 'I will not run from you this time, Hunter. We will finish it.'

'You will die,' I said, and it was not just my voice, but a chorus of voices, echoing behind mine. 'You will *all* die.'

Ahsen faltered. 'The veil is falling, Hunter. You have no concept of the army that waits and burns.'

'They have no concept of *me*,' I breathed, and slammed into her body – like a bomb, I slammed. And though my flesh should have been vulnerable, I felt nothing of the impact – nothing, not even when she tried to stab me with her fingers. My skin did not break.

But Ahsen's fingers did – and she howled. I reached down and grabbed her hair, yanking. Dek slithered down my arm, fire screaming from his mouth, enveloping that sharp silver head.

She shimmered – breaking her word, trying to escape – but I tightened my grip and felt the power inside me reach out and surround the Avatar, binding it, as though in a cage. Her skin shriveled, flaking in strips. Hunger roared through me. Endless, violent. Sucking her dry.

So easy. Like breathing. Death passed through me. I felt no pity, no mercy. The creature inside me eased into my heart like a missing key from a piano, sliding home to make a perfect sound. One clear tone that shivered.

It was the music that brought me back. I remembered Grant. And when I remembered him, I recalled my mother, too. I heard her voice.

Nothing so bad you need to be cruel. Tough, yes. You'll have to kill, yes. But there's a difference in the heart. One makes you mean. The other keeps you going.

Ahsen screamed. I let go of her, but it was too late. She grabbed my arm, and her bones fractured, her skin disappearing entirely from the dried strips of her muscle. Zee pulled her from me, and the remains of her flesh turned to dust in his claws.

I stood back. In that moment I did not know myself. All I felt was hunger. All I could remember was that backwoods Wisconsin bar, the memory of a body turning beneath my skin, a creature that I felt now, again.

A creature that wanted free. And I suddenly knew exactly what my mother had been afraid of, what she could not tell me. What my grandmother had tried to explain.

Veil gets weak, so do parts of us, I heard my grandmother say. *Walls around our hearts that were never supposed to come down.*

And then: *Stay true.*

'We're done,' I whispered, and the dark creature inside me protested. I pushed it down, gently, and the gentleness seemed to surprise it. The darkness faltered, then retreated, softly, with a hush. Sinking into the roots of my heart; the shadow, waiting.

I tried to drop the sword. I tried to shake it loose, but it was bound to the ring, and the ring would not come off my finger. I thought – *Do it now; be small* – and the sword flashed, once, and when my vision cleared, there was nothing but the ring – larger now, encasing more of my finger, with a curious little hinge for my joint. I looked at the rest of my hands, turning them, aching. My body hardly felt real. Nothing felt real. I heard gulls. Cars honking. Around us the night was calm.

'What am I?' I breathed.

'You are the Hunter,' whispered Oturu. 'You are the last.'

I stared at him. I could not hear my heart. I could not hear my thoughts.

'Hunter,' whispered Oturu, his cloak extending around me. I leaned into him. I could not help myself. His hair caught my shoulders, and the abyss of his body – however briefly it touched my skin – was an odd comfort. Tracker crouched, trailing a finger through the dust of Ahsen's corpse. Zee and the others crowded close, pushing him aside. Licking the ground. Queasy, I had to look away.

'So,' Oturu murmured, 'you are awake now. You have released the promise captured in your heart.'

343

I felt Ahsen dying. I felt the taste of her life in my veins. I closed my eyes and saw her withered face – but when I opened my eyes, I found Tracker, staring. Searching.

I was afraid of his scrutiny. Afraid of myself. I turned to look at Oturu. 'Was this the Hunt? Was this what it was all about?'

The demon bowed his head. 'There are many kinds of Hunts. It is what defines us, renews us. It is the same for you, Hunter. We are born in blood, and we will die in blood, but in the interim, we must put fire to our veins and find new paths to tread upon.' Tendrils of hair tapped his head. 'Paths, up here. It is what your mother wanted.'

Tracker stepped close and held out his hand. I took it. He rubbed his thumb over my palm, his gaze inscrutable. Zee wrapped his arms around my legs, as did Raw and Aaz. Purrs sank into my bones.

We went home.

EPILOGUE

TWO days later I found myself in Jack Meddle's downtown office, buried in a stack of books. Grant and I were there, helping him clean up.

Just that morning, Suwanai and McCowan had stopped by the Coop – but oddly enough, not for anything to do with Sarai's murder. As far as anyone was concerned, the woman was still alive. Off . . . traveling.

Badelt's killer, they had informed us, was at large. But I was off the hook. No evidence. A good alibi.

I was not comforted. A man was still dead. Sarai, though Jack assured me otherwise, was also dead. At least on this plane of existence. Which made me think of my dream. Sarai, as the unicorn, in flesh. I could almost believe it. Almost.

'Cops were called to the art gallery,' I told Jack. 'I was here. I left her body.'

He held up a piece of broken pottery, peering at its underside. 'Don't ask too many questions, my dear. Suffice it to say, the situation has been handled.'

'That seems vaguely menacing,' Grant said, struggling to keep a three-foot pile of texts on Mesopotamia from falling over. He pushed them once, then again, harder, but they kept tilting. I nudged him aside and started unloading the pile.

'I did warn you book stacking is an art,' Jack said to him. 'You have yours; I have mine, lad.'

Grant grunted, giving him a suspicious look. As did I.

I sensed movement on my right, and found Byron hovering in the doorway. The teen had tagged along, without much prodding. Another surprise, another surreal stitch in my life. He was living at the shelter, in his small studio. Grant had managed to divert Social Services. For now.

The eternal child. Your greatest mistake in the divine organic. Doomed to live as a boy for eternity, forever forgetting, forever wandering.

I did not know what that meant, but it haunted me every time I saw the boy. I could hear Ahsen's voice.

I stood, rubbing my hands on my jeans, and made my way to Byron. He did not leave the doorway. He held a pink box in his hands. Snack run. There was a bakery down the street. His face was still cut and bruised, his eyes hollow. But for a boy

346

with broken ribs, he was moving around well – perhaps too well – and he was here. He had not run, despite everything.

He was more than human. And he did not realize it.

'Um. I got doughnuts.' Byron shoved the box at me and reached into his pocket. He dropped a crumpled wad of change on top.

'Thanks,' I said.

'It's all there,' he replied, distinctly uncomfortable. 'I have a receipt if you want to count it.'

'I believe you.' I punched his shoulder, very gently. 'Relax, kid.'

Byron shrugged, glancing at Grant, then Jack.

I said, 'I appreciate your helping out today.'

He shuffled his feet. Shy, pained, thoughtful. 'You helped me.'

'I got you hurt.'

'You helped me.' Byron looked into my eyes, then faltered, swallowing hard. 'I . . . saw some things I don't understand. But it wasn't you who hurt me. Not you.'

It was my turn to feel awkward.

Byron said, 'The old man knew Brian?'

'Jack's business partner was married to him.'

The boy nodded, chewing his bottom lip. 'He's familiar to me. I don't know why.'

I hardly knew why. Jack had explained nothing.

I stepped aside, glancing deeper into the room, where Grant and Jack were stooped over a growing stack of books. Arguing softly with each other.

347

'You want to talk to Jack?' I asked Byron.

'No,' he said, already backing away. 'I think I'll go downstairs and look at the paintings.'

He fled. I let him go without a word, noting his speed, the stiffness of his shoulders. Something in him, an instinct. Made me afraid to tell the boy who Jack was to me. As proud as I was, it felt like it should stay a secret. Even more than my boys, my purpose, the prison surrounding the world. Jack Meddle: a grave and deadly riddle.

I carried the doughnut box back to the men, sliding the change into my pocket along the way. I felt the outline of my knives beneath my jacket. My mother's jacket. Oturu had left it behind, on the apartment roof, along with the weapons. Small things.

He had not done the same with the seed ring. I had let him take it into his keeping while Ahsen lived, but now that she was dead, I wanted it back. I needed it, even just to hold. My mother lived in the seed ring. Her ghost. Her thoughts. Her memories of my grandmother.

But Tracker and Oturu were gone. I had not seen them since that night.

'Byron,' Grant said, digging into the doughnut box. 'He slipped away again?'

'Downstairs.' I shot Jack a long look. 'Ready yet to explain who he is, how he's connected to you?'

The old man's jaw tightened. He gave Grant a gruff gesture. 'Into the kitchen with you, lad. I won't have your crumbs or sticky fingers around my books.'

Grant's gaze flicked to Jack's aura. I thought he would say something – and there was plenty to remark on, from Byron to Mary – but his shoulders settled, and he bent down and kissed my mouth. He tasted like sugary glaze. I hung on. Grant sighed against my mouth, pulling away with a solemn expression ruined by the warmth in his eyes. He jammed the half-eaten doughnut into his mouth, gave Jack a hard look, and took the pink bakery box in one hand. He limped away toward the kitchen, his cane clicking loudly.

I watched him go. When he was out of sight, I very quietly said, 'Jack, why was Ahsen afraid of Grant?'

'Why are you?' replied the old man carefully.

I flashed him a scathing look. 'I'm not.'

'But you're wary. You think about possibilities.'

I took a deep breath and counted to three. 'She called him something.'

'Names are meaningless,' Jack replied brusquely, and shoved a book at me. 'Here. I believe you admired this before.'

I wanted to keep arguing with him, but I looked down and found the text on the Wild Hunt. I almost laughed when I read the title. It felt like a lifetime since I had seen it, another Maxine Kiss.

I rolled up my sleeves, getting an eyeful of Zee's tattooed backside as I sat down on a stack of encyclopedias. I opened up the book, inhaling the scent of old leather, and within moments found the handwritten note I had started reading only days before.

It is of us, I read, *this hunt, this wild raging hunt that takes upon itself the nature of an Age, and destroys so that others may be reborn. It is why, I think, the leader of the hunt must so frequently change, because Ages change, and what defines one era cannot be relied upon to characterize the next. A new voice is required, a new heart.*

The hunt is defined by hearts, for good or ill. We have learned that lesson in the most brutal ways imaginable, and we will learn it once more. We have no choice. This fearful omen, so deep in our memory it has become sunk in human blood, has opened and closed, again and again. Faster now, like the hum of wings. And when it stops, we shall fall.

We cannot begin again. Risks will be involved. But it is as Tacitus said, 'No enemy can withstand a vision that is strange and, so to speak, diabolical; for in all battles, the eyes are overcome first.'

The eyes are overcome first. Yes. Or perhaps . . . just maybe . . . the eyes will be opened first. And with them opened . . . hope. We must have hope, and faith. We must. No one is more terrible than the leader of the hunt. No one is more feared. Her desire is her outcome. Her wish is the command.

And so her heart must be strong. The end of the world sleeps within her breast. The wyrms who will devour themselves in darkness.

I read the page twice, unable to help myself, those words sinking into me like each letter was made of heat. I felt terrified, exhilarated. Lost.

I looked up and found Jack watching me. Grant was still in the kitchen, out of sight.

'I'm scared,' I confessed to the old man. 'Where do I go from here?'

'Forward,' he said loftily. 'As your mother and Jeannie would have wanted. With strength and honor and goodness.'

'Old Wolf,' I said. 'It's not that easy. The prison is crumbling. The world as we know it is going to end. And I'm the *last*, Jack. I believe it now. When the veil comes down—' I stopped myself, thinking of my grandmother, feeling her hands, hearing her beneath the backdrop of wild sky and wind.

You dig deep inside that heart of yours and push the cutters back. You take care of what you can, when you can, but you don't give up.

Don't give up. Don't.

I gritted my teeth and met Jack's gaze. 'There's something inside me. I felt it, when I fought Ahsen. It was hungry. It was strong. It wanted death. And if I keep fighting, if I can't control it . . .'

I could not continue. I had tried not to think of it. *It* . . . Nameless, formless. The more I remembered, the more I felt a creaking inside my chest, like a door pushing open – and a presence inside, peering into my mind with a cold, hungry eye.

We are one, said that quiet voice.

No, I told it. *Never*.

Jack stood, stepping around books and pushing aside paperwork. He crouched in front of me. He held

351

my hands, very carefully, and said, 'The world is shaped by hearts. Look deep. Trust yourself, Maxine. Trust, like your mother trusted you. Like your grandmother, and every woman who has come before, who trusted her daughter to stay true. Don't listen to what your eyes tell you. Check here.' He laid his hand over his heart. 'Like the storybooks say.'

'That won't stop the walls from falling.'

'No,' he said kindly, 'but you'll have the right kinds of friends at your back when they do.'

Jack kissed my hand, but when he tried to stand, I held him.

'You're mine,' I whispered, full of wonder. 'Grandpa Wolf. Meddling Man.'

His smile deepened, and he pressed my hands to his wrinkled cheek. 'I have always been so, even before you were born.'

And that was enough. That was all I needed.

extras

www.orbitbooks.net

about the author

Marjorie M. Liu hails from both coasts of the USA, but currently resides in the Midwest. Having studied and practised law, she now writes full time. When not writing, she enjoys listening to music, painting, designing websites and returning to old movie favourites, some of which involve light sabres, various applications of the Force and small green men with pointy ears. She is also, occasionally, commandeered by poodles. For more information, please visit her website at www.marjoriemliu.com

Find out more about Marjorie M. Liu and other Orbit authors by registering for the free monthly newsletter at www.orbitbooks.net

interview

What turned you from the law and to writing? Was a career in writing something you always wanted to pursue?

I always wanted to be a writer, and I reached a certain point in my life where I felt strongly that it was 'now or never'.

Does your legal training consciously inform your work, or is it something you've left behind?

Once you're a lawyer, you never leave behind the law, though I can't say that it consciously informs my work. Studying and practising the law, however, provides a rather unique insight into human behaviour that I'm sure has played a role in my writing. Either way, I wouldn't give up that training for anything.

Your life and work has taken you to some interesting places. How much has your travelling and experience abroad influenced your writing?

It has certainly influenced my love of setting books in unique places. Every country – and town, and city – has its own personality, its own rhythm and mysteries. When you plunk the reader, or a character, into a place that is unfamiliar, the world becomes new. You don't need to devise some fantasy landscape to tell a story in – the truth can be strange enough.

How important is your Chinese heritage in your character and world building?

It's not something I consciously think about. I'm a human being first and foremost, and the human experience is what books, in general, are all about. Having said that, though, I have been exposed to cultures, places, and history that others have not (though every person has a life experience that is unique and wholly individual) – and yes, in retrospect I can think of some definitive examples of that influencing my work.

How extensively do you plot your novels before you start writing them? Do you plot the entire trilogy/series before you start writing or do you prefer to let the story roam where it will?

I prefer to let the story roam. Which isn't to say that I don't plan, because I do – or rather, I try to – but most of my books start out with an idea or an intriguing first line, and from there I just play things by ear.

Do you have a set writing routine and if so, what is it?
No set routine – just a flexible habit. I get up in the morning and write before and after breakfast – stop for a couple hours – and then pick up where I left off. I probably work about twelve to fourteen hours a day, but that's cut with email, reading, watching television, etc.

You've described authors such as Charlie Huston as both 'edgy and lyrical'. Do you have any particular favourite authors – SFF or in other genres – who have influenced the tone of your work?
Too many to mention. Every book I read influences me to some degree, though I remember being especially taken with Kelly Link, Isabelle Allende, Borges, Neruda, Frank Miller, Sara Donati and others. As I said, many others.

Some authors talk of their characters 'surprising' them by their actions; is this something that has happened to you?
All the time.

What is the most rewarding aspect of being a published author?
I do what I love for a living. Every part of that is a reward.

if you enjoyed
THE IRON HUNT

read on in

DARKNESS CALLS

by

Marjorie M. Liu

ZOMBIES had a bad habit of shooting me in the head. Most of them knew better, but there was always that one who wanted to get lucky.

It was a wet Monday morning. Almost dawn. Broken streetlights and glass in the road; and the hulking shadows of abandoned warehouses towering above me. Dead city, dead hour. Seattle was a dark place, even with the sun. Some days felt like living in the aftermath of a nuclear winter; as though a mushroom cloud had blown over and never left.

Quiet, too. Nothing to hear except harsh breathing, a soft whine; my cowboy boots scuffing concrete and the sharpening of claws; and the rumble of the freight trains at the rail yard across from the docks, mingling with the growls vibrating softly in my ears: baby symphonies of thunder. Good music. Made me feel safe.

I rubbed wet hair out of my eyes. 'Zee. Hold him tighter.'

Him. Archie Limbaud. Scrawny man, sinewy as a garter snake, saddled with a crown of short brown hair plastered to his soaked skin and flecked with enormous flakes of dandruff. He was a fortysome-thing man who smelled like the private bathroom of a teenage boy: unwashed and vaguely fecal.

He was also a zombie. Not the brain-eating, sham-bling kind, either. Not a corpse. Just a man, possessed by a demon – who was using his body like a puppet. Practically the same as being dead, if you asked me.

I did not want to touch him. He sprawled on the edge of an empty parking lot, crammed against the bottom of a chain-link fence, the contents of his wallet scattered on the ground in front of me. More condoms than cash, along with one credit card, and an expired driver's license. Minutes ago, there had been a gun – a .40-caliber pistol, pointed at my head – but that was gone now. Eaten.

I hated guns. I hated zombies. Put those together with what I knew about the possessed man at my feet, and I didn't know whether to cry, scream, or kick the fuck out of his testes.

I eased off my gloves, shoved them in my back pocket, and extended my palm. A sharp little hand passed me a switchblade. Pretty thing, with a mother-of-pearl handle and silver accents. Razor edge, still wet with blood. Engraved with the initials A.L. I waved it in front of Archie's ruddy face, and his dark aura fluttered wildly around the crown of his head.

'Some night,' I said quietly. 'I found the body.'

Archie said nothing. Part of that might have been the aluminum baseball bat pressed down on his throat. Stolen from the Seattle Mariners, if I had to guess. I could see the stadium walls of Safeco Field from where I crouched, and Zee and the others were going through a baseball phase. Babe Ruth was in; Bill Russell was out. Which pained me. At least my boys were still obsessed with Bon Jovi. I couldn't have handled that much change.

Zee, Raw, and Aaz were down on the ground, pinning Archie to the pavement. Little demons, little hounds. Rain sizzled, trickling down bony backs the color of soot smeared with silver, skin shimmering with a muscular fluidity that resembled water more than flesh. Razor-sharp spines of hair flexed against chiseled skulls while silver veins pulsed with slow beats that, if I had pressed my ear close, would have sounded like the steady thrums of bass guitars.

Red eyes glinted. I used the switchblade to tap Aaz on the back of the head, and his hair cut through the steel as if it were butter. Raw caught the bits of blade before they hit the pavement and stuffed them in his mouth, chewing loudly.

'Ease up on the windpipe,' I said to Aaz. 'I don't want the host harmed.'

Aaz blew a kiss at the zombie and removed the baseball bat from his soft, bruised throat. Archie started coughing, fighting to move his legs. No luck. Raw was sitting on his ankles, and Zee had his wrists pinned to the pavement. Not quite crushing bone, but close. My boys were strong.

'Please,' Archie whispered hoarsely. 'I want to convert.'

'Liar,' rasped Zee, before I had a chance to tell the zombie to go fuck himself. The little demon leaned close to lick the air above Archie's brow. 'Cutter lies, Maxine. He still hungers.'

'He murders,' I said, gripping the remains of the switchblade in my fist as a young face flashed through my mind, bloody and sliced, long brown limbs naked, splayed. Torn doll. Torn in places I did not want to remember. 'She was just a kid.'

'She was a prostitute,' Archie said. 'She was already prey.'

Dek and Mal, coiled heavy on my shoulders, peered from beneath my hair and hissed at the zombie. Unlike the others, they were built like snakes, with two vestigial limbs good only for clutching my ears. Heads shaped like hyenas. Sharp smiles. Fire in their breath. Archie stared at them, and trembled.

I reached through his thunderous aura to place my

hand on his clammy brow. He shied away, but the boys held tight, and in that last moment before I touched him, his eyes rolled back, staring at the delicate armor surrounding the entire ring finger of my right hand: a slender sheath of quicksilver, replete with a delicate joint at the knuckle, which allowed my finger to bend. Fit like a skin. Sometimes I forgot it was there.

'Prey,' I murmured. 'And what does that make you?'

'One of a million,' he whispered, shaking; staring at me with hate in his eyes. 'You can't kill us all. When the prison walls fail—'

'You'll be rat meat to the rest of the demons,' I interrupted, still thinking of the girl I had found in an alley only blocks from here, summoned to her still-warm body by Zee and the others, who had roused me from bed to hunt her killer. 'Your kind will be slaughtered, just like the humans. You're nothing to the others. Even your Queen has said so.'

'Hunter—' Archie began, but I didn't let him finish. I knew everything he was going to say. I had heard it thousands of times since my mother's murder, and thousands of times before that, as well.

I was going to die. I was never going to reach old age. The world was going to end.

All of which was true. But, whatever. His voice hurt my head. His sour scent, hot and prickly, made me want to vomit. I was tired, and cold all the way through to my soul, and there was a girl who had lost her life tonight for no good reason. She had suffered a bad death – and only because the parasite possessing this man had wanted to feed on her pain. I did not even know her name. No ID, no nothing. Lost forever.

Not the only one, either. The world was a big place. Too many predators: human, zombie, or otherwise. And just one of me. Nomad, born and bred, who had settled in this city longer than any other. Abandoning all others, so I could have some semblance of a normal life.

Right. Normal.

I ground my palm even harder against Archie's brow, and exhaled a soft hiss of words: sibilant and ancient, a focused tongue that made my skin tingle, and my hand burn. Archie's breath rattled, and he strained upward as his aura swelled, trying to escape me.

No such luck. The demon was young. Easy to exorcise. I drew it out, watching the passage of its wraithlike body churn through the human's open mouth like poisoned smoke. Archie went limp. Raw and Aaz released his legs, while Dek and Mal slithered off my shoulders, winding down my arms to be near my hands. Their tiny claws pricked my skin like kneading cats, and their soft, high-pitched hum of Bon Jovi's 'Social Disease' filled the air.

When the last trail of the parasite's writhing body was free of the human man, I held it in my hand with that soft, shrieking darkness spilling through my fingers, and felt a cold bite in my skin, like a glove of frozen nettles. Zee stepped over Archie's still body, and the others extended their razor-tipped claws.

I gave them the demon. I did not watch them eat it.

I knelt by Archie and checked his pulse. Strong, steady. His eyelids fluttered, but he stayed unconscious, and I backed away quickly, rubbing my sweaty palms on my jeans. I had no way of knowing what this man had been like before being possessed, though I guessed he hadn't been the happy type. Stable, mentally robust people did not get possessed by demons. Too much work. No cracks to exploit.

But this man, Archie Limbaud, would wake up a murderer – and never know it. Demons left no memories in human minds. Just chaos, ruined lives. Friends and family who would never look at you the same way.

'Maxine,' Zee rasped, rubbing his mouth with the back of his sharp hand. 'Sun coming.'

I knew. I could feel the sun, somewhere beyond the black skies and rain, slowly creeping up on the cloud-hidden horizon. I had minutes at most.

'Pay phone,' I said to Zee, and he snapped his claws at Raw and Aaz, who were prowling the edges of the dark lot, slipping in and out of shadows. Both of them loped close, graceful as wolves, and whispered in Zee's ears. Zee cocked his head, listening; and after a moment, pointed.

I said nothing. Just walked away from Archie. I did not rush. I did not look back. I held the handle of the switchblade and slid it into my hair. Listened to metal crunch as Mal chewed and swallowed. I could have left it. Evidence.

But I wanted the man to have a second chance. I wanted him to wake up, confused and amnesiac, but without the burden of murder. No one deserved that – even though there was a small part of me that felt like his hands were dirty. Dirty as mine. I could not stop rubbing my palms against my wet jeans. Felt as though Archie Limbaud's stink was all over me.

Early morning continued to be quiet, the drizzling mist softening the streets and rough, broken edges, and I drank in the cold air, savoring the chill of wet hair curled against my flushed cheeks. The boys moved through the shadows, invisible except for brief glimpses of their red eyes. I kept wiping my hands and thinking about the dead girl. And my mother. She had warned me before she died. She had warned me it would be like this. Always, victims. Victims, everywhere. And me, never fast enough. Always playing catch-up.

I found a pay phone two blocks away. Battered relic, covered in graffiti. I dialed 911 and left a brief message with the operator – teenager dead, murdered, several blocks south of Safeco Field – and hung up. Wiped off my prints, then remembered I could have worn my gloves. I was still rattled, not thinking straight. I wanted to go back to the dead girl and wait with her body – as if that would make a difference. Ease, somehow, the pain and loneliness of her murder.

Instead, I kept walking, taking a westerly route away from the rail yards, toward Chinatown. I saw no one but caught glimpses of headlights crossing distant intersections. The rumble of the trains seemed louder. The air tasted sharper, and suddenly electric, as though a city full of alarms had just gone off and I was feeling the pulse of thousands of eyes opening at once. In my ear, Dek and Mal began humming more Bon Jovi. 'Have a Nice Day.'

'You, too,' I said hoarsely, reaching into my hair to scratch their necks. 'See you tonight.'

I stopped in the shadows, well off the street, and the rest of the boys slipped free of the darkness to gather close, hugging my legs, running their cheeks against my knees. The boys liked to be tucked in. I slid my knuckles against their warm jaws and savored the rumble of purrs. Their skin steamed in the rain.

Zee peered up at me and tugged on my hand until I knelt before him. Very carefully, he cradled my face between his claws, searching my eyes with a sad compassion that made my throat burn.

'Maxine,' he rasped gently. 'Sweet Maxine. Be your heart at ease.'

We had seconds, nothing more. I kissed my fingers and pressed them against his bony brow. I thought of my mother again and caught myself in heartache. She had said good night to the boys like this, for all the years they were hers. I could not stop thinking of her tonight.

'Dream,' I whispered. 'Sleep tigh—'

I never finished. I got shot in the head.

Just like that. Right temple. Not much sound. The impact shuddered through my entire body, every sensation magnified with excruciating clarity as the bullet drilled into my skull – the inexorable pressure of a small round object, crushing my life. I could feel it. I could *feel* it. My brain was going to explode like a watermelon. I had no time to be afraid.

But in that moment – that split second between life and death, the sun touched the horizon somewhere beyond the clouds—

—and the boys disappeared into my skin.

The bullet ricocheted, the impact spinning me like a rag doll. I fell on my hands and knees, and stayed there, stunned and frozen. I could still feel the punch of the shot – the sensation so visceral I would not have been surprised to reach up and find the bullet grinding a path into my skull.

I touched my head, just to be sure. Found hair and unbroken skin. No blood. My entire right arm trembled, and a dull, throbbing ache spread from my sinuses to my temple, all the way through to the base of my skull. My heart pounded so hard I could barely breathe. All I could see was pavement and my hands.

My transformed hands. My skin had been pale and smooth only moments before, but tattoos now covered every inch: obsidian roping shadows, scales and silver muscle shining with subtle veins of organic metal. My fingernails shimmered like black pearls, hard enough to dig a hole through solid rock. Red eyes stared from the backs of my wrists. Raw and Aaz. I closed my eyes, trying to steady my breathing, and felt five corresponding tugs against my skin. Demons, inhabiting my flesh. Minds and hearts and dreams, bound to my life until I died.

My friends, my family. My dangerous boys.

Somewhere distant I heard police sirens wailing. My 911 call, coming this way. I had to get up. I tried, and fell. Gritted my teeth and dug my nails into the concrete. Tried again.

This time I managed to stand. I started walking, stumbling, but did not go down. My head pounded. I bent over once, still moving – afraid to stop – gagging uncontrollably. Felt like my stomach was going to peel right up through my throat, but instead of making my head hurt worse, the pain eased.

I touched my right temple with a trembling hand, savoring the smooth, unbroken skin. Momentarily in awe that I still lived.

I had been shot before. Frequently. All over. Never felt a thing. Bullets bounced off me during the day. A nuclear bomb could hit me in daylight, and I would survive – without a scratch. Might be a different story at night, when the boys peeled off my body, but I never underestimated their ability to keep me alive.

But no one – no one – had ever had the foresight – or the balls – to try killing me in that moment between night and day, caught in transition between mortal and immortal.

Near-perfect timing. Any earlier, and the boys would have killed the shooter before the bullet could be fired. Any later, and I would have been invulnerable. Which was exactly the case. Saved by a fraction of a second.

Too damn close. I scanned the shadows but saw nothing except for warehouses and dark windows, and the glitter of downtown Seattle to the north, all the lights of the city frozen like the unwavering pose of fireflies. Nothing unordinary. No shooter, waving a flag. But I felt watched. Someone, somewhere, out there in the darkness. Long range, or else the boys would have felt their presence well before the attack.

Zombie, I thought. Had to be. No one else who knew what I was would try to hurt me.

'You almost died,' I said out loud, needing to hear the words, to hear myself – as though I required some proof of life. Maxine Kiss. Almost taken out, just like my mother – with a bullet through the brain.

A zombie had killed her. But that was different. It had been her time to die.